AID AND COMFORT

AID AND COMFORT

Ted Allbeury

Hodder & Stoughton

First published in Great Britain in 1997 by Hodder and Stoughton
A division of Hodder Headline PLC

British Library Cataloguing in Publication Data

Allbeury, Ted, 1917–
Aid and comfort
I. Title
823.9'14 [F]

ISBN 0 340 69643 5

Typeset by Hewer Text Composition Services, Edinburgh
Printed and bound in Great Britain by
Mackays of Chatham PLC, Chatham, Kent

Hodder and Stoughton
A division of Hodder Headline PLC
338 Euston Road
London NW1 3BH

DEDICATION

One of the pleasures of being a writer is to be able to dedicate a book to a particular person or group. When I was writing this book an eleven-month-old baby was rushed to the local hospital at Pembury, seriously ill. The staff there feared that the baby may not survive the night. They appealed for the urgent help of a specialist team from Guy's Hospital. This meant a fifty-mile ambulance journey through heavy traffic both ways. The Guy's team didn't wait for the baby to be brought to Guy's but went down in the ambulance so that they could be treating the baby during the return journey to London. Cutting a long and harrowing story short, they saved the baby's life. The specialist team were Dr Andrew Durwood, Dr Cleave Gass and Staff Nurse Eliza Matthews. The Caleb Ward for Intensive Care at Guy's was their support unit. This is their book as a thank you to the team, Guy's and the NHS. And a small cuddle for the baby – my grandson Sam Parfitt.

AUTHOR'S NOTE

I can still remember vividly the months after the surrender in 1945 when my unit and I were combing our area of Germany for Nazis and other naughty boys. We were very busy. But I can remember having to give up fifteen minutes of my precious time to an elderly German lady who was protesting about the arrest of her grandson. She gave me a picture of an ideal son, husband and grandson who wouldn't hurt a fly. She was wearing one of those toque hats with a bird's feather and a bunch of cherries on it. And it dawned on me that she was the spitting image of my grandma and if the war had gone the other way it would have been me the elderly lady was talking about. Incidentally, her grandson was in the Gestapo and a pretty nasty fellow.

I suppose the most enduring lesson I learned from those days was that there wasn't all that much difference between German intelligence officers, KGB men and me. We had all been recruited and trained in much the same way. (Give or take a few national idiosyncrasies.) And this was underlined in my mind by the fact that for some years after the war and after I had left the services I got more Christmas cards from men I'd arrested and interrogated than from others. Could be a reflection on my character of course.

So I've written this novel to illustrate this point, to show the relationship between three men. One a renegade CIA man who sold the secrets of the CIA to the KGB for $4,000,000, the second a CIA officer trying to convict him, and the third the KGB officer who 'ran' the 'mole'. Some aspects of this novel are loosely based on the real-life case of the traitor, Aldrich Ames.

The central strand of this book, and some aspects of the characters of Art and Maria Jarvis, reflect the case of Aldrich Ames. But the book is a novel, and I would like to make it clear that the characters and incidents are my own invention, not based (beyond that starting-point) on any real persons and events. In particular, those of my characters who are depicted as holding official or diplomatic positions in the USA and other countries are not intended to depict the people actually holding these positions at the time, nor are my characters' actions to be attributed to those people.

Treason against the United States shall consist only in levying war against them, or in adhering to their enemies, giving them aid and comfort. No person shall be convicted of treason unless on the testimony of two witnesses to the same overt act, or on confession in open court. The Congress shall have power to declare the punishment of treason; but no attainder of treason shall work corruption of blood, or forfeiture except during the life of the person attainted.

CONSTITUTION OF THE UNITED STATES
Art. III, 1789

The right of the people to be secure in their persons, houses, papers, and effects, against unreasonable searches and seizures, shall not be violated, and no Warrants shall issue, but upon probable cause, supported by Oath or affirmation, and particularly describing the place to be searched, and the persons or things to be seized.

CONSTITUTION OF THE UNITED STATES
Amendment IV

PART ONE

Chapter 1

Yuri Volkov was thirty-nine and undoubtedly handsome. He had just been promoted and that meant he could choose to drink genuine Glenfiddich instead of vodka. The pretty stewardess had brought him an extra miniature whisky as soon as they were airborne. Because of his good looks he would have had much the same treatment from the Aeroflot cabin crew even if they hadn't been tipped off that he was a KGB VIP. It worked even with men. His mother and several of her women friends had said, when he was younger, that he was the image of Cary Grant. Despite his looks he was not a vain man and if he had to decide then he saw himself as more of a José Carreras. But for him what really mattered was what Fomenko thought of him. Fomenko had listened intently to his report on the 'agents of influence' that he had cultivated in Washington and New York. But Fomenko could only be described as an aggressive listener. Never a sign of his reaction to what was said. Not a raised eyebrow, not even pursed lips, but just that magnificent head that looked as if it had been sculpted out of granite and which never responded. When Volkov had said his piece Fomenko had stood up and rung for his assistant to take him back to the hotel. But the next day he was notified of his promotion and was taken that evening to a reception at the French Embassy where he had been introduced to Gorbachev who shook his hand but barely glanced at him. But it wasn't the men in the Kremlin who mattered these days. It was the men in Dzherdzinski Square who knew how the levers of power were manipulated. He wasn't going to disappoint them.

Like a good many charmers Volkov was very perceptive and aware where people were concerned. He would have made a successful con-man but he used his talent patriotically. He used it to find people of influence who might be persuaded, but not overtly, to adopt a sympathetic attitude towards the Soviet Union, its policies and its people. He himself had become very partial to blueberry pie and maybe he could make his American contacts discover a taste for *piroshki*. His predecessor had been a disaster. He had carried out the instructions they had given him at the training course in Moscow. It was the hard-sell route and it didn't work. It never had worked. Volkov had done two years in the States as a Fulbright scholar nominated from Leningrad University which he had never even visited let alone attended. After the Fulbright he had toured the country, working in bars, delis and drug stores with a little money and full blessing from Moscow. Americans, he knew, were masters of the hard-sell. They knew it inside out and could recognise it a mile off. And they didn't like it done on themselves. The hard-sell was for suckers and country bumpkins. His way was very soft-sell. There were good points to every political system he would say, and anyway people had a right to choose for themselves. OK, capitalism could cause unemployment but you can't be right all the time. Even Moscow Dynamo don't always win.

He had slept for most of the flight after the stop-over at London and they'd had to queue to land at Dulles because of snow, but eventually he was presenting his passport at the Immigration desk. The INS officer leafed carefully though the pink pages of the Russian passport whose cover still displayed the gold-blocked CCCP despite the fact that the Soviet Union no longer existed. He could have claimed a diplomatic passport but all KGB officers avoided them. Russian diplomatic passports were gone over in fine detail at Immigration desks all over the world. The Soviets had routinely abused them in the past and they now merely attracted official attention without any privileges. Not even courtesy. Customs were their usually bloody selves. Despite only having two cases they'd made him open them and take everything out. When they saw the three film cans they perked up but couldn't read the labels because they were in Russian.

'What are these?'

'A film.'

'You mean three cans for one film?'

'Yeah. It's 35mm. Black and white. It's a classic film.'

'What makes it a classic?'

'It's very old. It was made in 1925. This copy is only on loan. It was made by a guy called Sergei Eisenstein.'

'That the guy who invented the thing about space?'

'No. That was Einstein.'

'Let's have a look at it. Just open the top one.'

Carefully Volkov broke the tape and eased off the lid, uncoiling a few feet of the film. The Customs man held it up to the light. 'What's the film about?'

'A battleship. The film's called *The Battleship Potemkin.*'

'What's Potemkin mean?'

'It was a Russian admiral's name.'

'Why are you bringing it in?'

'It's for showing to the Arts Club at the Library of Congress.'

'OK. Wrap it up again.'

And the magic chalk marks went on both bags. It passed through his mind that you could electronically print information in the space under the film sprockets but it faded from his mind as he waited for a taxi to the embassy. It was 9 a.m. when he got to the embassy. The ambassador wanted to see him immediately.

For over an hour he sat retailing the bits and pieces of Kremlin gossip. Watching his words carefully and omitting the more scabrous episodes so that neither he nor His Excellency could be accused of plotting revolution if some creep had activated the bugs in the private office.

Back in his own office Volkov went through his diary for the week ahead. Lunch was with the secretary of a Republican Senator and in the evening there was a cocktail party at the British Embassy, followed by dinner with a congressman from one of the mid-west areas who was interested in an exchange visit between Soviet pig-farmers and his farming constituents. Volkov's cover function was as Senior Press Attaché to the embassy and that gave him considerably more freedom of movement and contacts than any other members of the embassy staff. The routine of actual press contacts and supplying of information were handled by his assistant who was not KGB.

It was just after 4 p.m. when he got the call from Komsky.

'Yuri. We've got a dangler.'

'What kind?'

'American. Middle-aged. Says he's CIA.'

'Where is he?'

'In the reception hall.'

'Put him in the annexe and I'll look him over.'

The annex was a small room full of concealed mikes and a wide-angle video camera concealed in the ornate central chandelier. Volkov stood at the spy-hole looking at the man. The dangler. The name all intelligence agencies gave to people who walked into embassies or offices and offered their services as informants or agents. The man he watched was seemingly at ease, with no indications of nervousness. That was a bad sign. Bogdanov was going to deal with him and see what it was all about. It was routine procedure to treat all danglers as plants, but Moscow had made clear that they were very interested in getting a mole established in the CIA or the FBI.

Chapter 2

Art Jarvis stood looking in the mirror at his face. Dulcie had sometimes called him 'rat-face' when she was in one of her tantrums. Poking fun at the glasses that gave him an owl-like look and the carefully clipped moustache that he felt gave his nondescript face a touch of character. He and Dulcie had had a twelve-year childless marriage. She too had been part-time employed by the CIA. But the short spell that he had spent in Mexico City had solved that problem. It was in Mexico City that he met a Colombian woman – Maria dos Santos. They would marry as soon as his divorce was final. He moved away from the mirror and looked out of the window at the dreary landscape of houses and apartment blocks that was Falls Church, Virginia. He had no choice. He had to do something fundamental about his life. Living in a one-bedroom apartment was not Maria's idea of how life should be lived. It wasn't his either, but the divorce settlement had been devastating. 300 dollars a month for the next four years, 33,500 dollars to pay off their outstanding debts. All out of a salary of 60,000 dollars a year at the CIA. No house, still paying off the car and he and Maria had already accumulated thousands of dollars in bills. He wanted out from this life. He needed fate to wave its magic wand and fate had never waved much in his direction. But at last he knew exactly how to get what he wanted. His meeting with Bogdanov at the Mayflower Hotel would be the start of the new life.

By lunch time, in his office at Langley, Art Jarvis had convinced himself that he was capable of deceiving both the CIA and the KGB. Two KGB men had recently approached the CIA offering to work for the agency. The agency had immediately classified them as 'plants' by the KGB. But they could be his passport into the KGB. Revealing them to the KGB would be doing no harm to anyone. The KGB

7

already knew they were 'plants'. They had 'planted' them themselves. But it would show that he was offering real information that they knew was true. That would be his entrance fee into the KGB.

The meeting with Bogdanov was arranged for 4 p.m. that afternoon and he left Langley an hour early and after parking his car at a garage he had a couple of drinks at a bar to boost his courage.

At the Mayflower Hotel's bar he had waited until 5 p.m., sustained by a couple of vodkas, and half angry and half despondent he finally decided to go ahead by the direct route. To the Soviet Embassy itself.

Several FBI agents who continuously monitored the comings and goings at the embassy saw him enter the ornate doorway and go into the reception hall. None of the FBI men recognised him.

Inside the embassy he gave a sealed package to the duty officer at the reception desk. It was addressed to Bogdanov and contained three documents. The first was a report on the two KGB officers who had offered their services to the CIA. The second document was a photocopy from the personnel directory of the Soviet division at the CIA. His own name and status as 'chief, counter-intelligence branch' was highlighted. The third document was a request for 50,000 dollars. He left immediately after he had handed over the package.

As he crossed Sixteenth Street to get back to the garage he looked at his digital watch. It was 5.25 p.m. and the date was 16 April 1985.

It had been nearly three weeks before he was contacted again by the KGB and it was 15 May 1985 when he visited the embassy for the second time.

He was shown into an annexe and after a five-minute wait a man came into the room. He put his fingers to his lips and handed him a note. The note said that they agreed and that the man with him would be his controller. They would contact him the following day to arrange a meeting. His controller would be a senior KGB officer named Volkov. Yuri Volkov.

Chapter 3

They had met as arranged in the Club Car lounge at the Howard Johnson's Motor Lodge and then moved to the hotel's Lamplighter Room. As they ate they exchanged gossip about people they knew in the intelligence agencies. Volkov was surprised at the knowledge his contact had of KGB men in New York and Moscow as well as those in Washington. They agreed a meeting place in two weeks' time and they discussed in detail their means of communication. The Russians were obviously wedded to their traditional trade-craft of chalk marks on fences, derelict buildings, toilets and brick walls. Volkov had already checked out suitable sites and provided a list with black and white photographs and a variety of recognition signals and acknowledgments of receipt of information. They had agreed that their code-names would be BELL for the American and Volkov's code-name would be THRUSH. Just before they left Volkov passed over a cigar box with its Cuban seal intact.

Volkov took a taxi back down-town and Jarvis had driven to his apartment. When he opened the cigar box he carefully counted out the money. There were five hundred 100-dollar bills. Fifty thousand dollars. They'd paid what he asked for. The plan had worked. So simple and yet so effective. He'd say nothing to Maria about it and put it into a separate account. Suddenly the dark clouds hanging over him had cleared and at last the sun was shining. Arthur Jarvis went to bed that night a happy man.

It was 3 a.m. when he woke and reached for the bedside lamp to look at his watch. He rubbed his face and swung his legs out of the bed and stood up slowly. There was something wrong. Something to be worried about. Something different. And then he remembered Volkov and the money. And as he walked slowly into the kitchen he said in a whisper, 'For Christ's sake. What have I done?' And suddenly the significance of what he had done made him close his eyes, his hand reaching out to the refrigerator door to steady himself. He'd gone over that line that marked the difference between foolishness and treason. He'd done it deliberately, but what scared him was the realisation that there was no going back. He'd done it. He'd taken their money and they had him now. He took a deep breath, opened the refrigerator door and took out the pack of milk and poured out half a glass and pulled up a chair to the kitchen table. He could keep it under control. He was smarter than both agencies. He saw their stupidities every day. He was swilling out the glass at the sink when the real blow fell. The CIA moles. KGB and GRU men who were working for the CIA. There were at least a dozen of them and they were bound to hear the news, the rumours, the hints that a top CIA man was doing a double-cross with the Soviets. No matter how tight the security one of them could pick up his name and pass it around. And that would be it. Finish, kaput. He knew from experience how the word would have got around in the CIA if it had been the other way round. When James Angleton had been the Director of the CIA he had been paranoid about his theory that there was a KGB mole inside the CIA.

The more he thought about it the more obvious the solution appeared. He must get those CIA moles exposed and dealt with immediately. Volkov would be staggered by the names and his own standing with the Russians would be rock-solid. He looked at his watch. It was 4 a.m. He dressed, left a note for the sleeping Maria and drove to Langley.

Volkov had a new office. A suite in fact. A fair-sized room with a table and chairs for meetings, a smaller, private room with armchairs, a small refrigerator, bookshelves and an ICOM R9000 multi-band radio with an aerial off the main feed. The third room was an office with computer, modem, three phones, one of them internal and the red one with a high-grade scrambler, a metal desk and folding chair for an assistant.

He sat at the table in the meeting room with the report on Arthur Jarvis, material that had been thrown up from surfing through Moscow's database on CIA personnel. Most of it appeared to be no more than gossip but the KGB were as keen on gossip as the

National Enquirer. Experience told them that gossip was a good source of information if the reader or analyst knew the background well enough.

The full name was Arthur Casey Jarvis. Born June 1942, the son of a CIA man, he had worked for the CIA all his life. He had been some sort of clerk when he joined in 1957 but after ten years in one job or another Arthur Jarvis had become a fully-fledged spy in the service of his country. He had been posted to Ankara, Mexico City and New York in counter-intelligence sections, but both the local and Moscow KGB reports had merely registered his existence. The official analysis pointed out that his lack of impact in the agency was mirrored by the fact that the CIA itself had been going through a bad patch during those years. With Directors of widely different attitudes appointed, the agency had suffered disorganisation and low morale. The main area to suffer was counter-intelligence and it had become a dumping ground for misfits and those who were reckoned to not have what it takes to make it in the world of actual intelligence. In the fall of 1983 Jarvis had been appointed as head of counter-intelligence in the CIA's Soviet division. There were no reports in the KGB files of anything more than his various appointments. He was not reckoned to be of any real danger or significance to KGB operations in the USA. The only personal items were that he had an unhappy marriage and a serious drinking problem. A hand-written note claimed that Jarvis spoke some Russian.

The only up-to-date item was a grainy black and white photograph of the building that housed Jarvis's rented apartment in Falls Church, Arlington.

There was a separate sheet with a single paragraph about a woman who had been seen with Jarvis, named Maria, which also recorded that the KGB office in Mexico City was sure that she did part-time work for the local CIA group.

Volkov pushed the report to one side and lit a cigarette. He hadn't found Jarvis an easy man to deal with. Volkov was used to more sophisticated Americans, people who could talk and argue. Nevertheless the wretched man had delivered the goods. The information had been of no positive use to them but at least it had established the man's knowledge of what went on in the CIA and the potential value of other things he could tell them. Fifty thousand bucks was way over the top but Moscow had seemed desperate to recruit a potential mole in the CIA.

The other thing that he needed to find out was Jarvis's motivation. He was almost certain that it was solely money. Jarvis had shown no interest in anything ideological. It would be interesting to see how long it would be before Jarvis came back for more.

He reached across for the personal letters that had come from the diplomatic bag. One was from his mother. She was a doctor specialising in what people referred to as 'women's problems'. His father had been an administrator with the Bolshoi ballet company for some years but was now a well-established film director specialising in historical romances which left him free of the hazards of whatever was the current political correctness. With his father frequently away on location and his mother occupied at the hospital, the marriage was successful by virtue of its lack of domesticity. Neither of them had commented on his choice of career but his mother still referred to the KGB as the Cheka, the name of its terrifying predecessor. He guessed that the snub was intentional. The family home was an apartment over an art shop in the Arbat and despite the cracks about the Cheka his mother knew that without the influence of her son they would never have got such a large, central apartment. She was diffidently reminding him in her note that their residency would need renewed approval in a few months' time. He made a note to get his secretary to phone the ministry in Moscow direct.

The second letter was confirmation from Personnel at Dzherdzinski Square of his promotion and the last one was a hand-written note from Fomenko, instructing him to report to him directly on his handling of their new recruit. It confirmed that there was no limit to payment if the man produced what they wanted. Volkov's reports to Ambassador Komsky should be diplomatic but uninformative. This was a Moscow operation and Komsky had been notified of its top-secret status.

By the time Arthur Jarvis had driven to Langley and made his way up to his office, the edge had gone off his panic and he cleared his desk carefully to accommodate the files. He decided to limit his first revelations to only two of the KGB's defectors. Oleg Gordievsky working for SIS in London and Sergei Bokhan in Athens, who was GRU not KGB. His package included a variety of documents, some were copies but many were originals. They were all top secret. At lunch-time he put a mark on the mail-box at the corner of R Street and Thirty-Seventh and then drove to a stone bridge off the Little Falls Parkway leaving the package in an empty packet of Kellogg's All Bran covered with a stone and a few twigs. He drove back to his office and three hours later he checked the mail-box and saw that the check-mark had been removed, and when he was almost home he drove slowly by the row of small garages and saw that the door of the second garage was half-open. They had already picked up the package.

There was a routine prearranged meeting with Volkov at a coffee shop near the National Theatre three days later and Volkov was obviously pleased with what was in the package.

'Tell me something, Art. Why are you helping us? You don't strike me as a convinced Marxist.'

Jarvis smiled. 'Let me ask you a question that answers your question.'

Volkov shrugged. 'OK. Go ahead.'

'Have you got a package for me?'

'Yeah.'

'How much is in it?'

'A hundred grand in bills.'

'I've got another nine or ten names with documentation if you're interested.'

'We're interested, Art. All the way.'

'I need money, old pal. A lot of money. And I need it soon.'

'Have you got a problem, Art? Maybe we could help.'

Jarvis laughed. 'I just need the cash. I got commitments.' Then his face was solemn. 'Say three times today's packet. How would that be?'

'No problem.'

'How long after I pass you the documents?'

'Four, five days. Just enough time to make a rough assessment. Not longer.'

'How about we meet here in two weeks' time? Same day, same time?'

'Let's make it same day, same time but at the Hampshire. In the bar.'

'OK by me.'

'The brief-case is by the leg of my chair. You take it and leave. I'll settle the bill.'

Volkov sat and drank another coffee before he left. Jarvis had obviously been drinking before they met and that could be a problem. Drinking because you liked the booze was one thing, drinking because you were under stress was dangerous.

Gordievsky in London and Bokhan in Athens were both ordered back to Moscow for urgent meetings. Bokhan didn't go back and was believed to have taken a flight to Nairobi. Gordievsky went back and was arrested and interrogated for several days. He managed to get news to his British intelligence controllers who smuggled him out of the Soviet Union via Finland in the boot of a car.

Jarvis used three discarded plastic bags with Safeways logos to hold the thick batches of documents. Again many of them were originals rather than copies and he had difficulty in getting the plastic bags into his brief-case. The CIA had stopped searching employees several years earlier when some barrack-room lawyer had claimed that searches were an infringement of individual rights, and the top brass had gone for peace at any price. So he walked with his precious load to the carpark, with no expectation of being stopped and searched. It was incredible that the agency responsible for the security of the United States could be so naif and irresponsible.

When he handed over the plastic bags to Volkov in the wash-room of the Hampshire Hotel he was sure that he was from then on part of the KGB rather than the CIA. And for the first time in his life Arthur Jarvis felt that at last he was being fully respected and valued.

Even without knowing what was in the plastic bags Volkov knew instinctively that he was handling and controlling the most valuable asset the KGB had ever had.

Fomenko was sitting in the VIP section at the Moscow Dynamo ground. Moscow Dynamo, both the team and the grounds, had always been owned by the KGB and Fomenko was watching a night game. A 'friendly' international between Russia and Georgia. He was annoyed as his assistant shuffled past the others and bent to whisper in his ear.

'What is it, Josef? Can't I even watch a bloody football match in peace?'

'There was a package for you in the Washington diplomatic bag. Jaworski had a look at the contents. He says it's so good you won't believe it until you see it. He says it can't wait.'

Fomenko cursed softly as he eased himself upright and nodded to people he knew as he made his way along the row of seats and out of the stand, down the concrete stairway to where a car was waiting for him.

It was late Spring and there was still snow piled up in the gutters but Fomenko had been born and brought up in Novosobirsk, the capital of Siberia, and he was barely aware of snow and cold. He wondered what was in the stuff from Washington. He hadn't met the man but his instinct and experience told him that Volkov's new man was going to be a winner.

It was 6 a.m. when Fomenko drank his last cup of coffee and waited until the signals section confirmed that his orders and comments had been received in Washington. It was two closely-typed pages but when it had been encoded and they used the fast transmission tapes, the whole lot only took four seconds on air.

The stuff from Volkov was incredible. Actual original reports and operational details, copies of signals and evaluations of results and methods of operation of eight men. Eight traitors. Six in the KGB and two with military intelligence, the GRU. No doubt about any of it. Barely any need to interrogate the bastards. The men stationed in Moscow were already under arrest and he had sent trusted operators to bring back Smetanin from Lisbon and Varennik from Vienna. There were two others whom he would leave in place until the dust had settled from the first arrests. They were too near to the Washington operation to deal with now. But they could stew.

It was getting light when he was driven through the Moscow streets to his apartment behind the Manege Museum. By the end of the week all but two of the CIA's moles exposed in Volkov's material had been executed in the cellars of the Lubyanka, the KGB's own prison that had once been the head office of an insurance company.

Fomenko's quick reaction and retribution on the traitors was understandable but ill-thought out. It was bad trade-craft. It could give a signal to watchers on the other side. A bad decision was made worse when Fomenko's most senior assistant misunderstood Fomenko's restriction on dealing with the two KGB traitors in the USA. This meant that Sergei Motorin at the Washington Embassy never got the hi-fi set-up that was to be part of his reward, and Boris Yuzhin, a KGB colonel whose cover was as a journalist in San Francisco, was lured to Moscow and spent five years in a Gulag camp near Arkangelsk.

Chapter 4

Walker picked up the phone and pressed the security button.

'Yeah.'

'Billy, I think you'd better come over and have a look at one of the airport videos with us.'

'Is it urgent?'

'I'm not sure. I think so.'

'OK. I'll come over.'

Walker closed and locked his safe and looked around the room. There was a drive on personal security at the moment. As he walked along the corridor he wondered what they'd got. It could only be an Aeroflot flight for them to draw him in. All passengers on Aeroflot flights and landings were covertly videoed and where possible identified from the passenger manifest. Collins did the job very thoroughly but had a tendency to zoom in on pretty girls with big boobs. He claimed it was one of the perks of the job.

The lights were on in the small projection room and Collins was checking the connection from the camera to the TV. When he saw Walker he pointed to one of the empty chairs.

'What have you got this time?'

Collins frowned. 'There's a guy I've got down as notifiable to you. A guy from the Soviet Embassy named Motorin. I've checked his file and he's listed as a Special.'

'What flight is he on?'

'It was the evening Aeroflot flight to Moscow.'

'Does it stop at Shannon?'

'Yeah, but only for refuelling.'

'So what's the problem?'

'He's with another guy from their embassy and it looks to me as if the Motorin guy is being hijacked.'

Walker said quietly. 'OK. Run it through.'

When the lights went down the video came up. The first shots were of passengers checking-in at the desk and then seated passengers in the flight-call waiting area. A different camera came on covering the Aeroflot VIP lounge. Finally continuous shots of the passengers handing over boarding-cards and entering the access tunnel to the plane. Sergei Motorin was in all the sequences and looked as if he had been drugged. Walker didn't recognise the man with him but he was built like the proverbial out-house and he stayed close to Motorin all the time. There was no doubt that Motorin was under close escort. He even gave one brief despairing look over his shoulder before his companion hustled him into the tunnel.

Motorin had been supplying Walker with information for about four months. Mainly technical stuff on new tank designs. They had obviously rumbled him, and Walker had no doubts about what the Russian's fate would be when he got to Moscow. Arrested at Sheremetyevo and a car to Dzherdzinski Square. Four days of rough stuff and then the chop. He'd need to let Getz and the others know what was going on. Getz might want to have a brain-storming session on where Motorin's security had broken down.

When Moscow Dynamo lost, Fomenko would dismiss any criticism on the grounds that they just didn't get the run of the ball, and although it didn't seem like it, the ball didn't run for Fomenko himself ten days after he got the package from Volkov.

Just after dark three men seized a man who was loitering in a Moscow park. His name was Paul Stombaugh, he was an American and a CIA agent who had been waiting for his asset, a top Soviet scientist, to meet him in the park. The CIA unit at the US Embassy heard the news on the grapevine an hour after Stombaugh was thrown into the Lubyanka. For the CIA it was a disaster, and when the coded message was passed to Langley everyone went on high alert.

The information that led to Stombaugh's arrest had not come from Arthur Jarvis's material but the loss of two informants in a couple of weeks had made the protagonists of 'the KGB mole inside the CIA' theory win the day at the rather scrappy meeting that had been cobbled together to consider the situation.

*   *   *

Larry Getz was looking for a copy of *The Catcher in the Rye* at Crown Books' place on K Street when his pager blipped. Friends kept telling him he ought to have read it years ago. He looked at the digital display and said 'Shit' but not out loud. He walked back to the street and dialled the number on his mobile. It was the DO's direct line, and it was O'Hara himself who answered.

'Yeah.'

'Larry Getz, sir. You paged me.'

'Where are you?'

'Downtown. K Street.'

'I wanna talk with you. Let's make it about 5 p.m. In my office. OK?'

'I'll be there, sir.'

O'Hara, Director of Operations, looked like someone put up by Central Casting to play the part of the white-haired sheriff who drove the villains out of town. Rumour had it that he was one of Ronald Reagan's buddies when the President was active in union politics and O'Hara was at the FBI's Los Angeles office.

He waved Getz to one of the visitors' chairs in front of his desk.

'What are you dealing with at the moment, Larry?'

'I've almost completed a survey of our security – physical, telephonic, documentary and communications in general.'

'What's it look like?'

Getz shuffled and hesitated and O'Hara said, 'Don't edit for me. I want the truth.'

Getz shrugged. 'It's a miracle we survive. There's not a single area in which our security is even adequate. We leak like a sieve all over the place.'

'Where do you put the blame?'

'All over, but especially at the top. Morale is bad, even among the old hands.'

'Why?'

'No clear policy, policy changes that throw the whole machine into confusion.' He shrugged. 'Conflicting orders. A classic case of too many cooks.' He paused. 'And of course the constant rumour that there's a Soviet "mole" right here in Langley.'

'Are you making any recommendations?'

'No. That's not in my brief.'

'Are you quoting examples and naming names?'

'Examples, yes. Names, no.'

'What about the Congressional Intelligence Committee?'

'Nothing to complain of there. It's just that their quite sensible recommendations don't get carried out. The faults are inside here, sir. And widespread.'

O'Hara sighed, and nodded, pausing before he said, 'I want you to take on a new job.' He smiled wryly. 'It doesn't even have a job title but the specification is quite clear.' He paused. 'As you've said there have always been voices, quite influential voices, claiming that there must be a KGB mole somewhere in the agency.' He shrugged. 'I can't believe it but I'm not going to ignore it.' He looked at Getz. 'Forget everything else. Just find me that mole. Take as long as you need. There's no sweat. But if there is a mole I want that asshole skinned alive. You understand?'

'Yes, sir.'

'If anybody gets in your way, tell me. If there are resources you need, tell me and you'll get them.'

'When do you want me to start?'

'You've started.'

O'Hara stood up and walked round his desk. 'You know we just lost two of our Soviet assets?'

'I heard rumours.'

'Well it's a fact.' He smiled. 'But we'll stop the bastards one way or another.'

'Where shall I work from?'

'See Facilities and pick whatever facilities you want. But don't hang around.' He held up two crossed fingers. 'We need some luck. Not much. Just enough.'

O'Hara's luck was at that very moment making his way cautiously through the crowded streets of Rome to the capital's main railway station, Stazione Termini, hoping to lose any pursuers in the throng of early-morning travellers. Another half-mile and he would be safe. The half-mile stroll took him to the Ambasciatore Palace Hotel on the Via Veneto. In the hotel lobby he dialled the number of the US Embassy which was directly across the street from the hotel. The man was Vitaly Yurchenko, recently promoted to deputy chief of the First Department of the First Chief Directorate of the KGB, and in charge of all operations against the United States and Canada. He spoke passable English and looked more American than Russian.

As always with a potential defector the CIA man who interviewed him at the embassy asked him right away if he knew of any KGB penetration of the CIA. When Yurchenko said yes, a call went through within minutes to Langley. He said he also knew of an informant inside the NSA, the US radio and telephone monitoring agency.

The Rome report was read over to O'Hara who issued orders for Yurchenko to be flown over to the States by the US Air Force via Naples and Frankfurt to Andrews Air Force Base near Washington. O'Hara decided to stick to the rules and notify the FBI, and then wondered who should handle the Russian for the debriefing. He chose Arthur Jarvis because he spoke some Russian and ordered him to meet Yurchenko at Andrews Base and take him over.

Jarvis was horrified when he got the news of a top KGB officer defecting and apparently ready to talk about a KGB mole inside the CIA. He tried not to envisage the scene at Andrews with the Russian pointing him out as Moscow's mole in the CIA. With his high position in the KGB Yurchenko could well have been told in confidence of the CIA man who was feeding them information by the bagful. Arthur Jarvis took his usual route to oblivion and went to bed so drunk that he nearly missed the alarm-call the next morning for his drive to Andrews Air Base.

As he drove to Andrews, Arthur Jarvis wondered why he had been chosen to debrief Yurchenko. A few days ago the divorce from Dulcie had come through from New York and in just over a week he would marry his new love, Maria. And already he had stashed away nearly 200,000 dollars. Was it all going to end just because some KGB idiot had decided to defect? Just for a moment Jarvis wondered if it could possibly be Moscow deliberately throwing him away because they'd got all they wanted from him. But it didn't fit. They were constantly pressing for more. Anything, however routine or trivial. And Yurchenko was too important for the Russians to put him at risk as part of a game. Yurchenko was, after all, in charge of all KGB espionage in the USA and Canada.

There would be FBI men at the safe-house as observers, but he would be responsible for the debriefing. He would need to arrange some free time for himself so that he could keep regular contact with Yuri Volkov.

The plane from Frankfurt was a little behind schedule and as Yurchenko walked unsteadily down the passenger steps he looked tired and jet-lagged.

Jarvis walked forward and they shook hands, Jarvis greeting the KGB man in rough but fluent Russian with the Russian responding in good English.

They left in a convoy of four cars, a lead and a tail car for security, then Yurchenko and Jarvis in the second car and three others in the third car. As the convoy threaded its way through the traffic, on the Capital Beltway, Jarvis swung between calm and cold fear as the Russian sat silently beside him. He could not say anything aloud or the driver might understand it, so he pulled out his notebook and wrote out a message in Russian and handed it surreptitiously to Yurchenko. The note said, 'If you have any information that you would like to tell only to the director of Central Intelligence, or some other senior US government official, tell me, and I'll take you to him'. When the Russian passed back the note he shrugged and shook his head as if he didn't understand what it was all about, and Jarvis almost wept with relief.

The safe-house was a suburban town house – 2709 Shanon Leigh Drive in Vienna, Virginia, about twenty minutes drive from CIA HQ at Langley. Oddly enough it was never CIA policy to provide any touch of luxury for a potential defector until he had been debriefed for several weeks. And the house in Vienna was furnished only to meet the practicalities of long hours of intense talking and questioning.

For three weeks Yurchenko followed the pattern of all defectors, talking incessantly about himself, about his humble parents and his struggle to improve his lot. He had married young, at barely eighteen years old, and the marriage had broken up in a matter of months.

Day after day Yurchenko and Jarvis sat at the small table with a tape-recorder between them, grinding away hour after hour of details of the inner workings of the KBG and its operations in Canada and the USA. Jarvis took a few hours away from the debriefing in the second week to get married at a modest ceremony with only immediate relatives of both parties attending, at a small Unitarian church. A compromise between Maria's Roman Catholicism and Jarvis's atheism. For Jarvis a snatched meeting with Yuri Volkov was even more vital than the marriage. They met at a gas station not far from the church. Jarvis was on edge again and Volkov could smell the beer on his breath as Jarvis said, 'You know about Yurchenko defecting in Rome, don't you?'

'I read the report. Is he here yet?'

'Yes.' He sighed. 'And I'm debriefing him. I'm his handler.'

'You're kidding.'

'I'm not and I need to know a couple of things.'

'Like what?'

'Is he genuine or a plant from Moscow?'

'The way our friends in Moscow are panicking I'd say he's genuine. Can't you tell from what he's telling you?'

Jarvis shrugged. 'That could be rehearsed.'

'What's the other thing you want to know?'

'Does he know about me?'

'There are only four people who know about you. And two of them only know you by your code-name. He couldn't possibly know about you.'

'You're sure of that?'

'Yes. Quite sure.'

'Will you check?'

'Yes. But I know the situation. We aren't going to risk compromising our most valuable CIA asset.'

'What about administration? People who file documents and pay my money . . . people like them.'

'Your documents are treated on an "Eyes Only" basis and not connected with their source. And Fomenko himself draws your money and it comes over double sealed in the diplomatic bag addressed to me. I keep no records of any kind.'

'I can't get away for long from the safe-house but I need to contact you. I can tell you what he's telling us and you can analyse it for me. How do we keep contact?'

'There's a small bookshop on Prospect Street in Georgetown. Near the ministry. It's called Kay's Bookshop. An old guy runs it. He's there all the time – lives there.' Volkov closed his eyes for a few moments, thinking, and then said, 'Ask him for a first edition of *Gone with the Wind*. He'll ask you your name. You say you're Max. If he's got anything from me to you he'll hand it over and if you've got material for me you just say it's for Max and hand it over.' He paused. 'You got that?'

Jarvis nodded. 'Yeah. I'll have to go.' He paused as he turned to leave. 'Does the guy at the bookshop already know of this arrangement?'

'No. But he will in about an hour's time.'

Jarvis was satisfied as he drove away that he had nothing to fear from Yurchenko. He was tempted to go for a drink to celebrate but decided against it. By the time Jarvis got back to the safe-house his elation had gone. There was a question he needed to have answered and only Yurchenko could supply the answer. But he couldn't ask him that question. The question was simple enough. If Yurchenko was in charge of all KGB operations in the US and Canada, why *didn't* he know about him. Maybe what Volkov had said about the tight security of the operation in Moscow was the answer but it seemed odd that the man in charge of all US operations of the KGB was not kept informed.

Day after day sheets of questions from the assessment team at Langley arrived at the safe-house for the day's session, and thousands of details were being compiled and compared. And as the days went by Yurchenko gave more, and finally he revealed the information about two Americans who were working for the KGB. They were only known by code-names but eventually one of them, already under suspicion, was identified in a matter of hours but escaped to Austria the day before he was due to be arrested. Jarvis had kept Yuri Volkov as well informed as he could of the debriefing sessions. The KGB were as well informed about the debriefings in the safe-house as the CIA themselves.

In their handling of Soviet defectors the CIA, including Jarvis, seemed unaware of the stresses and strains on a man who had just left his country, his background and security, and sometimes his family too. Getting information and providing tight security were what mattered for Langley. There was little appreciation of human factors. To them both sides were professionals, getting on with the job. In Jarvis's case he was never able to establish a real understanding with people, neither with his colleagues in the CIA nor those in foreign intelligence circles with whom he had contact as part of his job.

Arthur Jarvis was a man of moods. Moods that were affected by incipient alcoholism and self-interest. He was not touched by humanity and the human condition. Yurchenko was a professional problem not another man, a man who had a life and emotions beyond a CIA safe-house. He had mentioned many times his unhappy marriages and Jarvis had crassly interpreted this as a request for sex and had been surprised at the Russian's angry refusal of a session with one of the girls on the CIA's facilities' list. But out of this misunderstanding there came a request to be allowed to visit a Russian woman, Valentina Yereskovsky, a very attractive Russian doctor married to a Soviet diplomat in Montreal. He had known her some years back and was in love with her. He wanted her to leave her husband and join him in his new life with the CIA.

Some routine checking confirmed that there had been some relationship in the past that was construed as romantic but platonic.

A CIA officer and two CIA security guards flew Yurchenko to Plattsburgh, New York, and drove to the border where the Canadians took over. Valentina Yereskovsky lived with her husband in an apartment building in Montreal and the Canadians had kept her and her husband under surveillance to establish when he was likely to be away from the apartment. When her husband was known to be attending a luncheon engagement, Yurchenko phoned her from a call-box in sight of the apartment. She hung up on him but he persuaded the Canadians to take him up to the apartment. She didn't want to see him but reluctantly allowed him in for a few minutes. She was obviously disturbed by the meeting but flatly refused his suggestion of any further relationship. Yurchenko was obviously distressed when he came out of the apartment. None of his CIA handlers had shown any real sympathy for him. So far as they were concerned the whole thing was crazy, and a sign of Yurchenko's weak character.

Back in Washington Yurchenko was angry to read in the newspapers that his defection had been leaked to the press along with a number of his revelations about the KGB. Top brass somewhere in the CIA were boasting openly of their successful operation. There were equally counter-attacks in the media from cynics in the intelligence services who claimed that Yurchenko was obviously a 'plant', a double-agent.

In the next two weeks the atmosphere of the debriefing was relaxed and Yurchenko was left at weekends in the charge of a young and not very experienced CIA guard. He was allowed to go out with him on shopping trips to local department stores in nearby Manassa. On one of their Saturday trips Yurchenko casually suggested that they should have dinner in Georgetown. They had dinner together at *Au Pied de Cochon*. The dinner seemed to cheer up the Russian. While his CIA minder was settling the bill, Yurchenko strolled out of the restaurant and hailed a taxi which took him to the Russian compound on Wisconsin Avenue. It was less than a mile from the restaurant.

Two days later, at the Russian compound, Yurchenko was presented to the media at a press conference. He spoke in English and then in Russian. Describing how he had been drugged and kidnapped in Rome by the CIA. He claimed that the things that he had been reported as telling the CIA were fabrications that he knew nothing about, apart from reading them in the newspapers. The reports of the press conference all emphasised that the Russian appeared to be in a highly nervous state, talking volubly until his KGB minders shut him up. Some people suggested that he appeared to be high on drugs. But intelligence professionals reckoned that the Russian's hyperactive and nervous state was a strong indication that he had been a genuine defector who for some reason had decided to head back home and face the music. There were hints that maybe a deal had been done between the KGB and the CIA.

Three months after he had arrived at Andrews Air Force Base, Yurchenko boarded an Aeroflot jet at Dulles Airport accompanied by Lt.-Col. Valery Martynov, who specialised in collecting scientific and technical information for the KGB in Washington. Martynov seemed, to people in the business, to be a strange selection as Yurchenko's guard. Arthur Jarvis was the only American who knew why he had been chosen. Jarvis had given his name as a CIA collaborator to Volkov several months earlier. The colonel was on his way to the Lubyanka prison and execution but didn't yet know it.

Chapter 5

Way back before his contacts with the Russians, Jarvis had applied
for the post of the Soviet slot in the US embassy in Rome and shortly
after Yurchenko's departure for Moscow Jarvis's Rome posting came
through.

Before he left for Rome he had to attend language classes and
undergo a polygraph test. Yuri Volkov saw it as an opportunity for
a visit to Fomenko to lodge some complaints. They were neither of
them looking forward to the next few weeks. Jarvis was scared of the
polygraph test and Volkov was angry about Fomenko's handling of
the Moscow end of the operation.

Volkov landed at Sheremetyevo in the early hours of the morning.
Strong head-winds had held up the plane's arrival. And to boost his
flow of adrenalin Fomenko had sent only an assistant to meet him in.
To add to his bad temper the duty KGB security officer had queried
his ID card and insisted on phoning the KGB's new HQ on the ring
road. It was two hours before the official car dropped him at the
installation at Yasenova. He was taken straight up to Fomenko's
suite of offices and Fomenko had been waiting for him, taking his
arm to lead him into his private rooms. When he was comfortably
seated in a black leather chair with a cup of coffee on a table beside
hm Fomenko sat down opposite him.

'You look full of complaints, my friend. Let's get them off your
chest before we get down to business.'

Volkov shrugged, impatiently. 'I was shocked when I heard that
eight of the moles that Jarvis gave to us had been arrested and
executed in a matter of weeks.' He shook his head. 'That could
have given the clearest possible sign to the CIA that we had
a mole inside Langley. When the penny drops they're going to

spend a lot of time and money trying to find out who our mole is.'

'Go on.'

Volkov shrugged. 'That's it. To me it was reckless and impetuous. It's bad enough operating against the CIA but to have them alerted by my own people seems crazy.'

Fomenko sat in silence, his face, as always, revealing neither pleasure nor displeasure. Then he said, 'Seems to me you're jumping to conclusions, my friend.'

'No way. It happened. It's fact.' Volkov was almost shouting at his superior.

'Would you like to say your piece to the man who gave the orders?'

'I assume I'm talking to him now.'

'Like I said – jumping to conclusions. I certainly didn't give the orders. I was heading that way but on reflection I decided against it. When others insisted I raised hell about it but I was overruled.'

'Who can overrule you on an operation like this?'

Fomenko shrugged. 'His name's Gorbachev.' He paused. 'He has given me everything I asked for on this operation and I've had to report to him myself every day. Even when there was nothing new to say. When your package came through with the details of the CIA moles he was beside himself with anger.' He paused and shrugged. 'Personally I don't blame him, but the action against those bastards was precipitous. I give you that.' He sighed. 'Do you think it *has* made Langley more suspicious?'

'I'm sure it has. They're stupid, but not that stupid. I daren't raise it with our man.'

'Gorbachev apologised to me later. He knew that he had done the wrong thing. We should have spread it over at least a year. But you have to remember that when you're President of the USSR these days you can't be sure you'll even be in the Kremlin in a year's time.' He paused again. 'Any more complaints?'

'No. I guess not.'

'This move of Jarvis to Rome, do you think they suspect him?'

'No. It's something he put in for before he came over to us.'

'You must be tired. I've booked you a suite at the National and you'll have a driver and car all the time you're here.' Fomenko stood up. 'I'll contact you this evening. There's a lot for us to go into.'

The car and driver were waiting for Volkov and there were no problems at the hotel. They had given him a double suite. The hotel was in walking distance of the Kremlin and not too far from Dzherdzinski Square. The rooms were well-furnished, old-fashioned but comfortable. Instinctively he looked in the obvious places for bugs but if there were any he didn't find them. There was a central fitting on a massive chandelier that could be the lens of a camera but it was too high for him to check.

After a couple of hours on the bed, he bathed and shaved and unpacked his two bags. Then he dialled Fomenko's private number. There was a message for him. Fomenko would eat with him in his suite at 8 p.m. The thought passed through his mind to phone his mother but he decided to leave it. He would be here for a few days. It could wait.

He went down to the bar and already the place was full of *novy russky* types, Russian yuppies complete with bleepers and cellular phones. He had a vodka standing at the bar and looking over the girls who were already hanging around, obviously on offer. And they weren't just the usual hustlers that haunted every hotel in Moscow. These girls were elegantly dressed and extremely attractive. He was approached by two of them and he bought them a drink. The dark girl was from Kiev and the other was local. They had marked him as an American and had been amazed when he responded in Russian. They were in their mid-twenties. One had qualified as a doctor and discovered that cleaning-women in hospitals earned more than she could. The other had been a budding film actress until she realised that working first-class hotel bars paid better than casting-couches. They pointed out for him some of the men in the bar who were leading lights in the Moscow Mafia. He identified at least a couple of genuine Armani suits worn by the men who apparently controlled Moscow crime.

He explained that he was expecting a friend and bought them another drink, paying the bill before he kissed their cheeks and said his goodbyes. He found it oddly refreshing to find elegant and really beautiful hookers flourishing in Moscow. It was all very American.

Slightly old-fashioned like the days of gangsters in black and white films, but somehow cheering all the same. Far from the days when you could get six months if some miserable cop caught you doing it in the back of a taxi parked down a back-alley.

In his sitting room he stood at the window looking out at the lights on Red Square and the floodlit Kremlin buildings with the big red star. There was a knock on the door and he walked over and opened it. Fomenko was giving instructions to a man who was obviously some sort of KGB guard. A chair had been provided so that the man could sit on guard in the corridor. Fomenko turned to Volkov. 'Just a routine precaution.'

Fomenko had already ordered their meal and a waiter brought in a trolley loaded with food and bottles, setting the table in the next room before leaving.

They ate their way through *Staromoskovsky* soup full of tender pieces of veal, chicken and pork, and moved on to Siberian *pelmeni*, meat-filled dumplings from Fomenko's birth-place. The pastries were French and the fruit was from Georgia.

When they finally got to the coffee, Fomenko said, 'Tell me about Jarvis.'

Volkov looked puzzled. 'But I've sent you written reports about him regularly.'

'I know. So tell me again. What sort of fellow is he? What's he really like, inside?'

'You've seen the photographs of him that I sent over?'

'Yes. He looks like a ticket collector on the railways. How the hell did he make it into the CIA?'

'I've no idea but it may be because his father got him in. His father was said to be a good CIA agent but that was in the Far East.'

'Do you have any doubts about the stuff he's sending us?'

'I don't have time to read it properly. I get it over to you immediately.' He shrugged. 'What I've seen looks the real thing to me.' He paused. 'Do you have any doubts?'

'I don't. But others do. When you get a defector there's always some who swear he's a plant.' He sighed. 'They don't know anything about the operation or about Jarvis but they criticise what he gives us.'

'On what grounds?'

'They say it's too good. That nobody could get that sort of stuff out of Langley without being discovered.' He shrugged. 'They say he's too good to be true.'

'And what do you think?'

'I'm sure it's genuine but I wonder why he does it. You tell me he's not interested in politics.'

'He does it for the money. No doubt about that. That's his only motive.'

'D'you talk to him about KGB matters?'

'No way. I feed him some low-grade gossip about unidentified people just to make him feel that he's part of the inner circle.'

For a few moments Fomenko was silent, then he looked across at Volkov and said, 'You realise you'll have to go with him to Rome.'

'Not at the embassy I hope.'

'Why not?'

'It's too small. I'd be under constant surveillance.'

'You don't need anything other than basic equipment, so rent yourself some rooms. Choose an apartment block, then he can meet you there.' He paused. 'I'll tell Admin and Supply to fund you for whatever you want.' He looked at Volkov intently. 'You seem bored with this operation. Are you?'

'He's a very boring man and I'm not much more than a delivery service.'

'Let me tell you something, my friend. What you are delivering is priceless. I've got thirty people analysing and recording everything. What you're getting from Jarvis is rather like having our own office in Langley. It's invaluable. We *know* what they're thinking. We *know* what they're planning.' He paused. 'Your work won't be so intensive in Rome but you're our link with the most valuable asset we've ever had. And don't you forget it, my boy. Philby and his pals are nothing compared with this guy.'

'You seem to be worried about something.'

'I am. Too true I am.'

'What?'

'I too find it hard to believe that the Americans are so stupid as to let our friend get away with this.' He paused. 'Can you imagine a top man in Dzherdzinski Square or at Yavenova just walking out with shopping bags crammed full of top secret documents?'

'Jarvis has always said that they're stupid. I've asked him point-blank and he shrugs and says the people at the top don't know what they're doing. They don't exchange information with one another and they see the FBI as more of an enemy than us.'

Fomenko nodded and stood up. 'I'll leave you to it, but remember – we want that pipeline into Langley open for as long as we can. He's not so bright himself. So don't let him take unnecessary risks.'

When Fomenko had left, Volkov checked his watch and dialled a couple of numbers. Both girl-friends from last year. There was no answer from the first number and he hung up when a man answered the phone at the second number. He went down to the bar and picked up the dark girl and took her to the new disco on Nevsky Prospect and then back to his room in the early hours of the morning.

Chapter 6

The man said, 'My name's Friedmann.' He pointed at the chair. 'Make yourself comfortable and take off your shirt.' As he waited he said, 'There's no record of you ever having taken a polygraph test before. Is that right?'

Jarvis nodded. 'Yeah. That's right.'

Friedmann pulled up a stool and sat alongside Jarvis as he talked.

'I'm sure you know that lay-people call this thing . . .' he pointed at the equipment on the trolley '. . . a lie-detector. And I'm sure that you know that it's no such thing. The polygraph is an imperfect machine. It does not detect lies. What it does do is measure physiological changes in breathing, blood pressure, heart-beat and sweat. The theory is that when people knowingly lie the stress will cause physiological changes that the machine can measure and indicate.' He paused and looked intently at Jarvis. 'You understand what I have said?'

Jarvis nodded. 'Yeah. I understand.'

'Right. Now before we get to the actual test I want to ask you a few questions. No machine. Just you answering some questions much like the questions I shall ask you in the actual test. OK?'

Jarvis shrugged. 'I guess so.'

For fifteen minutes the questions were routine. Name. Status. Background, etc. Then the questions moved to finances. He said that he had outside income claiming that the source was from his wife's mother in Colombia. In addition he claimed that he had made shrewd investments that were beginning to pay off handsomely. That was the end of the first session.

After the patches had been placed on Jarvis and the machine calibrated the second session started. The routine questions were put more slowly this time. But this time the questions about Jarvis's finances were more specific. Did he have any financial problems that he was concealing. Jarvis said 'no' and he was telling the truth. The KGB had solved all his financial problems. There were no other questions about his finances. But the final question was a new one. The first part asked if he was working for a foreign intelligence agency. And he said 'no'. There was no reaction on the polygraph. But the second part of the question asked if he was hiding any contacts with foreign nationals. The machine reacted immediately and when the operator treated the response seriously Jarvis explained that what had confused him was the fact that his mother-in-law, a foreign national and a wealthy woman, frequently made cash gifts to his wife.

The operator extended the test for another hour and noted that the polygraph responded whenever the subject of contacts with foreign nationals was touched on. The examiner broke off the test and asked Jarvis to come back in four days to complete it.

At the second session it was a different polygraph operator carrying out the test and Jarvis answered all the questions, including the one about contacts with foreign nationals, without the polygraph registering a response. The examiner signed the report to say that Jarvis had passed the test.

Chapter 7

They'd booked a window table at the Key Bridge Marriott and Tony Parsons looked at his guest as he looked through the menu. He and Larry Getz had been born and grew up in the same small town in Vermont. They had gone to high-school together and then Larry had done two years in the US Army in Vietnam. Before he'd been recruited to the CIA Getz had been a lawyer in the DA's office volunteering to handle most of their pro bono cases.

When they had given the waiter their orders, Parsons said, 'I always wanted to know why you gave up your law career. I know that pro bono cases never got anyone promotion but I'd always understood that you'd volunteered for it. Almost made it a condition of taking the job.'

Getz smiled. 'I found I wasn't as nice a guy as I thought I was.'

'What's that mean?'

Getz shrugged. 'I was sorry for all those people who were being done over by bureaucracy. Shoved into a ball-game where nobody had ever told them the ground rules.' He shrugged again. 'People who'd never had a chance. People who'd given up all hope of ever getting a square deal from anyone.' He smiled wryly. 'In the end I came to the conclusion that I wasn't good enough for them. Just the wrong sort of guy.'

'But everyone said you'd got a fantastic record with your cases.'

'Yeah. Maybe. But I fell out of love with them. I was on the side of the down-trodden in general, but when I came face to face with some of them I ended up thinking that at least half of them deserved what they got.'

'In what way?'

Getz shrugged. 'They were lazy. They didn't want work, they wanted hand-outs. They produced kids but didn't care about them.

They were born with chips on their shoulders. They were ruthless with other people and only shed tears for themselves. I began to see them not as victims but as predators.' He smiled wryly. 'So I called it a day.'

Parsons paused and then said, 'And how's it turned out in the CIA?'

'Suits me fine.' He laughed softly. 'I guess I'm an old China hand now.'

'How long have you been with them now?'

'Just over five years.'

'Is yours the James Bond bit or behind a desk?'

'A bit of both I guess.'

'Do you carry a gun?'

'I've got a licence to carry a weapon, yes.'

'Have you got one on you at the moment?'

Getz frowned and then half-smiled. 'What is this? Are you interrogating me?'

'In a way. Joan's lawyer is going to use your job as grounds for opposing access to Bobby.'

'Jesus. They ought to make it compulsory for potential new CIA employees to have a couple of hours with that woman before they sign up.'

'I'll give you a copy of their statement and it might be sensible to show it to one of your CIA attorneys.' He paused. 'I put it to them that you were willing to give her the house and support for Bobby and to split possessions down the middle.' He sighed. 'But they want to play games on that too.' He reached for his brief-case and took out a single sheet of paper, glancing at it before he spoke. Then, 'She wants the Technics hi-fi set-up.'

'I bought that before we were married for God's sake.'

'All the LPs, cassettes and CDs.' He looked across at Getz. 'She also wants the E-type Jag, the computer and your golf clubs.'

'What did you tell them?'

'Nothing. We don't have to respond at this stage.' He paused. 'As a matter of interest who are the insured drivers of the Jag?'

'Just me. They wouldn't extend it to her because of her bad claims record with cars.'

'Good. The sub-text to all this stuff is that they'll fight about access all the way if we don't go along with them, no matter what they demand.'

'So. What do I do?'

'Right now, nothing. Let her stew. It's being done as a threat. Just to rile you.'

'Are you sure?'

'Absolutely.'

'How do you know that?'

'In the statement I'll give you she claims that your job involves you in violence and that you are a violent man. A bad influence on a boy.' He paused. 'She adds for good measure that you're a drunk.'

'But I virtually don't touch alcohol. I never have. She knows that.'

'So do any people who know you. It's there to get you worked up. I don't think her lawyer likes it very much himself. He says he's just working to instructions.'

'How about access to Bobby meantime?'

'Once every two weeks. Saturdays. Nine to six. Pick up at her mother's place. Is that OK with you?'

'No. But I'll take it. Any more surprises?'

'No.' He paused. 'They're not surprises, Larry. She's a very embittered woman. In her eyes she gave you the choice between her and your job. And you chose the job.'

'She had all the standard chat from our personnel people about the disadvantages of the job before I signed on. No problem, she said. My country needs me.'

'Don't rise to the bait. I've had dozens like her in my time. The steam goes out of them if there's no response. Just ride the punches and no counter-punches. That drives 'em crazy.'

'Ah, well. Another lesson learned old pal.' He smiled. 'I've got a spare ticket for the Bullet's game on Saturday. You interested?'

'Yeah. Let's go together.' He smiled. 'Be like old times.'

Larry Getz had an apartment now that he lived alone, in one of the converted town-houses in Harbour Square. The prints in the living room were typical of the man. Reproductions of Norman Rockwell paintings and two or three Ansel Adams prints. The furniture came with the apartment and was modern, mainly polished teak and leather.

39

There were few personal possessions. A photograph in a frame of his son, a silver cigarette-lighter in the form of an eagle, and a Sony 2001 radio, a portable, permanently pre-set to a local FM classical music station.

He sat on the side of his bed and read the two pages that Parsons had given him. The claim made by his wife for the break-up of their marriage. It portrayed him as selfish, unloving, seldom at home, employed in an agency that fostered ruthlessness and violence, an uncaring father and a monstrous husband. He opened the cupboard by his bed and shoved the papers inside, and as he slowly closed it he realised that he was closing the drawer on his previous life as well. He lay back on the bed and closed his eyes, thinking about her.

They had known one another since high-school and when he came back from 'Nam she had been both proud of him and helpful, providing a down-to-earth balance to the things he didn't want to remember. They had married when he finished law school but she had been against him taking on the pro bono law cases. Saying quite rightly that it was a dead-end job. She had been right too and he'd never been able to bring himself to explain that it was a kind of expiation, a cleansing from what had gone on in Vietnam. It had neither logic nor sense but he knew he had to do it. When the CIA approached him he had already had enough and he leapt at the chance. And it awakened his enthusiasm so that he did well, with two speedy promotions and finally, his present job co-ordinating the agency's fight against the men in the Kremlin and particularly those in Dzherdzinski Square. Senior Agent in charge of co-ordinating counter-intelligence against the KGB and its operations in the USA. It had meant a lot of travel both in the States and overseas and it had no formal working hours, and all too often the demands of the job were, by normal standards, totally unreasonable. Especially for a married man. It was true that he saw very little of her and true that he found his job more absorbing than his domestic life. But she had the benefit of a nice home, his good salary and some special privileges. And he'd never gone in for other relationships. And it was she who had made it an issue. Her or the job. It was a stupid choice to confront any man with who was successful and satisfied in his work. And it was still she who had made the decision when he had said that he didn't accept such a choice. The note blu-tacked to the refrigerator door had been final and spiteful. He had done what she asked and moved out two days later. Sorry for her, understanding her feelings, but resenting the ultimatum. There were other solutions if she had really cared about him but maybe she was right and they *had* come to the end of the road. But when the chips were on the table he had to admit that *she* hadn't changed. She was still the girl from the small town in Vermont. It was he who had changed. Not intentionally. It had just happened.

Chapter 8

Larry Getz parked his rented car outside his mother-in-law's house in Foxhall Village, a twenty-minute drive from his own place in Georgetown. He had always got on well with Mary Curtis. White-haired and looking rather like Barbara Bush she had always been supportive and helpful in her advice when she was told about the impending divorce. She was close to her daughter but not uncritical of some of her attitudes to the marriage. She always made it pleasant and easy when he picked up his son every other Saturday.

She opened the front door of the house as he walked up the short path from the street, smiling as she said, 'He's just finishing an ice-cream. Come and have a coffee with us in the kitchen.'

'Thank you Nana. How are you?'

'I'm fine. A few aches and pains but nothing to complain about. He's looking forward to his trip with you to the science place.'

He closed the door behind him and followed her into the kitchen. Bobby looked over to him, smiling. 'Hi, dad. How're you doing?'

'I'm OK. And you?'

He beamed, showing the gap in his front teeth. 'I got two As. English and Math. But I flunked History.'

'Well done. Don't worry about History. Most of it's a pack of lies anyway.' He smiled. 'Sounds like next time we ought to take a trip up to Baltimore and see how the Orioles are making out.'

Mary Curtis kissed them both as they left. They did the ritual tours that fathers do with their kids on 'access' days. The Museum of Natural History and the National Air and Space Museum and had then gone back to his apartment in Georgetown to freshen up before going for a meal in a nearby restaurant he used regularly.

They had gone to his parked car to check that it was locked and as they were walking away a white MGB backed into his rental car

43

with the sound of crunching metal and breaking glass. A girl got out of the car and looked at the damage. The MGB had taken the brunt of the collision, smashed tail-lights, badly crumpled rear wing and a sprung boot-lid. He walked over to the girl. She was in her late twenties and very beautiful. Black hair and big dark eyes. She looked at him.

'I'm terribly sorry, the floor mat got pushed over the accelerator so when I pressed the brake it accelerated. I am properly insured.'

Getz smiled. 'My car's rented and insured and there's not much damage. But I'm afraid your MG is going to be very expensive. You'll need to have it towed to a garage. The rear wing is hard against the tyre.' Still smiling he said, 'We can just exchange details. No need to make a song and dance about it. OK?'

'Yes. Thanks for not getting angry.'

'Have you got a note-pad or something?'

'I don't think so. Have you?'

'No,' he laughed. 'By the way this is my son, Bobby, my place is just around the corner. We can do the formalities and you can phone from there. Where do you live?'

'1601 Fuller Street.'

Getz frowned. 'Why do I feel I know that number?'

'It's the Italian Embassy.' She shrugged, almost apologetically. 'My father is the ambassador.'

'That's it. A very pretty old building. Let's go and do our stuff.'

'Do I have to notify the police?'

'No. It's damage only. Have you got a diplomatic number plate?'

'Yes.'

'Then you're OK anyway.'

He left her using the telephone in the living room and made coffee for the two of them and opened a can of Diet-Coke out of the fridge for Bobby who was watching cartoons on the TV.

The embassy were going to take over recovering her car and were sending a car for her in twenty minutes. Her name was Gabriella. Gabriella del Rossi and she was divorced, twenty-eight and taught Italian at the Italian Institute.

When the embassy car came he accompanied her down to the car and then went back to play Scrabble for an hour with Bobby.

He was always conscious of how ineffective his time was with

Bobby. If he asked questions it could seem that he was checking on Joan. If he didn't ask it could seem that he was indifferent to what was going on. And the various museums were full of lone parents with their offspring on Saturdays and Sundays. Whatever you did you couldn't be right. You were suddenly a kind of domestic line-crosser, a defector. Trusted by nobody.

Two days later he received a charming hand-written letter from Ambassador del Rossi and an invitation for himself and partner to a cocktail party the following Saturday evening. It was an RSVP invitation and the following day he phoned the social secretary to accept.

Arthur Jarvis and Maria had been on the Rome posting for almost six months when he decided that he'd got a problem. A money problem. The kind of money problem that he'd never envisaged having. What to do with all the money? He had deposits in several countries and four or five deposits in Swiss banks. They lived a life of luxury with private trips to several European cities. It was a man at an embassy cocktail party who had made him realise that people were noticing his life-style.

The man wasn't CIA and he was only a junior on the embassy staff. His name was Cooper and he'd been chatting to Jarvis about the forthcoming Italian elections and had changed the subject.

'You seem to live better than the ambassador himself. How the hell do you do it?'

Jarvis smiled. 'Wise investments way back that are now paying off.'

'What do you invest in?'

'I pay for my advice.' He grinned. 'You should try it some time.' He shrugged. 'And marry into a rich family – that helps.'

Jarvis turned his back on his interrogator and walked through the groups to his wife. He said quietly, 'Let's get out. I'm bored.'

She could smell the whisky on his breath and she knew it would be unwise to disagree with him.

Back at their apartment Jarvis could hardly keep awake and his speech was slurred.

'How long before the baby?'

'Early in November.'

'Next year we'll be back in the States.'

'What's worrying you?'

'Money,' he said, closing his eyes and resting his head against the back of the armchair.

'But we've never had so much money.'

'That's the problem. One of those bastards at the embassy asked me how we got so rich. I told him what I always tell them.'

'What's that?'

'I tell 'em it's investments paying off and that your family are very rich.'

'That's stupid. Anyone in Bogotá could tell them my parents are influential but they have no money worth talking about.' She sighed. 'You told me the money was paid by an old friend who owed you favours for various things, like getting his girl an abortion.' She paused. 'You know what your problem is, it's spending too much time with the Russians.'

'That's part of my job for God's sake.'

'That story's getting a bit thin, my dear.'

Jarvis knew then that she had at least a vague idea of where the money came from. The following day, as if in a gesture of defiance, Jarvis arranged a meeting with a senior diplomat at the British Embassy who was being posted as ambassador to Venezuela and was selling his Jaguar car before he left, because he would have an official car in his new post. The diplomat was amazed when the nondescript American just looked at the car, said he wanted it, and made out a cheque on the spot. But he remembered the strange little man saying, 'I always wanted a Jaguar.'

The black Fiat pulled up just past the Post Office on the Via della Mercede and Jarvis eased himself into the back seat. For most of the drive he stayed crouched down as they made their way to Villa Abamalek, the Soviet ambassador's house in the western suburbs of Rome. The meetings with Yuri Volkov were as friendly as always although the information he could now pass to the KGB had little to do with KGB men collaborating with the CIA.

In his job in the Rome detachment of the CIA, Jarvis had sight of hundreds of copies of general information from CIA detachments all over the world. Documents that gave the analysts in Moscow first-hand information of CIA operations and intentions.

Now that his time in Rome was almost through, the KGB wanted to establish better methods of passing information. The idea of plastic shopping-bags bulging with top-secret documents was not Moscow's idea of how such a high-grade operation should be carried on. But they wanted to reassure Jarvis of his status and value to the KGB. They had never had an intelligence asset of such magnitude and they were determined not to lose him. One of their problems was that neither they nor Jarvis knew what Jarvis's new post would be with the CIA.

There were only two more meetings at Villa Abamalek planned before Jarvis returned to Washington and at this meeting Volkov gave Jarvis a letter from Fomenko himself.

Jarvis read the letter as Volkov poured him a drink. It was an extraordinary letter, as if the KGB could read his mind.

'Dear Friend,
    This is your balance sheet as on May 1. All in all you have been appropriated $2,705,000 . . . we have delivered to you $1,881,811. On the above date you have in your account (including $250,000 in bonds) $1,535,077 . . .'

There were five coloured photographs included and the letter went on to say . . .

'PS. We believe that these pictures would give you some idea about the beautiful piece of land on the river bank, which from now on belongs to you forever. We decided not to take pictures of housing in this area with the understanding that you have much better idea of how your *dacha* should look like. Good luck.'

The inference was that he would always be welcome if he ever wanted to retire to the Soviet Union or escape.

He read the letter again and looked at the photographs, as he reached for his drink, raising the glass to Volkov.

'*Na zdrovie.*'

Volkov smiled. '*Na zdrovie.*'

Jarvis put down his glass and looked at Volkov.

'You must have talked to them about me having a *dacha.*'

'Of course. They were delighted to be able to give you something you really wanted.'

'You really think they mean it?'

Volkov looked shocked. 'Of course they mean it. That letter was signed by Fomenko but the whole thing was approved by Gorbachev himself.'

'I'm flattered.'

'How's that small boy of yours?'

Jarvis smiled. 'Peter? He's doing fine.'

Larry Getz felt slightly ashamed of what he was doing as he went through the file records of the Italian Embassy diplomatic staff. But he did it all the same.

Her father was Mario del Rossi, a career diplomat whose interests were recorded as tennis and chess. He was fifty-two years old. Two years older than his wife Giannetta, who had taught music at Milan University and now lectured on Cinquecento chamber music at Washington University. They had only one child, a daughter, Gabriella Maria. It recorded only that she had married aged twenty, a captain in the Italian army. And the marriage had been annulled two years later.

He sat looking at the file, trying to recall what had affected him so. She was more than pretty, with black hair and big dark eyes. But it was her voice that had mattered most. Deep and soft and gentle, with only the trace of an accent. As strikingly beautiful as she was, she must have been aware of men looking at her. But if she was aware she appeared not to notice it. He kept the file on his desk until he left in the evening when he handed it back to Records. It was crazy. He'd only been with her a couple of hours and they'd talked of practically nothing but the problem of driving a car in Washington DC. Take a wrong turn and you could get locked in the one-way system for hours. And on the strength of that you did what no decent CIA man would ever do – use the agency records to check on someone for personal reasons. What a creep thing to do.

*   *   *

48

Volkov was a skilled operator and had a natural talent for manipulating people but he knew that he didn't understand Jarvis. He had grown to accept that Jarvis's only motivation was simple greed. He seemed to have no doubts about what he was doing and was unconcerned that he was routinely passing over information that led inevitably to the deaths of many men. He never asked what the Russians did with the information he supplied, nor did he ask about the fate of those he exposed. He seemed to have no moral scruples. It was just business, and like any other tradesman he was only concerned with his reward. He had never attempted to justify what he was doing. For Jarvis that was not his part of his deal. Volkov often thought of those plastic Safeways bags bulging with top-secret information as being typical of the whole set-up. They were so ordinary; vehicles for taking home groceries, now carrying death-warrants for unknown men.

Many times as they chatted together Volkov had tried to find out what had made Jarvis a virtual alcoholic. Once when he had asked him directly Jarvis had laughed and said, 'I just like the booze. Always did. Always will.' Russians were never averse to the bottle but at least it usually made them either wildly belligerent or uproariously happy. But he had never seen Jarvis happy. He smiled, but it was the smile of a used-car salesman. He seemed to have no interests apart from expensive possessions. The Jaguar, the Rolex watch, the expensive clothes and jewellery for his wife. Jarvis maintained that Maria knew nothing of his relationship with the Russians but although Volkov had only met her once at a party at the Egyptian Embassy in Rome, he had got the distinct impression that she was far more intelligent than her husband. The records said that she'd had some sort of relationship with the CIA's office in Mexico City. And that was before she even knew Jarvis. Volkov had had several long talks about Jarvis, without giving his name, with KGB psychologists but the attitude was that either his observation of the subject was inefficient or he was mistaking what could be described as no more than exaggerated greed on the part of a weak and feckless man. They suggested that the subject would have indulged in some kind of fraud or theft no matter what kind of business he was employed in. One of them had pointed out that there were hundreds of similar men with their little scams operating on the fringes of Red Square. One of them had smiled and said it just epitomised the American way of life – the free market. Who paid the top buck? The other one had hinted that perhaps it was he, Volkov, who had problems. To them the subject was just a normal man on the make who'd found he owned a gold-mine. The male equivalent of an exceptionally beautiful hooker.

Volkov had asked Fomenko about the psychologists' backgrounds and Fomenko had said that they were highly regarded in their circles, with the highest honours that the medical faculty at Moscow University could award. He added drily that they earned twice what a well-qualified surgeon made, and that well-qualified surgeons made rather less than bus drivers made.

Larry Getz wasn't a man for Washington-type cocktail parties. In fact he'd never been to one and almost the only impression he had of what went on was from old black and white films. Vaguely Fred Astaire and Ginger Rogers, or Jimmy Stewart standing up for the common man. He decided that his dark blue suit was about right but he put it into the cleaners for a clean and press.

A security guard at the embassy showed him where to park his car and when he had handed over the keys the guard took him into the mansion. His invitation note was checked and he was led over to where a tall man was talking animatedly with a group of people. The tall man was His Excellency himself and he shook hands enthusiastically, leading Getz away from the group to an alcove beside one of the big windows.

'I was looking forward to meeting you to say how grateful my wife and I were for you being so kind and so helpful to my daughter.' He looked around. 'Is your wife here this evening?'

Getz smiled. 'I don't have a wife I'm afraid.'

'But Gabriella said you had a splendid little son named Bobby.'

'I do. But the wife part's over.'

'I see. I see. Now help yourself to a drink and I'll find Gabriella and she can be your hostess.'

Getz helped himself to a glass of red wine, and hanging around at the back of his mind was the fact that the girl and her father must have talked about him and the fact that he had a son. Then she was heading towards him, smiling as she took his free hand.

'It's great to see you again. And how's Bobby?'

He smiled. 'I only see him every other week. I'm sure he's OK.' He paused. 'And how's the car business?'

She shrugged. 'They're repairing the MG and it'll be another ten days. Daddy says I ought to be patriotic and have an Italian car.'

'A nice Alfa-Romeo perhaps?'

She laughed. 'I'll suggest it to him. But more important, how are you?'

'I'm fine.'

'It's probably very rude for me to ask but is your apartment permanent or temporary?'

He shrugged. 'More or less permanent. Why do you ask?'

She hesitated and blushed. 'I think it needs a bit of caring. It's just a bit too masculine. Too . . . too.' She shrugged. 'It lacks the imprint of a personality.'

'I'm sure you're right.' He smiled. 'Maybe you'd tell me what I should do to humanise it.'

The dark eyes looked up at his face and she nodded slowly. 'Why not?' She smiled. 'Consultancy fee, a dinner at La Brasserie?'

'It's a deal. When do we start?'

She thought for a moment and then said, 'Let's make it tomorrow, Sunday.' She sighed. 'Now let me introduce you to some of the less boring people. By the way, may I ask what you do?'

'I work for the government.'

She laughed. 'Daddy was right. He said you'd be CIA or FBI. Was he right?'

'Why did he say that?'

'Because when I gave you my address it was a number you had obviously come across before.'

'It's CIA but I generally just say the government.' He smiled. 'Avoids frightening people.'

'Are you allowed to tell lies about what you do?'

He laughed. 'What kind of lies?'

She shrugged. 'Well, can you say you work for the Treasury or State if you want to?'

'I can. But there's not much point. If people really want to know what you do it's easy enough to find out. Washington's quite a small community. There's always someone who can tell you what you want to know.'

'Let's do the rounds.' She tucked her arm in his and led him from one group to another. The people she introduced him to were mostly in their late thirties and were mainly academics and creative people. She was surprised and quite pleased that her protégé could hold his own on politics, Hockney, Yo-Yo Ma and John Updike.

Eventually she had walked him into the small garden at the back of the house. It was beginning to get dark and when she shivered he put his jacket around her shoulders.

'What time do cocktail parties finish?'

'Oh, they're pretty well movable feasts. About eight o'clock is a happy medium. Are you bored?'

'Can I ask you a personal question?'

'Try me.'

'Tell me about your ex-husband.'

She stopped and looked at him. 'How did you know I had an ex-husband?'

'You said you were divorced when you were at my place after your car was messed up.'

'What do you want to know about him? I was very young when we married. He was a quite handsome young *capitano* in the *Bersaglieri*. I grew up and he didn't. I think he was as glad to be out of it as I was.'

He turned her so that he could look at her face, his hands on her shoulders. 'I'm sorry. I told a bit of a lie. I'm ashamed. I looked up the embassy and your family in the CIA files.'

'Why? Why were you so interested?'

Getz looked up at the sky, sighed and said quietly, 'I found you attractive. The way you look, the way you speak . . .' he shrugged. '. . . I wanted to know about you.'

She smiled. 'You should be ashamed. But I should be too. I liked you. I wanted to see you again so I asked my father to invite you this evening.' She laughed. 'Both as bad as one another. What time shall I see you tomorrow?'

'Say I pick you up here about noon and we can have lunch first.'

'That would be fine.'

She walked with him to his car and waved to him as he moved off.

As he drove back to his apartment he was vaguely aware that he was behaving like a teenager.

*   *   *

52

They both had *sole meunière* followed by La Brasserie's special *crème brulée* and were waiting for the coffee when she said, 'What went wrong with your marriage?'

He hesitated for a moment then said, 'Two things I guess. We both grew up in the same small country town in Vermont. She didn't like cities, especially Washington DC. And my kind of job doesn't fit well with a domestic life unless the spouse is very flexible and understanding, or has an interesting career herself. I guess we grew apart anyway as time went by and in the end she made the job an issue. Either I gave up the job or she would divorce me.' He paused. 'You don't do things like that in my book if you really care about someone.' He smiled wanly. 'I think I'd just worn out my welcome.'

'Was it messy, the divorce?'

'It got messy. One fight after another. I took my lawyer's advice and stopped fighting. It was good advice. In the end it was sorted out. I got a bad deal financially to get access to my boy.'

'Do you miss family life?'

'Sometimes. It's depressing sometimes coming home from some foreign trip and everything's just as you left it. The dishes still in the sink where you left them and nobody to ask how you got on. But I think when she married me she got a bad deal too. She married a good old country boy and in her terms he turned into a city slicker.' He smiled. 'For once the prince turned into a frog.'

'How long ago was the divorce?'

'Nearly two years now from when it started.' He paused. 'And you?'

'A long time. It was an annulment and it wasn't painful. He was as relieved as I was to call it a day.'

'What went wrong?'

'We married far too young. I did anyway. Looking back I think I was not only a fool but I was irresponsible. I should have known better. It was almost the reverse of your situation but the same ending.' She shrugged. 'And fortunately nobody got hurt . . . much.'

The coffee came and, changing the subject, she said, 'We can do a lot to make your place more comfortable and more human.'

He smiled. 'Have you got it all worked out?'

'More or less.' Then she said softly, 'Maybe I should ask you if you actually want it fixed. Am I being too pushy?'

'I'd be very grateful if you'd take it in hand.' He paused. 'May I ask why you are willing to bother about it at all?'

She looked down at her coffee cup and then back at his face, smiling as she waved his question away and said, 'I'll tell you one day.'

She settled Getz down in the single armchair to watch TV. She had brought a small notebook and a tape measure in her handbag and for an hour she measured and contemplated and made notes. Using the phone in the kitchen she called two stores in the suburbs that were open on Sundays and checked the going rate for a number of items.

Back in the living room she switched off the TV and sat on the floor beside the armchair.

'Facts of life first, Larry. How many dollars are you willing to spend?'

'Whatever you say!'

'You're not broke? The alimony and all that.'

Getz smiled. 'No. I own a couple of quite nice rented holiday houses in Vermont. And my parents' house. And a majority holding in the agricultural business my father built. Tell me what it's gonna be.'

'You speak as if your parents are dead. Are they?'

'Yes, they died in a car accident visiting friends and relations in Germany. That was about four years ago.'

'I'm sorry. Do you miss them?'

He nodded. 'Yes. We were very close.' He sighed. 'Let's get back to the decorations.'

'It'll be somewhere between four and five thousand dollars to do the real thing but I could get by on three thousand. That includes some equipment and some furniture.' With her head appealingly to one side she said, 'It can be very nice.'

'I'll sign you a blank cheque and let me know the final figure so I can move the money to the bank.'

'Larry. Don't be so idiotic. A blank cheque. You barely know me.'

'I know you very well, dear girl.'

She laughed. 'The CIA files can't be that good.'

'You're right. But I've been around a long time so I know you where it matters.'

'Is that part of your job – judging people?'

He shrugged. 'I suppose it is.'

'I feel I know you too. As if we've known each other all our lives.'

He smiled and stood up, reaching for her hand and hauling her to her feet. Looking at her face, he said softly, 'You make me feel very young but I'm ten years older than you.'

She nodded slowly. 'That's just about right.'

And when he kissed her she slid her arms around his neck and kissed him back. It was a long kiss and when it took its inevitable course she pulled back her head and looked up at him, as she said softly, 'Shall I stay the night?'

Chapter 9

Arthur Jarvis sat in his small study and read the nine pages of
instructions that Volkov had passed to him from Moscow.

It was all business. They were concerned with his protection and
they wanted all the usual trade-craft precautions to be invoked
immediately. And they had outlined specific targets for him.

He had sold the silver grey Jaguar just before he left Rome and
he missed the elegant car. He felt a surge of self-confidence and
decided that if things were hotting up so promisingly he could
give himself a treat. This time it would be a brand-new Jaguar.
And white. Volkov was horrified when he was shown the new
car. It was crazy to run a Jaguar and crazier still to have a
white one. Especially when you only earned $60,000 a year with
alimony, and a wife and child. But Jarvis had laughed at the
Russian's caution. What's the use of having money if you can't
buy nice things. His 'rich' relations in Bogotá were all the cover
he needed.

For the first time in his relationship with Jarvis, Volkov gave some
thought to what he himself should do if ever Jarvis was caught. The
usual drill was for the handler to sit tight and if pressure got out
of control he just used his diplomatic status and caught the next
plane wherever it happened to be going. But that drill was for
routine operations and if the Americans discovered what sort of
material Jarvis had been passing over they could be so shocked
and enraged that they might consider more drastic action. Arresting
him wouldn't do them any good. Even the Russians stuck to the
protocols of diplomatic immunity. Killing him wouldn't do them
any good either but it could well relieve the tension of the immediate
surge of anger. It annoyed Volkov intensely that he had to think
about such an eventuality solely because Jarvis was such a stupid

man. And he had no doubt that if Moscow had to decide who to smuggle out, him or Jarvis, it would be the American who made it to Moscow, while at best he'd be a virtual prisoner in the embassy.

PART TWO

Chapter 10

They had spent a week house-hunting when they got back to
Washington DC and the Jarvises had both fallen for the house
on North Randolph Street in North Arlington. It was a pleasant
ten-room house with landscaped gardens in one of the best sections
of the sprawling suburb across the Potomac from Washington itself. It
cost $540,000 and Arthur Jarvis paid in cash. He told the title lawyer
and the real-estate agent that the reason why he paid cash was that
the house was a present from Maria's father in Colombia to celebrate
their son's birth. Jarvis spent another $99,000 on redecorating. At
the same time he bought himself a new white Jaguar and a Honda
for his wife.

It was not a happy marriage, mainly because of Jarvis's drinking
and Maria had no interest in Jarvis after the birth of their son. There
were constant rows that were smoothed over with yet another piece of
expensive jewellery or clothes. But Maria no longer had any interest
in her husband. As she frequently said, 'He has his life and I have
mine.' At that time she had no idea of what his other life was. She
didn't care. She infinitely preferred her small son.

The report on Jarvis from the head of the Rome CIA unit was damning
and was summed up in the final sentence that stated 'Jarvis handles
no ongoing cases; his efforts to initiate new developmental activity
of any consequence have been desultory.'

In a personal telephone call he strongly recommended that Jarvis
should be sacked.

When the CIA personnel placement board met in July 1989 to
consider the status and fate of a hundred or so of its officers, Jarvis's name was on that list. The Soviet division chief,
Erikson, told the Board that he had sent Jarvis to Rome for

the sole purpose of being rid of him and would never take him back.

But Erikson was himself replaced a month later by Cassidy, a successful leader of active operations in the Middle East. A gung-ho man more used to running guns to partisans than running a division of the CIA. He saw the personal criticism of Jarvis as being made by the same old guard that had frequently criticised him and his operations. As a concession he agreed that Jarvis should not be sent overseas but should have a nice meaningless title at headquarters. With the collapse of the Soviet Union he decided that the old Soviet division was a backwater now. He made Jarvis the chief of the Western Europe branch. It was an incredible decision when the low morale and upheavals going on at Langley were taken into acount.

There was a news item in the *Washington Post* of a statement by a spokesman for the KGB that was being treated by the US media as a 'virulent attack on the CIA', but was seen as a kind of seal of approval by the CIA itself. Particularly the claims in the statement that the CIA was involved in 'a wide-ranging campaign of spy mania and brutal provocation employed against Soviet institutions'. There were those in high places at Langley who wondered if this wasn't a good time to ask Congress for additional funding.

One CIA man was disturbed by the report of the Moscow speech because it was reported as having been made by Gorbachev's newly appointed chairman of the KGB, Viktor Fomenko.

Jarvis checked his diary. There was only one entry for the whole week and the entry was just the letter 'R', the code for a meeting with Volkov whom he hadn't met for nearly five years. The 'R' code was for meetings with no particular agenda. Just keeping contact and as a security check.

He slowed down at the old bridge on his way to Langley and checked the chalk marks on the telephone pole that confirmed the meeting and its venue. Looking round casually to check that he was not observed he rubbed out the chalk marks and got back into his car. They were to meet at the bookshop that evening at about 6 p.m.

When he made his way up the wooden staircase at the back of the shop he had in his hand the key that the old man had given him. He had parked the white Jaguar several blocks away in a hotel parking lot.

The small room had no windows and was sparsely furnished. A single bed, an oak chest of drawers and two cane chairs with a lone picture on the wall of Marilyn Monroe smiling up at Arthur Miller. There was an old-fashioned electric ventilator set in the wall and Jarvis switched it on and then off as the clatter of the fan betrayed its decrepitude. Then he heard noises down below, followed by footsteps on the stairs, before the door opened and Volkov came in. He nodded at Jarvis and looked around the room.

'I think this is where he brings his little girl-friends.' He nodded at the chairs. 'Let's sit down.'

When they were settled Volkov handed over the usual envelope and said, 'What's happened now you're back at Langley?'

'The bastards put me on the Czech section. When Gorbachev made clear they were going to let the Czechs get away with independence, the section virtually folded. They've put me in charge of the Western Europe desk of the Soviet set-up.'

'Is that a promotion?'

'No way. Not as far as I'm concerned. But I'll have material for you covering all that the CIA is doing in Europe.' He shrugged. 'But otherwise it's a dead end for me.'

'Do you think they suspect you?'

Jarvis shook his head. 'No. If they do then they suspect everyone working on KGB operations.'

'What about that Jaguar, it's bound to be noticed?'

'There are seven other Jags in the parking lot at Langley.'

'But I bet the owners didn't pay cash for them.'

'So what? All my money comes from Maria's rich family in Colombia.'

Volkov was silent for a moment and then he said, 'Anything else you need from me?'

Jarvis smiled. 'I read in the papers that you've got a new boss in Moscow. How does that affect me?'

'Favourably.'

'Does he know about me?'

'He ran the Moscow end of this operation. He still does.'

'So why does he allow people to make statements about the CIA and a campaign of brutality against Soviet institutions?'

Volkov laughed. 'That's just Fomenko's idea of lashing out before you get hit. Arrest one of our people in the USA and you make his point.'

'I've got a feeling you're annoyed at something. Are you?'

Volkov shrugged. 'I'm worried about your security. You're our most valuable property. We don't want to lose you by being careless.'

'Look, Yuri. I do it for the money. I don't give a shit about the politics or who rules the world. And money's no use if you can't spend it and have the things you want.'

Volkov gave up and smiled. 'OK. You win. Have you got anything for me?'

Jarvis passed him an envelope. 'This is an assessment of operations in Austria against the KGB in Vienna.'

Volkov took it and slid it into his jacket pocket, relieved that the meeting hadn't been entirely useless.

They had met in a private room at the Marriott. There was O'Hara, Grady, O'Hara's boss, Senator Powell and much lower down the scale, Larry Getz. It was O'Hara who got down to business.

'Gentlemen. I need some fresh thinking. Frankly, some inspiration.' He paused. 'We have recently lost two of our KGB assets. We haven't heard from at least half a dozen others in the last six months. We know that at least the two have been executed.

'Nearly a year ago I asked Larry Getz here to look into our general security at the CIA. His report was damning. Talk about the Keystone Kops. We were insecure in every area. I then ordered Larry to produce a list of possible "moles" inside Langley.

'Now gentlemen, we come to our first problem, *my* first problem I guess. Strictly speaking if we suspect one of our people of treason we hand the investigation over to the FBI. It's constitutionally their ball-game. As you can imagine, we don't rush into informing them that we've got a rotten apple in our barrel. Problem number two. I ordered Larry to produce a list of the people who could have blown our KGB assets and informed Moscow by one route or another. Larry's list consists of nearly forty names. But the suspicions are unsupported by any evidence. A court of law, even our own lawyer, would laugh at what we've got.

'Why do we have such an impasse? I'm afraid to say, gentlemen, that it's the law and the Constitution that protects these people.

We need to check their lives minutely, bank accounts, background, telephone calls, mail, garbage, neighbours, trades-people – the lot. And to do any of these things we need a warrant, and in some cases the law says we have to inform them of what we're doing. In our game that's an impossible situation. Whoever our mole is he'd be off to Mexico City, Vienna and Moscow in a matter of hours. And we'd be back to square one.' O'Hara paused and looked at each one in turn. 'I'd like your views on my suggestions for a possible solution.' He wagged a finger. 'I emphasise that this is a chat between friends. With honest people, with no political axe to grind. No records, written or acoustic of what we all say. Just a shake of the head or a nod of approval. Yes?'

He looked down at a typed page on his desk in front of him and then looked up.

'I've had long talks with the Director of the FBI and he has agreed that Larry Getz can act for FBI interests in setting up a CIA unit for an intensive investigation of anyone we nominate. Their resources will be made available too, and that – gentlemen – is a valuable gesture. It's part of our rules that such information is pooled from both agencies, but for understandable reasons it rarely happens. The main reason for arranging this informal meeting was to get an outside view on what will inevitably be a ruthless check on the lives of a number of people, all of whom, except one, are entirely innocent of any treachery.' O'Hara looked at the Senator who shifted in his chair.

'What about the warrant problems in your scheme?'

Getz noted that O'Hara glanced briefly at Grady before he replied.

'I have had lengthy talks with our legal people and the courts are prepared to assist us on the question of warrants.'

Senator Powell raised his eyebrows and then turned to Getz.

'Tell me, Mr Getz. Are you happy about this arrangement?'

'Yes, Senator.'

'How long will it take you to find the mole in the agency?'

'I don't know, sir. I see it as a deep investigation but I have been promised all the staff I need. I should expect it to take at least a year.'

'When you identify the man, what then? Will you have evidence enough to prosecute him?'

'Yes, sir. That's why it will take a lot of work and a lot of time.'

Senator Powell pursed his lips as he thought and then, looking at Getz, he said, 'You can assure me that this is the only method to deal with this with any chance of success?'

'Yes, sir. That's my opinion.'

Senator Powell looked at Getz and O'Hara. 'You want my blessing to this?'

They both nodded their agreement and Senator Powell sighed and said, 'OK. You've got it.' He stood up and taking Getz's arm he said, 'Have a sandwich with me.' He turned and waved farewell to O'Hara and Grady. Picking up the phone he ordered sandwiches and coffee to be brought up to the private room.

There were several leather club armchairs and Senator Powell waved in their direction. When they were both seated he said, 'What do the Soviets get from a traitor? Is it worth all the song and dance?'

'They get a picture of our thinking. It's like putting them on the distribution list of top-secret documents. Our preparations to defend ourselves. Our morale. Our scientific programme. Our attitude to aggressive moves the Soviets make. Are we prepared to give them a bloody nose or will we back down and chicken out? They can know more about what's going on in Washington DC than the President himself.'

'But I'm sure we do the same to them, don't we?'

'We try to, but the KGB resources and training are far ahead of ours.' He smiled. 'They don't have to argue their way through Kremlin committees and party political dog-fights. If they want it, they get it.' He paused. 'And we're dealing there with a tightly closed society. Secretive by nature and with organisations that can bend any law to prevent a breach of security.' He smiled. 'It really is an Iron Curtain.'

Powell smiled. 'Sounds like you're pitching to the Congressional budget committee.'

Getz shrugged but didn't smile. 'I ought not to need to.'

'So why don't you get a bigger budget?'

'Two reasons. The first is that the top brass of the CIA are made to compete for resources against the FBI and the NSA. And secondly, we don't do a very good job.' He paused. 'If we catch a KGB spy the media just ask why we took so long.'

'Why don't we do a very good job?'

'Internal rivalry. Conflicting theories at the top. And we're a democracy. That makes life easier for people who want to destroy us. The Soviets sell a dream of equality and we sell "the market-economy". Neither of them work so politicians blame the executive. Makes life comfortable all round.'

'You sound rather cynical, Mr Getz.'

Getz shook his head. 'Angry, not cynical.'

'Sounds like you're the right man for this tough job.'

Getz smiled. 'I hope you're right.'

'Ah. Here come the sandwiches. Let's eat.'

Chapter 11

As a gesture of recognition Getz chose the FBI offices at Tysons Corner as his headquarters while keeping a duplicate base at Langley.

There were six other people, apart from Getz and his secretary, around the plain wooden table. Three were FBI and three CIA. The equilibrium was accidental rather than intentional. The FBI people were specialists in surveillance.

'This is our first meeting and I'm grateful to both agencies for making you available. On the cork board on the long wall there's a list of fifty-two names. All of them suspect for one reason or another. We can be pretty sure that fifty-one of them are entirely innocent. They may have drink problems, they may have money problems, they may have turbulent private lives or they may have sex problems.' He paused. 'But that's not our concern unless this problem shows an indication of character breakdown, unreliability or obvious breaches of security. They all have connections at one time or another, or currently, that give access to our KGB documentation. Many have job specifications that allow, or even encourage, contact with Soviets. Only four or five of the names are based outside the United States and they will be looked at by other staff.' He paused. 'Tom Welby, at the end of the table in the check shirt, will be in charge of allocating names. You each have your own two assistants and I shall want a daily report from each of you, even if it's a nil report. Understood?' There was a murmur of assent before he resumed.

'Then we come to the question of warrants. We don't go for warrants until we genuinely have reasonable doubts. Let's say two or three indications of unexplained items. I'll deal personally with all applications for a warrant.' He paused. 'I can tell you that if I am satisfied there will be no problem about warrants. This operation is for real and both agencies have pledged their total backing.

'In the early stages you need to go very carefully and discreetly. Outside this room there are no more than half a dozen people who know what's going on. And we don't want to give the game away by being noticed or all we have done is provide our target with an indication that the heat is really on. If we are obvious then we have given our fellow notice that it's time to do a skip.' He looked around the table. 'We'll have a meeting like this once a week until we've brought the suspect list down to around ten subjects. After that we'll meet every day.' He smiled. 'So. Best of luck and thank you all for the efforts you are about to make.'

With a scraping of chairs and a hum of talk, the meeting broke up and the two-man teams were given the single-page reports on two targets.

Larry Getz called out. 'Somebody has just asked me why two targets each, not one. Well it's a precaution. With two targets to go at you'll be less likely to be so occupied with one person that it's obvious to him that he's under surveillance.'

The only doubt in Getz's mind was about O'Hara's assurance that he could get warrants for anything they wanted to do. Getting warrants was always a hassle and when it involved house searches in the owner's absence the judges all too often refused.

By the end of August 1991 there were only twenty-nine names left on the serious subject list. The list was compiled from the reports of four different investigating teams each providing its own list. There were five names that appeared on all four lists. Arthur Jarvis's name was one of them.

Chapter 12

She had been looking in a closet for a dark red wallet of Arthur's. It was a small wallet that he seldom used and it fitted nicely inside the small purse she intended using that afternoon when she went shopping. The wallet was empty except for a torn piece of typewritten paper. She could hardly understand the very cryptic sentences but there was one that said, 'the city where your mother-in-law lives'. It both scared and angered her. She knew that his work had nothing to do with South America.

She confronted him angrily the moment he arrived home. 'I wanted to use that red wallet of yours. There was a typewritten page in there that mentioned my mother. What the hell does she have to do with your job? You know I don't want her or any of my family involved in your affairs in the CIA.'

He shrugged. 'It's nothing. Don't worry. Just forget it.'

'I want to know what it's about, Art.'

He shook his head. 'I told you – forget it.' He said casually. 'Where's Peter?'

'He's in his playroom.'

She was far from satisfied, but in Colombia a woman never questions what her provider might be doing. Nevertheless over the next ten days she asked him several times for an explanation. All her questions were ignored or brushed aside until one evening when they were having dinner together at a Washington restaurant.

When they got to the coffee she asked the same question but this time he answered her. Looking up from the wine glass he was touching he said, quite calmly, 'I'm working for the Soviets.' And he said it as casually as if he were saying that he'd taken up golf.

'What's that mean?'

He shrugged and passed her the cream for the coffee. 'I see them from time to time and . . .' he looked directly at her face '. . . they pay me money.'

'Is this part of your CIA job?'

He smiled and shook his head. 'No, honey. It's freelance work. It's why we are able to live as we do. What the CIA pay me wouldn't cover your dress allowance.'

For several days Maria was utterly confused about what she had learned. It sounded as if he was spying for the Russians but he hadn't said that in so many words. He had still implied that money came from an old friend who owed him favours. Finally she decided that she would do nothing. Just let things go on as they were. She wasn't interested in him as a man. They no longer had any intimacy. Neither did she want it. Neither did she want to disturb what was a very pleasant life-style. At least he was a spender and she had her share of what he was paid, whoever paid it.

Her submission to what was going on had no reward, their relationship was antagonistic because of Arthur Jarvis's drunken behaviour, not only in private but in public too. The few friends they once had had long ago faded away.

The Jarvises spent the Christmas holidays at Maria's parents' house in Bogotá. They saw little of Arthur Jarvis who spent most of his time at the Soviet Embassy with Yuri Volkov. He was able to warn the Russians that the FBI were demanding access to the confiscated Stasi files in Berlin but were being stopped by the Berlin CIA bureau refusing to give up the documents. It was just the normal inter-agency bloody-mindedness.

The news that worried Volkov was that Jarvis was being transferred to the CIA's Counter-Narcotics Centre. Volkov had one of his 'agents of influence' at the Drug Enforcement Administration, and he had heard about the CIA's drug centre. Apparently inside the DEA it was seen as a joke and referred to as the 'Gulag'. The DEA not only despised the CIA drug people but feared them on the grounds that they were suspected of murdering one of the DEA's agents in Mexico.

'Why do you think they moved you to counter-narcotics?'

Jarvis shrugged. 'It's part of the musical chairs that goes on all the time.'

'How long will you be there?'

'I've no idea but I've already got a trip to Moscow scheduled for next month.'

'How did you do that?'

Jarvis smiled. 'Liaison with your drug people in Moscow. Maybe arrange co-operation or even working jointly.'

'Has it been agreed, the trip, officially?'

'Yeah.' Jarvis smiled. 'I've already got my tickets. I'll be having lots of overseas meetings as a liaison officer.'

'Will this prevent you from continuing to give us your usual material?'

'No problem. I'll still have access to anywhere at Langley.'

'I've got a packet for you. I'll bring it tomorrow. OK?'

'That's OK.'

Volkov walked Jarvis down to the back entrance of the embassy building and locked the iron gate when Jarvis had left.

Volkov was disturbed by what Jarvis had told him. Why should they transfer an intelligence officer to an anti-drug set-up? It didn't make sense. Unless they were beginning to have suspicions about Jarvis. But in that case they surely wouldn't be letting him go to Moscow. Jarvis had always insisted that they were totally disorganised and that nobody in any section knew what he was supposed to be doing. Maybe he was right. But he must pass on the word to Moscow.

In fact, Jarvis liked his new job and, to the surprise of his new colleagues, he came up with several good ideas. But what he liked most was the prospect of going abroad to meet with other counter-narcotics officers. The trip to Moscow was his top priority.

There were several of his colleagues due to go on the Moscow trip with him and he'd given their names and backgrounds to Volkov at their last meeting before he was due to go.

'I've had strict instructions from Moscow that you don't make any KGB contacts while you're there. It's far too risky. Your Moscow CIA bureau will be watching every move you make and the same goes for your colleagues. We don't even trust our own drug people. So be very careful.'

Jarvis shrugged. 'That's fine with me.'

* * *

There was a party to mark their final evening in Moscow and Jarvis's colleagues had been shocked when he turned up already drunk. What was worse were the things he said when they were toasting the co-operation between the Soviets and the CIA. His toast was a long befuddled tirade against the inefficiency of the CIA and the stupidity of its top people. It was embarrassing for the Russians and even more embarrassing for Jarvis's colleagues. He ended up passed-out with his head on the table and two of his people had to carry him to his room. Nobody reported anything about the embarrassing display when they were back in Langley. But when Jarvis flew down to Caracas for a meeting with Volkov and several others it was obvious that Volkov already knew of the scene at the farewell party.

'What sort of trip did you have?'

Jarvis shrugged. 'Pretty boring.'

'I hear you had a pretty wild party the last night.'

Jarvis laughed. 'Not really wild. Just got shitfaced with your people.' He grinned. 'They're great guys. I like 'em. No glasses crap. Straight from the bottle. Great stuff.'

'What's your situation regarding our side of the fence?'

'Not much, my friend. But I've got a computer at home now as well as at the office and I can put my stuff on floppy disks and pass on the information that way instead of printing it out. You'd better warn your people. I'll just be able to give you a disk and you can send it on to them.'

'I think our computer back-up is pretty primitive.'

Jarvis laughed. 'They'll know what to do. They just type in my password and run it.'

'Let's go over the new dead-drops and contact signs and direct contacts. Moscow want us to establish an "iron contact".'

'What the hell's that?'

'It's a fixed and imperative contact. Every year without fail. Same place, same date, same recognition sign every year.'

'I don't get it.'

'It's a safety check. If something happens so that we can't make contact with an asset for a long period then we've got that set meeting at a set place and time which is compulsory. Even if we met a couple of days before we still keep that RV.' He paused. 'If the asset doesn't keep the RV we know there's real trouble.'

Jarvis looked suspicious. 'You got some reason for doing this?'

Volkov laughed. 'No. It's just routine with all our contacts and case-officers. Moscow kicked my butt for not having established it before.'

'Where is this meeting-place?'

'It's by a statue in a park in Bogotá. I've got the details for you. And a map and a couple of photographs.'

'Sounds crazy to me.' Jarvis shrugged. 'But if that's how they want it. So be it.'

They spent the rest of the day going over the format of the revised trade-craft details.

On the plane back to Washington Jarvis was worried about not being able to supply the same high-grade material to the Russians. Would they reduce his payments? Would they value him less? He coped with his problems the usual way. Oblivion, courtesy of Jameson 10-year-old.

A week after his return from Caracas Jarvis had logged onto his office computer and he couldn't believe the message that came up. It registered that he had been given access to a restricted message-delivering service originating from the Directorate of Operations. It was crazy. Even people who worked in the DO couldn't download information from the message system. There were messages about ongoing covert operations and he could just download them onto floppy disks. No Safeways shopping-bags needed to hide a floppy disk. He could access almost all of the CIA's most highly classified circuits and nobody would ever know.

He sat there for long minutes trying to absorb his good fortune. He was back in business. Back in the money. Just to check that it wasn't some computer error he logged in and there it was. The monitor was scrolling through a menu giving details of hundreds of files he could access. He filled two floppy disks in his lunch break and slid them into his jacket pocket. Showing unusual caution for Jarvis he checked for the next three days that he actually had got access to the DO's files. The checks confirmed that he had access without any problem.

Chapter 13

The work at Larry Getz's place had taken a week and he had stayed at his club until it was ready at the weekend.

The transformation was almost incredible. It looked as if it had been lived in for years. Bookshelves from floor to ceiling. A Sony Trinitron TV and VCR and Denon hi-fi. The pictures on the walls were his original choices except for a print of a house on the banks of Lake Champlain in the snow. She had arranged a reduction in the rent with the leasing company in exchange for returning their furniture and kitchen equipment.

The settee and armchairs were buttoned leather and old-fashioned with a circular glass coffee table in front of them. The two bedrooms were modern with bleached-pine drawers and wardrobes. The carpets in all the rooms except the bathroom and kitchen were wall-to-wall. There was a six-place set of KPM china and a seventy-piece cutlery set. The kitchen equipment was new and made in Germany. There were two racks of CDs, mostly classical and jazz and the Thirties ballads of Bing Crosby, Frank Sinatra and the big bands like Glenn Miller and Jimmy Dorsey. There was one disc on top of the hi-fi. A selection of the *Piedigrotta* songs done by Pavarotti. The title of the CD was *'Parla mi d'amore'*. All free walls were painted white which gave the whole apartment an impression of light and sunshine no matter what the weather was outside. The only concession she had made to her frequent overnight stays was a dressing-table with mirrors in the double bedroom.

She had insisted that he had his first look at the apartment on his own so that he didn't have to pretend if he didn't like it.

He walked slowly from room to room and as he absorbed what had been done he realised how well she had read him, and the care

77

and love that had gone into every detail. It wasn't a replica, it wasn't big enough for that, but it encompassed almost forgotten memories of the house he grew up in. But she'd never seen the house. She hadn't even been to Vermont.

When she arrived an hour later it was obvious that he was delighted with everything she had done. She was amused by his stumbling attempts to be grateful but she knew it was as much part of the man as she had tried to make the apartment. Larry Getz wasn't accustomed to people wanting to please him.

They were about to leave to go out to dinner and he stopped with the door half open.

'Something I meant to ask you.'

'Tell me.'

'Way back when we first talked about your taking this place in hand, I asked you why you bothered to do it, and you said you'd tell me one day. How about you tell me now?'

She smiled and said, 'I was being selfish because I hoped I'd be here with you.'

'Do you still want that?'

'Not in a formal sort of way.' She shrugged and laughed. 'After all I've got a key and I choose what goes in the refrigerator. What more could a woman want?'

He opened his mouth to speak and then closed it, putting his arm around her shoulder to ease her through the open door.

They had dinner at his usual Italian restaurant where she was always treated with the elaborate courtesy and respect that *il propritario* thought fitting for the Italian Ambassador's lovely daughter. It amused her but she obviously enjoyed it. She had once persuaded her father and mother to have a meal with them and the place had been bursting with Fiorello's friends. There were photographs of the event on the wall of every alcove.

His six section leaders had asked for a meeting and it was one of the FBI men who raised the problem.

'I'd like to suggest that we establish, say, four or five categories of prime suspicion so that we can begin to eliminate people who don't fall in any of those categories.'

Getz nodded. 'Are you having problems because of the numbers?'

'Yes, and it's like firing buckshot when we should be firing bullets. If we could eliminate those who don't come in our proscribed categories we could spend more time on more likely suspects.'

Getz looked around the table. 'Let's try it for a month and see where we get to. Any ideas of categories?'

The spokesman nodded and said, 'We've made a list. Five pointers.' He looked at Getz. 'Shall I read it out?'

'OK.'

'Not in order of importance.' He paused. 'Signs of living above income. Alcohol problem. Sexual problems. Direct contact with Soviets. Access to information on our Soviet operations.' He paused. 'We've counted unhappy relationships as coming under sexual problems.'

Getz shrugged. 'Let's separate them and make it six categories.' He paused. 'Is there any other help you need?'

'When we've got it down to those who fit our model we're going to need warrants covering a much wider area. Relatives' finances. House searches.' He looked at Getz. 'That sort of thing. Shall we get 'em?'

'Yes, once I've approved them.' He went on, 'What's been the main factor in the names you've put aside?'

'No actual contact with Soviets. Limited access to Soviet documentation and no booze or money problems.'

'Fair enough.' Getz looked around the table. 'Any other problems?'

There were none and the meeting broke up, but he'd expected to be asked about time off. They were working flat out and the early stages of a multi-target surveillance could become grindingly boring when the results were mainly negative.

He chatted with one or two of the group who were talking about some of the problems. The one that amused them all was the target who had everything on the negative list, particularly living a life-style far beyond his salary. He had quoted his in-laws as the source of his money and after checking the in-laws' bank accounts they had found that they were indeed millionaires many times over with the father-in-law a broker at Merrill Lynch, New York, and a loving and generous father to his three daughters. The family homes were a three-storey brownstone in Sutton Place and a mansion just outside Martha's Vineyard. The payments were made to the target's account as father-in-law felt it could seem insulting to pay the money to the wife even if she was the real recipient. They were all Louis Auchincloss characters. The only embarrassing incident was when after a month of carefully planned covert surveillance another target had reported to CIA security that he was being followed by some kind of gang including two men and a woman. He gave quite accurate descriptions of three of the surveillance team but hadn't, apparently, spotted the second woman. He had been told that it was just part of a surveillance training exercise for the benefit of new recruits.

Getz spent many hours reading the daily sitreps on two targets who he felt were highly suspect. One who seemed to spend unnecessary time with Soviet contacts. It was part of the man's job but the contacts seemed to be too frequent and too regular. The information Langley got from the man's contacts was mainly gossip but it had its uses. He had also failed a polygraph test on the questions of relationships with foreign nationals. The second target was Arthur Jarvis, but his failings were mainly social. A drunk and an incompetent, and with a seeming disregard for even routine security. Getz decided that he would take over both files and deal with them himself. He picked a small team of six people to help him with the leg-work. As he slid the two files into his brief-case, a call came through that O'Hara would like to see him at Langley as soon as possible. It reminded him of his 'letter of initial notification', a formality which had to be gone through when a CIA officer had to notify his superiors of his intention to marry a foreign national. It was a formality but it had to be accompanied by a signed letter of resignation that could be used by the top brass if they decided it was necessary for some reason. He had told O'Hara that the notification was likely to land on his desk fairly soon. But that had been a month earlier.

O'Hara was on the phone at his desk when Getz walked in and O'Hara waved to the chair in front of his desk. While he was waiting, Getz took out his notification and pushed it across the desk. When O'Hara hung up he reached for the letter and the accompanying resignation. He read it carefully and then put it to one side. Looking across at Getz, he said, 'When you mentioned this to me I put in a request for a check without mentioning your name but recording that you were employed on top-security operations.' He paused. 'I had the clearance in a couple of days, so there's no problem.' He smiled. 'The cheeky bastard who did the check had put a hand-written comment on a separate sheet. 'It said – "Who's the lucky Joe?".' Still smiling, he said, 'You must come and have dinner with Maggie and me, the two of you.' He sighed. 'That's the only good news and in the light of what you're up to I'd best put you in the picture.' He paused and stood up. 'Let's go sit in the armchairs. I hate sitting behind desks.' On the way over to the chairs O'Hara took two cans of Diet-Coke from the small refrigerator and put them on the coffee table between them.

'No glasses, I'm afraid. Drink up.'

When Getz put down his can. O'Hara leaned forward and said, 'How's it going?'

'We've eliminated half the suspects and we're concentrating on the rest. I've taken over a couple that I don't like the look of for myself.' He paused. 'Are you being hassled?'

'Not really. But I'm conscious of the fact that in a well-run intelligence agency none of this would be necessary.' He shook his head. 'We mustn't ever let it get like this again when we've got this asshole who's shafting us now.'

'It sounds like you've got more information. Have you?'

'We know that Sergei Motorin from their embassy was hijacked back to Moscow and executed there a few days later. But we didn't know that until months afterwards. Then there was Valery Martynov, ordered back to Moscow on the pretence that he was the official escort for Yurchenko. He was executed. No trial. The Brits managed to rescue Gordievsky but they blame the leak on us. There are seven or eight of our assets in Moscow we haven't heard from in nearly a year.' He shrugged. 'We might as well write them off. And any KGB or GRU guy who was vaguely thinking of working for us will have learned the two lessons. First, that if you work for the CIA you stand a good chance of being sold down the Swanee because of a KGB mole in Langley. And second, that if you're betrayed, it'll be the chop.'

'There's something else isn't there?'

'Yeah. It sickens me to think what kind of man can do this. Send people to certain death for money. It can't be ideology. Even the Soviets have given up on communism. It can't be that.'

'It may take us a few more months but we'll get this guy. We've learned a lot about what we're looking for in the last months of the operation.'

'What do the people think who are working for you?'

Getz shrugged. 'I've kept personal feelings out of it. No rhetoric. No emotion. Just plain police work. I don't want them turned on until we get to the real thing.' He smiled. 'Don't worry. It's just a question of time.'

'What makes you so sure?'

'Just that feeling in my bones.'

Getz went to his own set-up at Langley after the meeting with O'Hara. He knew he had overdone his confidence in the result when he had reassured O'Hara that all would be well, given time. From past experience operations searching for suspected moles just quietly petered out. But this time the stakes were higher and even eliminating suspects had given them new experience. There was something that O'Hara had said that stuck in his mind. He had wondered what kind of man could send other men to certain death just for money. Maybe they should look more at the characters of those still in the net. But look for what?

Borinski was forty-five and had specialised in the FBI on criminal-psychology. He had been useful in several cases of serial killers, and sat in his shirt-sleeves as Getz unfolded the background of the operation. When he was finished Borinski was silent for several minutes and then he said, 'You know when I first started looking at serial killers I was always looking for a motive. Revenge . . .' he shrugged '. . . against a certain kind of individual or even society in general. It was never money – there were dozens of easier ways to get money. Then there was the sex angle. There was often sex involved but not normal sex. All too often the victim was an elderly woman. That sends you back to looking at the relationship with their mothers.' He shrugged his shoulders. 'On the whole no better nor worse than a good many ordinary men.'

'Does that mean there is no common characteristic?'

'No way. But it takes time to realise that you aren't even thinking the right thoughts. You're looking for motives that you can understand yourself. One of my teachers said, "When you've looked at all the possibles, look at the impossibles". It was only when I gave up on the normal things that I made any progress.' He shook his head. 'Plenty of men have fantasies about raping a pretty girl. Men who wouldn't do it even if they had the chance. Plenty of us have hated someone enough – a colleague, a boss or even a spouse, and felt angry enough to do them violence. But we never did it.' He paused. 'You fancy a sandwich and a drink?'

'That'd be fine. Thanks.'

Borinski rang the FBI's cafe service and ordered sandwiches, beef, tomato and egg. He checked with Getz before ordering Bud Lights.

They chatted about the problems the Orioles had, and the perennial problems of driving a car in Washington DC. But when the waitress had left the tray of food and the bottle they got back to business.

'Can you give me any suggestions of what to look out for?'

Borinski frowned as he bit into his sandwich and was obviously thinking as he chewed it. He looked across his desk at Getz. 'I think I've got to tell you first what not to look for.' He shrugged. 'It takes time to realise that criminals don't necessarily look like criminals. Their eyes ain't close together and they don't have toothbrush moustaches. They may beat up their women but they can be quite good fathers. But on our side of the fence we have some prejudices built up from childhood of bad men looking and behaving like bad men.' He paused. 'So what is it you look for? Every serial killer I've had to deal with had several things in common. First of all they like what they do. Killing, violating, cutting people up are their prime purposes in life. They don't have any qualms about what they do. I've had men who talk like we could be old mates, calmly describing to me how difficult it is to cut a man's head off, or gouge out an eye with a spoon. I've listened to hours of that crap until I couldn't take any more. They have no regrets, no remorse, no feelings of any kind about their victims. They just happened to be there at the wrong place at the wrong time. Maybe they'd stalked the victim for weeks as part of the pleasure, or it could be just the spur of the moment. They don't blame their mothers or fathers, they probably had a reasonable upbringing. If you talk about a connection they don't get it.' He sighed heavily. 'So don't expect your guy to look guilty and furtive. He won't be. The rules of life are not for him. He's beyond all that. He probably never thinks about his last killing until the mood comes on him again. Believe me. Your guy who sends people to their death has never lost a wink of sleep about what he does. He won't be for or against the Soviets, they're just servants of a superior man who can defy the law at will. No. Not *defy* it. *Ignore* it. Completely. Could be the life and soul of the party in his ordinary life. He's untouchable. And when you put him in the slammer he won't understand what all the fuss is about.' Borinski lit a cigarette, and said quietly, 'I've probably confused you rather than helped you. Fortunately for me I don't have to catch the assholes, I just have to dissect them when they're up for trial.'

Getz smiled. 'You've helped a lot. I'm not sure how but you've made me look through a different pair of eyes. I'll let you know how it works.'

Borinski smiled and stood up, reaching out his hand, and as Getz took it Borinski said, 'I'll probably end up having to sort him out before you try him. He'll be full of his own importance and I'll be trying not to imagine what the KGB do to traitors before they put them up against a wall.'

Getz had fixed himself up with a camp-bed in a corner of his own office in the Tysons Corner building and he slept there most week-nights and took calls from those of his team who were in different time-zones or overseas. In the middle of the night he woke and pushed off the blankets. Still half asleep he dialled the number of Archives' Night Duty Officer.

'NDO. Please identify yourself.'

'Larry Getz. Special Operations. Could you pass on a message for me to your day staff?'

'Yes, sir. No problem. What's the message?'

'I'd like a complete list and appropriate files of all staff at the Soviet Embassy. ASAP.'

'It'll be on the boss's desk in ten minutes time.'

'Thanks.' He laughed. 'What do you say to NDOs? Have a nice night.'

The NDO laughed but not heartily. Getz made himself a cup of coffee and drank it sitting perched on the edge of his bed. It was more than likely that the mole was handled by somebody at the embassy. It was time they looked down the other end of the telescope.

Chapter 14

By midday Getz had had a quick look at nearly a hundred files of staff at the Soviet Embassy. It wasn't easy even to pick out the likely KGB and GRU people. They could be car drivers or maintenance men despite the importance of their real status. But a KGB man who handled a CIA traitor was going to have had long periods of training and service in Moscow HQ. This cut out more than half the personnel. The man would also need to have a job or cover job that allowed him to move as freely as the regulations allowed in the Washington area. Even the Soviet Embassy had to have senior staff who were capable of dealing with the normal business of diplomacy. Genuine diplomats would have worked at several embassies before being posted to Washington DC. Sergei Motorin had passed a lot of information about embassy staff before he was hijacked back to Moscow and these factors allowed Getz to bring the list of possibles down to seven. The diplomats who were responsible for Trade, Economics and Science had to have knowledge enough to be able to talk with their opposite numbers in Washington and were most unlikely to be used as a case-officer where their other experience would be wasted. That left the two Press Officers. A senior and a junior. And a travel official. According to Motorin's information it was the junior who did the hard graft of press releases and acting as spokesman when there were problems. That left the Senior Press Officer and the young woman who was responsible for promoting tourism to Russia. From the photographs she looked very attractive and the notes said that she got about a lot, talking to tour operators and social groups. The notes also said that she spoke fluent English and was very popular.

He wrote out a note for Anastasia Petrova and Yuri Volkov to be put under twenty-four-hour surveillance until further notice. He wanted reports on both of them every day. The surveillance teams must be the best they have. He wanted videos, and still-shots where videos would be too obvious.

As Jarvis sat watching the TV he could hardly believe what he saw. It was a CNN news report live from Moscow. It showed the building that housed the Russian parliament. A building that Muscovites called the White House. It was under fire from tank cannon ripping jagged holes in the structure with clouds of dust rising from the rubble. The almost breathless CNN reporter was claiming that there had been a planned coup against Gorbachev but the army had refused at the last minute to co-operate with the KGB who had planned the coup.

A local Moscow journalist had joined the CNN man and had been asked what it was all about. The journalist said they were witnessing the end of the old hands of the KGB. On the late-night news bulletins they showed a crane toppling the statue of Feliks Dzherdzinski, the founder of Soviet intelligence. An unnamed CIA officer, back to cameras, said that it was not only the end of the old KGB set-up but they were watching the Soviet Union crumbling to pieces. He said that the CIA were reliably informed that the former head of the KGB, Viktor Fomenko, who had only recently been appointed, had already been arrested.

To the top men at Langley the good news was tempered by the realisation that they had not had the slightest hint that such a coup was even rumoured. Once again the CIA had been exposed in its ignorance of impending events.

For Arthur Jarvis it was more proof of his instinctive theory that both the CIA and the KGB were hopelessly inefficient. And this time it would affect him. He switched off the TV and called out to his wife that he would be away for an hour or so. He drove to the drop at the old bridge that was the emergency site and put the two vertical chalk marks on the brick where the grassy bank started. An hour later he phoned from his house to the unused number and said 'Bell' three times. It was mid-evening when he took the lid off the toilet cistern at the cinema. The note was there, in a plastic bag. He read it carefully. It was from Volkov himself. It told him to arrange no contacts until he was given the clear and he was to meet Volkov at the 'iron' RV in Bogotá the following week. The Sunday at 3 p.m. He burned the note with his lighter and flushed the ashes down the toilet.

By the time Jarvis was reading the note Volkov was already on a TWA flight to Toronto where Aeroflot held the late evening flight for him for half an hour. He had no idea what sort of reception he would get. He had only got non-committal replies to any of his questions. It sounded pretty chaotic but they surely wouldn't risk upsetting the relationship with the best asset that Moscow had ever had. Apart from anything else they had invested a lot of money in Jarvis. After the fuelling stop at Shannon he had slept through most of the flight to Moscow.

As the plane approached Sheremetyevo one of the cabin staff gave him a radio message from the cockpit. A car and driver would be waiting for him and would take him to the Metropol where he would be awaited. He breathed a sigh of relief. At least they weren't taking him to the Lubyanka.

He was even more reassured when he found that it was a suite rather than a room which had been booked for him. As he booked in the receptionist asked him to wait for a moment while she telephoned. As she hung up she gave him his suite number and the keys. He asked where he could buy a razor and toiletries and the girl hesitated and then said quietly, 'I should go straight up. I think someone's waiting for you.'

He smiled, took the keys and headed for the elevators. He smelt the cigar smoke as he slid the key into the lock and let himself in. Fomenko was sitting in an armchair, his jacket on the floor beside the chair, a drink in one hand and a cigar in the other. The cigar hand waved him to the nearest armchair.

'Sit down, comrade. Sit down.'

Volkov sat down slowly. 'I thought ... the news bulletins said ...'

'You shouldn't take your time from the media, especially the Yanks, my friend.' He paused. 'There was a problem, but I did a deal.' He paused and half-smiled. 'I'm Minister of Special Projects covering the security of the State.'

Volkov smiled. 'I ought to have known better. May I ask what happened?'

'You may ask but I have no intention of discussing what went on.

Enough to say that my new job consists solely of seeing that our friend in Washington keeps sending us what we need.' He paused. 'So bring me up to date.'

'Since the coup business was on every TV screen I've kept away from him. We've communicated on an "urgent" basis and I've fixed to meet him next week in Bogotá. But I needed to know how things are at this end.'

'Nothing's changed. Well . . .' he shrugged. '. . . I guess a few things have changed. A few lessons have been learned all round. But nothing's changed with your operation, not with you, nor with me. We've got that funny little guy as our insurance.' He nodded. 'And don't let's forget it.'

'Tell me what happened – the coup.'

Fomenko shook his head and waved his hand dismissively. 'It's safer to know nothing,' he said. 'But I'll tell you this – it was the grave of the Soviet Union. Nobody will be able to put the pieces together again.' He sighed. 'Not that anyone will try.'

When Fomenko eventually left, Volkov walked down to the Arbat. It was a mild, sunny, spring evening and the people in the streets seemed better dressed than he remembered. He pressed the bell on the door of his mother's apartment and was surprised when it was answered by his father.

'Good God in heaven . . .' he called over his shoulder, '. . . it's Yuri, Maman.' He smiled. 'Our son has come a-visiting.' He moved aside. 'Come in, my boy, come in.'

His mother put her arms around his shoulders and kissed him on both cheeks. 'It's lovely to see you, boy.' She turned and pointed to a girl who was standing behind her. 'This is Sabine. One of my colleagues. She's from Paris. Isn't she just beautiful?'

The girl offered her hand, her beautiful face calm, serene. 'Nice to know you,' she said. 'Forgive my Russian. It's very primitive.'

Yuri laughed. 'So is mine.' He spoke in English.

The girl smiled. 'I can do better in English. I went to school in England.'

'How long have you been in Moscow?'

'A week only.'

His mother brought in coffee and cups. He had sent her airtight bottles of coffee from the States but he knew she only used it on special occasions. His father joined them, his personality overpowering even when he was just having a cup of coffee.

'What are you doing, Papa, at the moment?'

He laughed. 'It's a modern version of the Bible story of Solomon and the two women who claimed the baby. But this time it's a husband and wife quarrelling about a horse.' He paused, nodding towards the girl. 'This young woman wants to see the Bolshoi, the ballet company, they're doing *Swan Lake* tonight. Why don't you take her?'

Volkov looked at the girl. 'Would you like to go?'

'I'd love to go.'

Volkov looked at his father. 'Who's got most pull, you or me?'

His father laughed and stood up. 'After your lot's little effort two weeks ago I think maybe it should be me.'

It had been a special performance that night in honour of the Swedish ambassador and it had taken longer than usual. It was almost midnight when Yuri and the girl walked down the embankment beside the Moskva river. As they stood looking at the boats still carrying their patrons the music was just audible across the water.

The girl turned to look at him. 'Who was that man with all those medals who spoke to you in the first interval?'

Volkov shrugged. 'He's a colleague of mine.' He smiled. 'He likes showing off his medals. He's just been through a bit of a crisis so I guess he was giving his ego a boost.'

'He was very polite to you. You must be very important. Your mother said you worked in America for the Foreign Ministry.' She paused and laughed. 'She said she thought it was time you found a nice girl and settled down.'

Volkov smiled. 'Nice girls are boring, honey. But she's probably right.' He paused. 'How about you? You must have dozens of young men in tow in Paris.' He smiled. 'You've probably already got one here in Moscow.'

She laughed. 'You're a flatterer. And you're my only beau in Moscow.' She paused, smiling. 'So far. So you'd better stake your claim.'

'It's Sunday tomorrow. Would you like to go for a drive? We could go to see Peredelkino where all our famous writers had *dachas*. And still do for that matter.'

'But your friend with all the medals said he's seeing you tomorrow.'

Volkov smiled. 'He can wait.' It amused him to hear Fomenko described as his friend with all the medals.

'What time shall we need to leave?'

'How about I pick you up at eleven?'

'That would be fine.'

At the door of his mother's place they kissed goodnight. It wasn't a polite peck but it wasn't outrageous either. He watched her turn the key and go inside but he didn't follow her. He could hear 'In the Mood' from the radio in the sitting room.

They sat side by side on the fallen tree-trunk brought down in the winter storms. The hotel had made up a basket of sandwiches and drinks for them and they munched slowly on the sandwiches like children out on a picnic. They were looking out across the lake. It was still and calm and there were circles where fish were rising for flies.

'When do you go back to the States?'

'I'll be leaving on Tuesday. And you, how long are you staying in Moscow?'

'Not long.'

'Then where?'

'Back to Paris. I'm not medical you know. I'm a script-writer for a film company. I'm just doing research here.'

'How do you like Moscow?'

'Truth or polite?'

He smiled. 'Truth of course.'

'I find it terribly depressing. It's as if someone has cast a spell over all the people. Nobody smiles. There's food at last for people to buy and even luxuries. In bad times there are always luxuries. From what my parents tell me Paris was like this after the Germans marched in.' She paused and looked at him. 'I think it is even worse for all those people in other countries who were persuaded that communism was the answer to the human condition. It isn't of course. And it never was.'

He smiled and raised his eyebrows. 'As that anonymous French philosopher once said – "*tout passe, tout casse, tout lasse*".'

She smiled and clapped her hands. 'Very good, very clever. I can see why you are so successful.'

'Who said I was successful?'

'Both your parents. In their separate ways. Your father said that you should be in the Duma as a politician. Your mother said that you were far too intelligent for the job you do.'

He grinned. 'I'd better tell you that in my father's opinion politicians come well below used-car salesmen.' He paused. 'Tell me about your parents and your life in Paris?'

'My father is head of an independent film company and my mother is a TV producer on state TV. She covers current events. And I write scripts for feature films. Mainly with French settings.' She smiled. 'Very gentle and very romantic. Did you see the recent remake of *Un homme et une femme*?'

'Yeah.'

'I helped on that.'

'Apropos nothing at all. Can I see you every day until I leave?'

She smiled. 'Are you sure you want to? There have been lots of phone calls at your mother's from girls who've heard rumours that you're in town.'

'She didn't tell me. She knows I wouldn't be available.'

She smiled again. 'Why not? Is it because of me? Would you have been available if I wasn't around?'

He pursed his lips. 'I guess I would have.'

'At least you're honest.' She paused. 'But why me?'

'For about an hour it was because you're very beautiful. Those big dark eyes and that lovely calm face. After that . . .' he shrugged. '. . . after that I guess I just feel I've known you all my life. I don't have to play games. I can just be myself.'

'And what is "myself"?'

He thought for a moment and then shrugged again. 'I'm just an ordinary man. Fairly bright, quite good at my job and . . .' he hesitated '. . . and I like you very much.'

. She reached out for his hand and said quickly, 'You're a very modest man. I'll have to tell you about yourself one of these days.'

'There's something I'd better tell you. It's against the rules but to hell with that . . .'

She held up her hand. 'You don't have to tell me, I know.'

'How do you know?'

'Your mother told me.' She smiled. 'She said it was obvious that I was going to be involved with you and I ought to be warned.'

'It was a stupid thing to do. Irresponsible. It could have caused us both a lot of trouble. What did she actually say?'

'Just that you were a senior officer in the KGB.'

'She didn't talk about my work?'

'No. She obviously had no idea of what you actually do.'

For long moments Volkov was silent and then he said, 'Let's go back to Moscow and have a celebratory drink at the Metropol where I'm staying.'

She was obviously relieved. 'What are we celebrating?'

'You know as well as I do what we're celebrating. We're celebrating you and me.'

They had eaten in the restaurant at the Metropol, the most elegant and efficient hotel in Moscow and after their meal they went up to his suite.

They had talked about films they liked. He had talked about America almost as enthusiastically as any American would do, until he realised that he was becoming an 'agent of influence'. It was at this point that he broke all the rules of both commonsense and security.

'Have you ever been to South America?'

'No.' She shrugged. 'I haven't travelled much outside France.'

'When I leave here I won't be flying direct to Washington. I'll be flying to Colombia, to Bogotá. I'll be there for about four days. Would you like to come with me?'

For long moments she was silent and then she said quietly, 'I'd come with you but I think we're rushing things a bit. We've only known each other for a couple of days. I want to go on seeing you but . . .'

'But you don't want to be committed.' She could hear the disappointment in his voice.

'No. It's not that. I guess I am committed without having thought about it. But flying to Bogotá doesn't fit in.'

'Fair enough.'

'Are you committed?'

'Yes.'

'Would you like me to stay with you tonight?'

'As a recompense you mean?'

'No, you idiot. As a pleasure to us both.'

He sighed. 'You're absolutely right. I may be bright but you've got more commonsense than I have. And I'd love you to stay the night.'

She went with him in the car to Sheremetyevo where Volkov was surprised to find Fomenko waiting to see him off. He introduced him to the girl and Fomenko was barely polite in his response. He mumbled some excuse to lead Volkov away from the girl to the bookstall.

'Who is she, the girl?'

'A friend of mine. She's French.' When Fomenko still looked displeased Volkov said, 'And her father is making a film set in Moscow. Let's hope Moscow treats his daughter well.' He knew it was a lie but Fomenko's attitude angered him. Fomenko left, nodding condescendingly to the girl as he walked past her.

She was obviously amused by Fomenko. 'The man with the medals – a real gorilla? I guess he was the real KGB. The old ones that they try to keep in the background.'

'Forget him. He doesn't matter. I can handle bastards like him.'

The lie to Fomenko and his self-assurance about handling him were mistakes and Volkov knew it. He should have been cool and laid-back, not stung and angry.

She stayed with him until one of the cabin crew came for him to make sure that he had first choice of seats on the plane. They had kissed ardently and were not aware of Fomenko watching them from the Immigration office observation window. As he turned to go Volkov said, '*Do zvedanya.*'

She smiled and said, '*À bientôt.*'

Fomenko decided not to put Volkov in the picture about the diversion he had planned in Bonn. It was intended to take Langley's attention away from Washington and Jarvis and he knew that Volkov ought to have been told. But Fomenko had never liked the French and he didn't like Volkov's latest girl-friend. And apart from his existing prejudice the girl had looked him in the eyes. Not overawed. Not impressed. Almost amused. He had tried to stare her down but it hadn't worked. He would have her checked out.

Senator Liebman was no admirer of the CIA and that was why he had been made chairman of the small unofficial committee responsible for overseeing the agency with informal meetings from time to time. Senator Liebman loathed diplomats and anything to do with intelligence work.

He had listened with ill-concealed impatience while the Director of the agency gave the committee a verbal report that was a barely disguised litany of the agency's failures.

Senator Liebman sat sucking his back teeth and fiddling with the notes in front of him on the desk. From time to time he ostentatiously looked away towards the windows and sighed.

When the Director finished, the Senator leaned forward, his elbows on the desk.

'Tell me, Mister. I've listened patiently to your bullshit. A list of excuses. I want you to answer me a few questions. Yes or no – no bullshit, no flim-flam. OK?'

'Certainly.'

'Did you warn the White House that the Soviet Union was about to fall to pieces?'

'I gave some indication . . .'

'Yes or no.' The Senator's voice thundered around the room. 'Yes or no.' He barked again. 'The answer's no, isn't it? You didn't warn the White House because you didn't know a damn thing about what was going on in Moscow.' He was breathing heavily as he went on. 'Did you warn the White House that the Berlin Wall was coming down?'

'Even the East German government didn't know that.'

'Did you warn the White House that that asshole Sadam was going to invade Kuwait?'

The Director was silent.

'Did you warn the President of what was about to happen in Yugoslavia?'

'No. The Yugoslavs themselves didn't know.'

'Is it true there's a KGB mole inside the CIA?'

'If there was, Senator, and I knew it, he'd be in a Federal prison.'

Senator Liebman sighed heavily and leaned back in his chair until it creaked. He looked around the table at the other members of the committee.

'Anybody else got any questions?'

If there had been the others knew that this was not the time to ask them. The Senator looked across at his adversary.

'OK, Mister. I've finished. You can go.' Mentally he added, 'And the sooner I get you out the better. You asshole.'

There was a scraping of chairs as the small meeting broke up.

Chapter 15

When O'Hara got the phone call from the CIA bureau in Bonn he immediately contacted Larry Getz. Getz had wondered why O'Hara was insistent that they meet in the Langley carpark.

'Sorry to drag you away from your operation, Larry, but I've just had a call from our Bonn people. They say that one of their guys has got a KGB man who's been co-operating in the past who insists that he knows of a mole in Langley who's feeding Moscow with authentic information about our Soviet assets.' He paused. 'I'd like you to make a quick visit to Bonn and look at this guy yourself.'

'Is there any indication that the alleged mole has actually done any damage?'

'Yes there is. Not very positive but it seems he knew about the two KGB men here in Washington and that they were executed about a year ago.'

'So why isn't our guy in Bonn capable of dealing with the Russian?'

'Seems like the Russian says he will only talk to someone more important at Langley.' He shrugged. 'Two or three days should be enough.'

The mid-morning sun was lifting the mist that hung over the pine forest as the plane made the final approach to Wahn airport and there was a car and driver waiting to take him to the pleasant house on the river-bank where Maclean was waiting for him.

Maclean had introduced him to his man who had been handling the KGB man. He was very young and had done barely a year in the CIA and the KGB man was the first he had handled alone.

When they were settled Getz said to Maclean's man, 'Tell me about the Russian.'

'He works at their commercial section but that's just a cover for being KGB.'

'What's his name?'

'Levin. Andrei Levin.'

'Apart from the CIA mole story what else has he given you?'

'Mainly technical information about tank and armoured-car designs.'

'And how long has he talked about the CIA mole?'

'About a week. I reported it as soon as he mentioned it.'

'What has he told you about the mole?'

'That he works at Langley and was responsible for uncovering two KGB men working for the CIA.'

'Where?'

'In Washington.'

'Is that all?'

'He said he would only tell more to someone more senior than me. And it had to be someone from Langley.'

'OK. Bring him in.'

The Russian was in his thirties, but already balding with a moustache that was obviously intended to add strength to his weak chin. There were no introductions and Getz was to do all the questioning. The early questions didn't seem relevant to the issue of moles. How was he recruited? Where did he do his training? Who were his seniors in Moscow? Did he have a girl-friend in Bonn? Had he ever been promoted? What were his ambitions?

Then Getz said, 'It's Andrei, isn't it?'

'That's correct.'

'Tell me about the CIA man who works for the KGB?'

'He works here in Germany but he is controlled from Langley. He goes there a lot.'

'What section?'

'The section that operates against the KGB in Europe.'

'Do you know his name?'

'His code-name is Joe.'

'How did the KGB recruit him?'

'I don't know.'

'How do they reward him?'

'I think it's something to do with a girl.'

'What makes you think that?'

'Just odd things he's said.'

'How long have you been handling him?'

'About a year.'

Getz could see the beads of sweat on the Russian's forehead, and he was constantly fidgeting with his shirt and tie. He had done too many interrogations not to recognise the signs.

'Describe to me what this man looks like.'

'He's about forty, heavy build, blond hair, blue eyes.'

'What language do you speak with him?'

'A bit of German, a bit of English.'

'When were you last in Moscow?'

The Russian looked surprised at what seemed an irrelevant question. 'About ten days ago.'

'What were you doing?'

'I was on leave.'

'Who did you report to there?'

'Nobody.'

'You didn't even go in just to say hello?'

'No. Why should I?'

For long moments Getz stared at the Russian without speaking. Then he said quietly, but with a tremor of anger in his voice, 'Who briefed you with this mole story?'

'I don't know what you mean.'

'Either you tell me or I'll take you down to the BND offices and they can deal with you.'

'I don't understand.'

'I'm a busy man, comrade. You can talk to me or to German intelligence. One or the other.'

Getz saw the hesitation. 'I'll do a deal with you, my friend. Tell me about the briefing and I promise you nobody outside this room will know what's been going on. Not Moscow, not the Germans, not even people at Langley. I just want the facts. I shall take no action about what you tell me.'

The Russian was trembling and he couldn't keep still. He spoke in a whisper as he said, 'Is that a promise?'

'Absolutely.'

It was a pathetic story. His name was Glinsky. Nikita Glinsky. He had been on leave in Moscow and he'd been told there was a special mission lined up for him. They'd given him the 'mole' story and he'd had two days of mock interrogations about the non-existent CIA mole. Nobody had told him the purpose of the exercise but he had a Moscow man he could ring from the embassy if it got out of hand and the CIA man wanted some hard identity of the mole. It was his own idea to insist on only talking to someone senior from Langley. He didn't expect that they would do anything about it. Fomenko would have sent him to the Gulag if he'd known about his stooge's creative touch.

As the Russian told his story Getz was more friendly. Sympathising with the difficult position the man had been forced into. Critical of whoever had devised the operation in Moscow and then left him to get on with it. If ever he wanted some help, Getz said, pointing at Maclean, he knew where to come.

Maclean had got him on a direct flight to Washington and driven him to the airport. As they sat drinking beer in the bar, Maclean said, 'I was very impressed. What made you so sure he was lying?'

'I don't know, Mac. He had all the body movements of a liar. The story was pathetic. Any fool would have spotted that. It was full of holes.'

'I'm afraid my young fool didn't spot it.'

'He did the next best thing. He reported it right away to you.'

'How are things at Langley these days?'

'About the same as our friend described Moscow. Chaos. Stupidity and bloody-mindedness in about equal proportions.'

'I heard that your marriage went down the pan.'

'That was a long time ago.'

'Do you get to see your boy?'

'Every other Saturday.'

'Anybody new?'

Getz smiled. 'You're doing a soft interrogation on me, Mac.' He paused. 'Yes. There is somebody new. She's much younger than me. Italian and very beautiful.'

Maclean smiled and raised his glass. 'Better be lucky than rich.'

*   *   *

Fomenko still had to learn that time spent in preparation is seldom wasted. But it took him nearly three months to admit that his clumsy ploy to divert attention from Jarvis was a waste of time. Fomenko had a gift for rationalising his own mistakes.

Chapter 16

Volkov disliked Bogotá. He could never understand why tourists would visit a city where they were constantly warned that they were likely to be robbbed with violence. Where you daren't carry a camera or wear good jewellery. He settled himself in at the embassy and spent his time with the KGB staff. They were all well aware that the house opposite the embassy was occupied by CIA people photographing and filming everyone who visited or arrived at the Soviet Embassy. The CIA people were even careless enough to be seen setting up their zero-light cameras every evening to try and identify visitors after the streetlights were switched off. He had arrived two days before he was due to meet Jarvis and had enlisted the aid of the ambassador's secretary to help him choose a present for Sabine. The problem was that everything the secretary fell in love with was French and in the end he chose a locally made gold bracelet. It was elegant and expensive and the secretary assured him that any Frenchwoman receiving such a gift would realise that it was something both special and valuable.

On the Sunday Volkov strolled to the park and stayed in the vicinity of the statue that was the RV. By midday the heat was almost unbearable and Jarvis was already two hours' overdue. Cursing the American, Volkov waited another hour with no sign of Jarvis and then Volkov angrily made his way back to the embassy.

He spent a couple of hours trying to get through to his mother's number in Moscow in the hope that he might be able to speak to the girl. When he finally got through it was his father who answered. Sabine and his mother were at one of the hospitals looking at the intensive-care unit. But his father was able to give him Sabine's number in Paris where she would be returning in a few days' time.

The protocol of the 'iron' RV was that if the meeting didn't take place on the appointed day the case-officer should attend the same place and at the same time on the two following days.

The next day, the Monday, the skies were overcast and there were fewer visitors to the park apart from women with small children.

Volkov saw Jarvis strolling casually up the path towards the statue and went through the ritual of asking him for a light for his cigarette.

As Jarvis proffered his lighter, Volkov bent his head to the flame, and when he raised his head he said, with barely concealed anger, 'Where the hell were you yesterday?'

Jarvis looked surprised. 'I was at my in-laws. Why do you want to know?'

'Our meeting was fixed for yesterday.'

'No way. I marked it in my diary when I got your note.'

'Check it. Let me see it.' When Jarvis looked confused, Volkov said coldly, 'Show me your diary.'

Jarvis zipped open his carry-bag and searched for his diary. When he found it he turned the pages slowly and then stopped. 'Oh, shit. You're right.' He looked up, smiling, at Volkov. 'Sorry pal.' He shrugged. 'Anyway we've met now. What's it all about?'

'What do you think it's all about?'

'I hope you got us sorted out in Moscow now your guy has bit the dust.'

'He didn't bite the dust as you put it. He is now solely in charge of this operation and the analysis of the material you pass to us.'

Jarvis shrugged. 'So we're back to normal.'

'Not exactly.'

'Oh. What's different?'

'He wants to emphasise to you the importance we place on keeping to our signals system and the dead drops.'

Jarvis shrugged. 'Fair enough. No problem.'

Volkov was tempted to harangue him about his failure to keep the meeting but decided that with a man like Jarvis it would make no difference. But he went back to the instructions again.

'Fomenko sent me a message yesterday that he is carrying out an operation that he thinks will divert any suspicion there might be about you to another area. He's going to a lot of trouble to protect you and the operation and sticking to our communications protocol is virtually an order. He wants a hundred per cent compliance. You understand? No excuses. Agreed?'

Jarvis smiled. 'Don't get worked up, comrade. I'll be a good boy.' He grinned. 'You got time to have a tequila or something?'

'No. I've got to get back to Washington. I'm already a day late with my appointments.' Relenting slightly, he said, 'But at least you can be reassured that you are still in good hands in Moscow.'

Jarvis smiled amiably and patted Volkov on the shoulder and Volkov could smell the booze on Jarvis's breath. 'You go first and I'll admire the geraniums for five minutes.'

Volkov got the embassy to book him onto the next flight to Washington and to pack his belongings in his bag and bring them to him at the bar at the Hilton.

He ordered himself an omelette and as he ate it slowly he thought about the girl. What excuse could he create for a trip to Paris? Maybe they could meet half-way until he realised that half-way was somewhere in the middle of the Atlantic. One thing he must do and that was improve his elementary French. He must start cultivating a few people at the French Embassy in Washington. He even bought a two-days' old copy of *Le Figaro* at the hotel bookstall so that he could read it on the plane. He was more relaxed after the delicious omelette and he was faintly amused to reflect that he was beginning to pursue the girl as if he were running a new agent rather than pursuing a pretty young woman who probably didn't give a damn about her KGB acquaintance. There was a French girl at reception and he asked her who was the man who sang '*La Mer*' so beautifully. She told him it was Charles Trenet and he made a note to buy one of his tapes when he was back in Washington.

Chapter 17

Getz listened to the man and the woman who had been leading the surveillance on Volkov and the tourism girl at the Soviet Embassy. Her name was Petrova. Anastasia Petrova.

'She's twenty-five, Larry. There's a few still photos with my written report. She's all over the place. Drove me crazy. A dozen meetings a day but there's no doubt they're all work. Several guys made passes at her but she gave them polite brush-offs. Nothing suspicious. Never talks politics. All she puts over are the joys of visiting the Soviet Union and special deals for various groups – teachers, sports people, farmers and theatre people.' She paused. 'I'd say she's not a runner as a target.' She turned to her companion. 'Your turn, Johnny.'

'Volkov disappeared almost as soon as my chaps started. It took us a day to find out that he was in Moscow. Our people in Moscow were useless. They only caught up with him at Sheremetyevo when he was leaving. He had visited his parents who've got a good-sized apartment on the Arbat but he'd stayed at the Metropol. A suite. One of the cleaning women said he had had a long visit from someone whose car had a KGB number.' He paused. 'It seems he also had a woman visitor. Young, attractive and a foreigner but not English or American. She saw him off at Sheremetyevo when he left.' He looked at Getz as he said, 'Volkov's flight was a one-way flight to Bogotá. He sighed. 'Our people in Bogotá were hopeless. They got nothing on him but we found he'd travelled on an Air American flight back here to Washington. We've restarted the surveillance on him but like the girl he has a lot of meetings and it's our guess that he's just a propagandist, maybe on the look-out for "agents of influence". He had a prearranged meeting with some travel agency people and we got one of our girls into the meeting. Says he charmed the lot of them.

Lock, stock and barrel. Said he reminded her of Jimmy Stewart but brighter.'

Getz glanced at both of them. 'OK. Keep it going. If there's anything you need let me know.'

With the file on Anastasia Petrova put on the back-burner, Getz concentrated on the other file. The file for Arthur Casey Jarvis. After an hour's reading he reached for a scratch-pad and wrote out a list of things to pursue.

1. The Jaguar cars. How many?
2. Life-style.
3. Bank account at Northwest Federal Union.
4. Purchase of house at N. Randolph St. Arlington, VA. Mortgate. Lien.
5. Previous home.
6. Cost of renovations at new home.
7. Checking account at First Virginia Bank, Arlington.
8. Checking account at Dominion Federal Bank, Vienna, VA.
9. Check possible inheritance from death of Jarvis's mother. She lived in North Carolina. Employed one time as teacher in Fairford County.
10. Check financial status of wife's parents in Bogotá.
11. Check Jarvis's possible knowledge of all CIA Soviet assets now not operating.
12. Check general life-style and relationship with wife.
13. Check any polygraph tests.
14. Check locations and dates of non-official overseas trips.
15. Speak in confidence to previous bosses and colleagues.
16. Consider applying for search of house with 'in occupier's absence' warrant.
17. Consider warrant for phone tapping (Grade 1).
18. Consider warrant for bugging home rooms.
19. Check long-term work record.
20. Get woman's view on Jarvis (Gertie??).
21. Check Jarvis's status against PERSEREC Hearing's report on past defectors.
22. Check his father's record with CIA.

Getz had phoned Gabriella and they had arranged to have
sandwiches in the garden at the embassy as Getz would not
be able to get there before 10 p.m. and he would have to leave
before midnight.

There was a small pond with goldfish and water-lilies in the
garden and they sat with cushions on a stone bench beside it.
There was a light at one corner of the pond set unobtrusively
in a cluster of yellow celandine. It threw reflected light up at
Getz's face and she was aware that his thoughts were far away.
There was a pulse beating just above his cheek.

'Are you sure you aren't overdoing things, Larry? You look
very tired.'

He turned to look at her face. 'Don't worry, honey. I've
got a long messy job at the moment and . . .' he stopped.
'. . . I'd better not go on.' He smiled. 'Anyway, even if I
am tired, don't worry about me. I've had far worse times,
believe me.'

She smiled and kissed him. 'Any chance of you taking me to
the movies on Sunday?'

'Sunday afternoon.' He frowned. 'Could be. What's on?'

She laughed. 'There's a classic film club and they're doing *La
Dolce Vita* again. Have you seen it?'

'Is that the one that opens with the statue of Christ moving
slowly across the sky and the city?'

She nodded. 'Yes. At least you didn't say is that the one
showing Anita Ekberg's beautiful boobs.'

He smiled. 'I confess that that had also passed through
my mind.'

He reached down for the wine bottle and went to pour wine
into her glass when she put her hand out to stop him.

'What's the matter? You had enough?'

'No. But you mustn't pour wine backwards like that, it's a
porta sfortuna – a sign of bad luck.'

He laughed. 'You and your mother and your superstitions.'

'My father believes it too. About pouring the wine backwards.
Ask him.'

For a moment he was silent and then he said, 'Does your
father approve of our relationship?'

111

She shrugged. 'I've never discussed it with him. It's not his business. But he approves of you.'

'In what way?'

'Says you're a good man. Honest and thoughtful. And that's high praise from Papa I assure you.'

'He must find me a bit dull. He's such a lively man.'

'You're fishing for compliments, my friend. Anyway lively men like my father need an appreciative audience and you fit that nicely.'

He sighed. 'I've got to go, honey.'

Back at Tysons Corner, Getz drank a cup of coffee as he read through the PERSEREC Hearing's report that was number 21 on his Arthur Jarvis list.

The Defence Personnel Security Research and Education Centre had published a research paper based on a broad overview of the demographics of Americans who had committed espionage between 1945 and 1989. The findings of the report took up only a single page of double-spaced typing. He had skipped through it when it was first published because its contents had no relevance to his work at that time.

Most American spies have been Caucasian, heterosexual males. The spies are fairly well educated, generally married, and most frequently hold technical or intelligence jobs.

In terms of volunteering and recruiting, 73% of the spies were volunteers as compared with 27% who were recruited, either by foreign intelligence agencies or by fellow Americans. Patterns of volunteering and recruiting changed over the 44-year period with the large shift toward volunteering in the past 20 years.

As for motivation, money has been the major reason for espionage, followed by ideology and disgruntlement/revenge. When we look at motivation over the past 44 years, money had increased dramatically.

There are more long-term spies, here defined as those whose espionage careers lasted more than 2 years, among those to come to espionage at a later age. In other words, spies who begin espionage young are less likely to survive a 2-year career.

As Larry Getz closed the file and put it to one side he realised that he ought to have read it way back. It was a very revealing piece of research and something to use as a reference against the characteristics of their suspects. Especially Arthur Jarvis. It was then that he realised that he had never actually seen Jarvis. He'd seen a lot of grainy black and white 35mm surveillance still-shots and one or two short Hi-8 video clips. But he should have seen him in the flesh. He'd do it the next day. As he undressed slowly and arranged his clothes on the chair beside his camp-bed he wondered why she put up with him. He was doing it all over again. She'd had barely ten hours of his time in the last two weeks. The meetings were always at the last minute and timed to suit him and his work, not her. He resolved to do better in the next few weeks and then sighed because he knew it was no more than a pious hope. He started reading Martha Gellhorn's *The View from the Ground* and fell asleep ten minutes later, the bedside light still on.

It looked a pleasant enough house on the edge of Georgetown and the girl rang the bell and waited. The man who answered the door was obviously in the middle of eating his breakfast and when he saw the girl he wiped his mouth with the back of his hand.

'What can I do for you?'

'I'm trying to trace the history of a dark red Jaguar car with a Virginia licence number QH1319. The records seem to show that you were the owner until about July 1989.' She smiled up at him. 'Am I right?'

'You'd better come in.'

He took her into the kitchen and cleared a space for her at the table.

'A coffee?'

'Thank you. Milk but no sugar.'

'Milk but no sugar it is,' he said amiably as he handed her a large cup and saucer and a milk jug. He poured the coffee and watched her stir in the milk.

'Where are you from?'

'I'm a freelance journalist.'

'You thinking of buying a Jag?'

She laughed. 'No. I've got an old Mustang.'

'I wondered if you might be snooping around for the IRS.'

'Not me, sir.' She paused. 'Why should the IRS be interested in Jaguars anyway?'

'Just checking if I declared any profit I made on the sale of the car.'

'You'd only have to do that if selling cars was your business.'

'It *is* my business.' He roared with laughter. 'It's what I call a paying hobby but you know how those bastards can twist things.'

'You can't sell all that many Jaguars anyway.'

He shrugged. 'Jags. Rolls Royces – Silver Shadows mainly, and the odd Merc. Keeps me in pocket money.'

'How much did you sell the Jaguar for?'

He stood up clumsily and she was suddenly aware of the glass of whisky alongside the cruet.

'I'll go and check the records, honey. Wouldn't do it for anyone else but you.'

He steadied himself at the door and disappeared inside the house. He was away for nearly ten minutes and was reading a slip of paper when he came back.

'Yeah. I remember this now. Funny guy. Real weirdo. I wanted fifty thousand bucks and ended up taking five hundred less because he was paying cash. First time, no I tell a lie, the *only* time a guy has paid actual cash for a car like that. He'd got the money with him. Counted it out here on the kitchen-table. I gave him the documents and signed the transfer of ownership. Didn't want no receipt or anything.'

'Must have been a very rich guy.'

'Didn't look rich. I'd have put him down as an insurance salesman. But full of his own importance. Just drove off in the car. Said he was used to Jags.'

'What did he look like?'

'Glasses, bit bald at the front, moustache . . .' he shrugged '. . . drank whisky like it was water.'

She reached in her handbag and took out a photograph of Jarvis. 'Is that the guy?'

He looked at it and then at her. 'You *are* a cop, aren't you?'

She smiled. 'Kind of. But not to worry.'

'Yeah. This is the guy. What's it all about? This guy a crook?'

She stood up. 'You've been a great help, sir. I really appreciate it.'

He saw her to the door and stood watching as she headed for the ancient white Mustang. Trust a woman to choose the wrong colour.

'Was he friendly?'

She shrugged. 'He was at first. I thought he was going to make a pass but once I showed him the photo of Jarvis he wanted to know what it was all about.'

'Do you think he'd make a statement and sign it?'

'I don't know. He's cheating on the IRS and we'd probably have to give him some kind of indemnity.'

'What was the house like? Signs of money?'

'Nice house. Wasn't outside the kitchen much so I can't say. I'd say he's not hard up for a buck.'

'Does he have an office?'

'No, he seems to work from home. I made a few enquiries and it seems he rents a couple of garages where he keeps the cars he wants to sell. They said there was quite a bit of movement. Looks like he sells at least two cars a week.'

'Speak to one of our legal guys. Tell him what was said and ask him what we have to cover in the statement. And have we got enough? When you've done that, take a short break and we'll go together and see your Mr Helliwell.'

It was a couple of minutes before their ring on the bell was answered and Helliwell looked surprised and not too pleased when he saw them.

Larry Getz wasted no time. 'Mr Helliwell, my assistant was full of praise for the help you gave her this morning.' He paused, smiling. 'I wonder if I could have a word with you?'

Still rather reluctant the man took them into a pleasant living room and switched off the TV and waved them to a leather couch.

'Let me assure you, Mr Helliwell, that nothing we discuss with you will be available to anyone else. No government agency, no law enforcement agency. I give you my word.' He paused. 'In fact, the whole matter is so confidential that I must ask you not to inform anyone else about our talk.'

The two men talked about cars for a few minutes, both of them agreeing that if they wanted a Jag it would have to be an early E-type. Then they got down to business. The man repeated what he had said earlier that day and Debbie wrote it out by hand on statement paper.

He was ready to sign it as soon as she finished but Getz smilingly insisted that he read it carefully before he signed it. In the new statement he had been able to remember that Jarvis had told him that he had wealthy in-laws in Colombia.

The next target on Larry Getz's list was the cost of purchasing the house at North Randolph St. Arlington, Virginia.

There was a department that was responsible for maintaining the fabric of the sprawling HQ at Langley, and the responsibility included the maintenance of houses in Washington DC and in Virginia and Maryland that were used by the CIA as safe-houses or for covert operations. Sam Harris had been in charge of the department since it was first established.

Getz introduced himself and showed his priority card.

'I was told that you might be able to help me, Sam. A bit of detective work about a house.'

Sam Harris was not a conversationalist. He shoved a piece of paper across the battered table. 'Write down the address.'

Getz wrote the address of Jarvis's house and Harris read it and then looked at Getz.

'What about it?'

'Sam. I need to know who bought it. How much they paid for it. Mortgage details if any. Bank loan. Date of purchase. Who the vendor was. Any other details that refer to the purchaser.' He smiled. 'And when that's done I need to know how much money was subsequently paid for refurbishing the house.'

'What date are we talking about?'

'September 6th 1989.'

'Any idea of the purchaser's name?'

'Yes. It's Jarvis. Arthur Jarvis. But I definitely don't want him to know we've been making enquiries about the house. OK?'

Sam Harris nodded. 'How urgent is it? How long have I got?'

'Is a week enough?'

'Who knows. I'll get on with it and keep you in the picture.' He paused. 'This guy Jarvis, what's his job?'

116

'He's here at Langley. He's CIA.'

Sam Harris raised his eyebrows and folded the piece of paper before pushing it into the pocket of his blue denim shirt.

Volkov stood looking at himself in the tall mirror in his bedroom. His target was a man he had met before, at a cocktail party at the Norwegian Embassy. The man was genuine Ivy-League but didn't flaunt it. First and foremost he was a business man in the venture-capital field. Volkov wore a light-weight jacket with beige trousers and well-polished black shoes. Volkov always remembered a very successful tycoon who had told him that he didn't need to read a prospective employee's CV. He could tell everything he needed to know by the man's shoes. When he asked what a good guy's shoes should look like his question had been ignored.

Volkov got to the Marriott early and checked that the table he had booked was secluded but alongside the windows.

He breathed a sigh of relief when his guest appeared. Casually dressed and seemingly in a good mood. Volkov had learned that Europeans never discussed the business in hand until the coffee. But Americans got down to it with the canapés.

'Are you able to talk about the current business position in Moscow?'

'Of course. But I should point out that there are other cities with thriving businesses. St Petersburg, Kiev, Smolensk for instance.'

'Let's keep to Moscow. I'm always hearing and reading about so-called Russian Mafia, financial scams, threats of violence and protection money for successful businesses. What are the facts?'

'Since *perestroika* and *glasnost* we have had one main problem. The only people who knew how to organise a business and run a business were the civil servants who ran the Soviet economy. Some were very good, some hopeless. Foreigners always ask – "was this guy a commie?" – and more often than not the answer is "yes". Communist or not he knows how to work the levers of the economy. There's no room for political prejudice these days.'

The man smiled. 'You didn't say anything about the so-called Mafia.'

'They are just the remnants of the state system. Before the change they ran the black-market. You've got a nice little shop. OK. You pay us protection. They ran the prostitutes, they carried out small hold-ups. And they ran the black-market whether you wanted an orange or a Swiss watch. They are still there but still only at street level. OK. They shoot people. But mainly their rivals. The real smart ones are into drugs and technology. You don't need violence for that. The threats may be there but that's considered old-fashioned.'

'Not a very happy picture for an investor.'

Volkov shrugged. 'I just gave you the picture of the things you'd heard. That isn't where people like you go looking for investing.'

'Where do I go then?'

'First for high-tech. We have great engineers and scientists with lockers full of unexploited goodies. And then there's the other side of the coin – entertainment. Films, videos, CDs, pop groups. There's tremendous possibilities there. Our young people are hungry for the American Dream. They're a big market. And they've got a lot of money these days.'

'How do I get to look over those areas?'

'I can arrange a trip to Moscow for you and a colleague and you'll meet top people in both areas. People who know the market potential and who can indicate the possibilities.'

'Tell me, Yuri. Between friends, do I have to provide pay-offs for these people?'

Volkov smiled. 'These are people who have as much money as you and your company have.'

'So why do they need me?'

'Because despite their wealth the market is far too big for them to cover it. You have to remember that the old Soviet Union is twice the size of the United States. It's about the same size as Canada and the USA together.'

'You know, talking to you has been an eye-opener. It's not like talking to a Russian, it's more like talking to an American.' He smiled. 'And a pretty bright American too.'

Volkov smiled. 'I'm flattered.' He paused. 'That's about it, and contact me if I can be of help to you. Either here or in Moscow.'

The man said, 'I will. How long since you were in Moscow?'

Volkov laughed. 'A long time I'm afraid, but I have access to all the current information.'

They talked about the Oscar nominations and the poor showing of the European films that were being made to please the American market, but inevitably failing as miserably overseas as they did at home.

Getz drove across to Langley and checked that Art Jarvis was in the building. He was shown on the internal building plans the office that Jarvis occupied. There was a glass partition between two offices and Getz watched Jarvis working at the computer, looking at the monitor from time to time. When Jarvis turned to reach for a Diet-Coke on the table behind him, Getz saw his face and realised that he had seen Jarvis somewhere before. But he had no idea where. It wasn't a memorable face that might linger in the memory but Getz thought vaguely that it wasn't at Langley that he'd seen him.

When his guest had left, Volkov walked slowly out of the reception area. It took a few minutes to spot Vlasov who was half-hidden behind a huge palm. He walked over casually and very ostentatiously looked at his wrist-watch as he said, 'The table with the red carnations. A man and a woman. Who are they? And I'm in a hurry.'

Vlasov strolled away, stood for a few moments looking around the restaurant and then walked back to reception. Volkov watched impatiently as Vlasov languidly turned the pages of the booking diary. Finally he scribbled a note on a hotel card, walked back to Volkov and gave him the card.

Volkov looked at the card as he waited for a taxi. The card gave a name. Tom Laufer. Girl not known. Booking made from following number.

The following number Volkov knew was a CIA number. Not Langley but one of the out-stations. He couldn't remember which. He was sure that they were watching him and he was sure that he'd seen them when he was looking earlier at the cameras in the photographic shop windows. They were doing that old dodge of pretending to be a couple, but she didn't seem to know if he took sugar in his coffee and the man had always been looking at Volkov when Volkov turned his head to look at the couple. It was a reminder that Fomenko was right. Security of communication was going to be vital.

*　　*　　*

Getz's official mail was delivered to him at Tysons Corner but his personal mail still went to his apartment. Gabriella would collect it for him and give it to him when they met.

She had given him half a dozen letters when he came to pick her up to see *La Dolce Vita*. One was from the owner of his apartment who was pleased with the work that had been carried out. There were share offers from two different brokers, one letter was from a book-club he belonged to and the last was marked 'personal' on the envelope and he recognised the handwriting.

Dear Larry,
I have tried several times to contact you by telephone with no success. A bit like old times.
  I wanted to let you know that I have accepted a teaching job in England for a year and that Bobby will be going with me. I shall, of course, ensure that he keeps in touch with you but as you know he sees you very infrequently.
  We shall be leaving on the 2nd and I will let you know our address as soon as it is fixed.
  Yours,
  Joan

Getz read it again and looked at the post-mark. It was posted the day they left. He looked at his watch. It was the 8th of the month. For long moments he was silent and then he handed the letter to Gabriella and stood in silence as she read it.

She turned to him after she had read the letter and said, 'Did you have any idea she was going to do this?'

He thought for a moment. 'I had vibes that she was going to do something.'

'Tell me about the vibes.'

'It must have been three weeks ago and we, you, me and Bobby were at my place. You were in the kitchen and Bobby and I were looking at a ball-game on TV. He'd seemed a bit on edge that day and I wondered what it was all about.' Getz sighed. 'He turned to me and said, "Are you going to marry the Italian lady?" I said something non-committal but actually saying yes. I said something like "I guess so if she'll have me." Then he gave me the vibe clue. He said, "But that won't make her my mother." I said, "No. She'll be your stepmother. Nothing will change." Then I was unfair to him and I said, "But you like Gabriella don't you?" He went back to his usual self and smiled and shrugged and said, "Yeah. I guess so".'

'Why didn't you tell me about this?'

'I didn't think it had any significance until afterwards.'

'What was the significance?'

'Joan had obviously been talking to him about you and me getting married.'

She nodded. 'She took the answer as yes and this letter is her response, her get-back at you.' She paused. 'Can she legally do this – take him out of the country without your permission?'

'No. But if it went to court she could put up a pretty good case. It would mean doing things I wouldn't like doing.'

'Like what?'

'Attacking her in a foreign court. Demanding that she be extradited to stand trial here and to make Bobby decide who to support in court.'

'It's a kind of blackmail.'

'I had to go along with it when she sued for divorce. If I hadn't, her lawyer would have used my job as a means of making me look like something just short of the Mafia.'

'How do you know he would do that?'

'He told my attorney. He told him so that he could warn me.'

'An attorney? And he goes along with that? My God, lawyers are real blood-suckers.'

He smiled. 'I was a lawyer at one time as you know.'

She shrugged impatiently. 'Yes, but you were a kind of Social Services officer.'

He smiled and put his arm around her shoulder. 'Let's go or the movie will have started.'

Probably because of their mood the film was a disappointment. The excitement that was there the first time had gone and as they walked to his car he said, 'Was Rome ever really like that?'

'I'm afraid it was. It still is.' She linked her arm in his as they walked. All through the film she had tried to think of something she could do or say to cheer him up. But there wasn't anything.

They sat in the car, chatting, outside the embassy and then she kissed him and walked to the big doors at the top of the steps and waved to him as he drove off into the night.

As Getz took off his tie and then his shirt he walked over to the windows in the general office. There were slashes of rain on the window panes and there were no lights in the buildings across the street. For long moments he just stood there, aware that if he had been paying real interest to what was going on in Bobby's life he could probably have done something to at least prevent him from being removed from the US Court's jurisdiction.

This time they had eaten in a Spanish place down by the river.

When they had ordered, Tony Parsons said amiably, 'How are things with you?'

'You tell me.'

Parsons looked surprised. 'I don't understand.'

'What response did you give to my ex-wife's lawyer when he told you that she proposed removing my son overseas and out of US jurisdiction?'

'You're kidding. There has been no such conversation. I'm not even certain that she still has an attorney.' He frowned. 'Look. Don't let's play games. Tell me what's going on.'

Getz handed him his ex-wife's note. Parsons read it carefully then turned it over to see if there was any more on the reverse side. There was nothing and he pushed the note back across the table.

'I assure you, Larry. I had not the faintest idea that she even contemplated such a move. And if they had told me of such an intention I would have not only warned them of the serious consequences, but I would have told them that as an officer of the Court I had no choice but to report her intention so that a restraining order could be imposed.' He shook his head. 'She's a stupid woman.' He paused. 'You know, I see it time and time again in divorce cases. It's easy to deal with the two-timers and the philanderers male or female. They don't really care about what goes on apart from the financial settlement. They've got their next bits of life already going along nicely. It's the goody-two-shoes who are always the problem. They yell blue murder. They haven't committed any marital offence. They haven't screwed the pizza boy, they haven't got a lover. They've never said an unkind word about their spouse. They've been pure and faithful in word, thought and deed. So how can the bastard do this to me?'

'Is there anything I can do?'

Tony Parsons sighed. 'If it wasn't for your job I'd recommend you do a PR job on it. You'd have the sympathy of many people. Women as well as men. On the legal side you could make an ex-parte application for a hearing on care and control plus suitability of mother as law-abiding example.' He paused. 'But with your background she'll have offers from every sleazy lawyer in town and they'll take you and your job to town, Larry. You know how hard I had to work to persuade her to lay off that approach for the divorce.' He shook his head. 'Try and remember, Larry, she's not a bad woman, she's stupid and vengeful. Nothing more.'

'What do you advise me to do?'

'Nothing. Absolutely nothing. And don't let it get you down. In a few days time you won't remember this nonsense. Play it rough and she'll win. Just smile and take it, and she's got no prize. She'll know that she isn't going to get away with it. If she contacts you by telephone or letter, ignore it. Do nothing.' He wagged a finger. 'And you aren't able to send her any maintenance or there would be tax problems about sending funds not according to the Court's decisions. Don't be soft-hearted. She's got to learn.' He looked at Getz. 'You know the really shocking aspect of her move?'

'Yes. But tell me.'

'Forcing Bobby into deceiving you. That is not forgivable in my book.'

'I agree. I heard a rumour that you were likely to be a judge the next vacancy.'

'I heard it too. But nobody's approached me. I'm not all that keen anyway.'

'What does Michelle think about it?'

Tony Parsons smiled. 'You're a little behind the times, old friend. We parted up nearly two years ago.'

'I'm sorry, Tony. I had no idea.'

Parsons shrugged. 'Why the hell should you. More to the point, I saw you with a gorgeous girl in the restaurant at the Hilton a few weeks back. Who was she?'

Getz smiled. 'She still is. She's Italian. Gabriella del Rossi. We're waiting for me to clear up the job I'm on at the moment and then we'll be getting married. You'll get an invitation.'

'You lucky bastard. Like I always say. Better be lucky than rich.' He reached over and covered Getz's hand as he reached for the bill. 'No. My go this time.'

When Getz got back after taking Gabriella to the cinema, there were two notes on his desk. One, handwritten, asked him to phone Sam Harris the next day and the other was attached to the file on Jarvis's polygraph test. He made himself a cup of instant coffee and settled back at his desk. He looked at his watch. It was just after midnight. He was tired but not sleepy and he opened the file.

There was a typed transcript of two polygraph tests, the questions and the answers. He read them through twice before he realised that they were signed by two different operators with only a few days between almost identical tests. The covering note was from the Senior Polygraph Operator and suggested that Getz should call him.

'I'd like to speak to Mr Friedmann if he's available.'

'Friedmann speaking.'

'Hi. My name's Getz. You sent me two polygraph transcripts of a guy named Jarvis. Arthur Jarvis. Your note suggested I should call you.'

'Yeah. When I read through his stuff I realised that somebody else had done the test that gave him clearance. That was because I was whisked off to hospital before I finished the first test to have a hernia attended to. I didn't like the look of our friend Jarvis. I think he got through the second test and got a clearance because he'd had a dress-rehearsal with the tests I did but didn't complete. The chap who did the second test wouldn't know that Jarvis had already been done by me because the test wasn't finished and therefore not on file.'

'What were your doubts about Jarvis?'

'The questions about concealing contacts with foreigners. The needle jumped a mile but he said he was confused by what the question meant. Was it his in-laws being referred to. He must have known that they weren't a problem. He'd already mentioned them in terms of giving him and his wife financial support. So – who were the foreign nationals that he was really concealing? I had to stop the test at that stage because I was in pain. An hour later I was in hospital. I have to tell you, Mr Getz, that Jarvis would not have got a clearance from me.'

'You felt he was covering up?'

'I'm damn sure he was.'

'Could I ask you to put what you've just told me in writing and get one of our attorneys to notarise it?'

'OK. Will do. How soon do you want it?'

'Soon as you can. It's part of our operation.'

'Fair enough. I'll do it this morning before the week's work starts piling up.'

The call to Sam Harris had meant a visit to Langley, where Sam Harris was in his small office looking at samples of floor-coverings.

'Morning, Chief.'

'Morning, Sam. I gather from what you told me on the phone that you've got everything I need.'

'There was no problem. The house was sold to him by a retired naval officer. A real nice guy who also lives on North Randolph. Since retiring he's taken up real estate brokering.' He looked at Getz. 'Coke or a coffee?'

'Coke would do me fine.'

As Sam Harris opened the cans he said, 'Caused quite a bit of talk at the time. Paid the asking price $540,000 in cash. Just imagine it. Blocks like bricks of notes still in their bank wrappers. Just wanted the title. No survey, no bargaining – just the title deeds and here's the money.' He smiled. 'Just the same with the refurbishing. Bill was for a hundred grand reduced to ninety thousand when he offered cash. In both cases he kept saying that he paid cash because it was a gift from his rich in-laws.'

'Would he sign a statement, the broker?'

Sam Harris passed over several papers fastened together by a plastic paper-clip. There was a signed and notarised statement by both the real-estate broker and the builder who did the refurbishing. There was a photocopy of the title to the property, the receipt for the cash, a meticulously detailed summary of all the capital and labour costs of the refurbishing work.

After reading through it, Getz looked up at Sam Harris. 'You're a gem, Sam. You really are. Did you caution them about not talking?'

'I told them there was a family quarrel about who owned what and I was acting as a mediator.' He shrugged. 'They weren't all that interested. I played it pretty low-key.'

'Bless you, Sam. You've been a real help.'

'You're welcome.'

As Getz drove back to Tysons Corner he wondered if perhaps the quite open and almost blatant spending of cash wasn't proof that Jarvis had perfectly legitimate sources of money. Surely nobody who was actually involved in treason would live so ostentatiously, positively inviting comment and speculation.

Getz had asked O'Hara for a meeting and they had met in the restaurant at the Hilton. When they had ordered their meal and the starters had been served, Getz passed a typewritten sheet across the table.

'Would you have a look at that?'

'Now?'

'Yes please.'

O'Hara read the page carefully and then looked across at Larry Getz. The sheet gave details of ten bank accounts.

'Tell me more.'

'I'd like warrants to investigate those accounts and I'd like a specialist accountant with foreign banking experience to be seconded to me for as long as I need him.'

'What just cause can I put up?'

Getz reached into his jacket pocket and pulled out a small bundle of folded documents. They were the notarised statements covering the purchase of the latest Jaguar, the house on North Randolph Street and the work done on the house.

'That's the basis of my request. It doesn't have to be connected to suspected treason. I was deputed to check on any possible breaches of security. That's all I'm doing now. Looking for an acceptable reason as to why these large amounts have been paid in cash.'

'Show me.' O'Hara held out his hand and Getz passed over the bundle of documents.

O'Hara unfolded them carefully, flattened them so that he could read them and then looked at each page. When he had finished he looked up.

'Get me certified copies and I'll see what I can do.'

'And the accountant?'

'No problem.'

'How long before I can go ahead?'

O'Hara shook his head. 'I don't know. I'll have to step very carefully.'

'Why?'

'Because I'm sure that this is only the first of the warrants you'll be asking for.'

Getz smiled. 'You're right.'

'Is Jarvis your main suspect now?'

'He falls foul of all our negative indicators. But I can't be sure. We've got to provide evidence. Just strong suspicions won't run in a Federal Court.'

'What doubts do you have?'

'This ostentatious spending of money is so damning that one can't believe that a guilty man would behave like that. It's like waving a flag with "Guilty" written on it.'

'Certainly seems foolish . . .' O'Hara shrugged '. . . but who knows? It may be a form of arrogance.' He waved an arm. 'Gets so confusing you could even think the guy's so bright he thinks some blatant breach of security might be the perfect disguise.' He shook his head. 'I'll leave it to you.' He sighed as he stood up. 'Give me a week to get the warrants.'

Chapter 18

O'Hara had phoned Judge Klein's office and after some discussion had arranged a meeting in the judge's room for late afternoon the next day. He knew that it was a waste of time but it was a ritual that had to be gone through. It was for the record. Judge Klein had no party affiliations and was considered by most lawyers to be scrupulously fair. A judge who kept to the book and abhorred any tendency for the judiciary to do a bit of 'interpretation' to meet some transient public clamour. He particularly loathed politicians and law-breakers who still imagined that judges could be bought and that it was just a question of finding the right price.

O'Hara was ushered straight away into the judge's chambers and after a few banal exchanges about the weather, the judge said, 'What can I do for you, Mr O'Hara?'

'It's a request for search warrants, your honour.'

Judge Klein held out his hand and O'Hara handed him the papers. The judge read them carefully page by page. Turned back at the end to check something and then, still holding the papers, he said, 'Are you intending to notify the people mentioned here? Particularly Mr Jarvis.'

'No, your honour.'

'May I ask why not?'

'Mr Jarvis is suspected of treason, your honour. If we told him or he learned that we were investigating him, he'd be on the first plane out of the country.'

His Honour shook his head. 'I don't have to remind a man in your position that what you have here is entirely speculation and that what you propose is a clear breach of the Fourth Amendment of the US Constitution.' He shook his head slowly and pushed the documents back across his desk. 'You'll have to do better than that, Mr O'Hara.'

'Could you give me any guidance on what more I need to provide?'

Judge Klein smiled. 'I give judgments, my friend. You have attorneys at Langley who can give you the advice you need. I'd hazard a guess that they didn't go over this stuff before you brought it to me.' He paused. 'Am I right?'

O'Hara nodded. 'Yes your honour, you're right.'

'Ah well.' He looked at O'Hara. 'A lesson learnt.'

There was a little sunshine and O'Hara was attracted by the blossom on a group of trees in the Botanic Gardens. O'Hara didn't know one tree from another but as with philistine admirers of other types of beauty, O'Hara knew what he liked and had a soft spot for growing-things.

There was a bench not far from the trees and it was in the sun but there was a breeze and O'Hara turned up his coat collar and made himself comfortable. O'Hara was a good man. A caring man and a patriot, and he found this sort of thing over the warrants rather disturbing. All he had to do was go back with the documents to Richards at the Justice Department and quote Executive Order 12949, signed by Clinton himself, and the warrants would be in his hands the next day. He had been told by someone who was there in the Oval Office that Clinton had been reluctant to extend the powers of the secret court which had been created by the Foreign Intelligence Surveillance Act. But with mounting threats to national security he had finally signed away the rights of all citizens to the protection of the Fourth Amendment.

As a citizen O'Hara found it outrageous that a secret court could authorise actions that were demonstrably unconstitutional. But wearing his CIA hat it angered him that someone who was betraying the country to a foreign power should have any protection from the rights granted to loyal citizens. But O'Hara was a practical man, not given to philosophising. If the President of the USA had created a weapon that would enable him to combat what a suspected traitor was doing it was up to him to use it.

He strolled back to the Supreme Court building and made the arrangements with Justice Richards who seemed cheerful enough about destroying the rights of the citizens.

When he came out of the building he stood in the sun for a moment trying to remember where he had parked his car. Then he remembered that he'd used his official car and driver and pressed the appropriate buttons on his portable phone. He was back in Langley half an hour later. The warrants arrived late the next day and he gave the clearance to Getz on the phone. He also told Getz that he was going to keep the signed warrants in his personal safe in his office. Getz was too busy to speculate on why O'Hara was hanging on to the warrants and was grateful when the banking-accountancy expert arrived the next day. He had spent four years as a consultant to the FBI on investigating the laundering of Mafia money.

Volkov had spotted them as they followed him up 18th Street. It was the same couple but they were more casually dressed than when they were at the restaurant. Just to make sure that he wasn't getting paranoid he turned into Borders bookshop and browsed through the table display of new paperbacks. He moved to the non-fiction shelves and searched for something suitable. He chose a paperback, paid for it at a cash-point and walked through to the cafe, picked up a cappuccino and moved to a table. They appeared a few minutes later, ostentatiously not looking in his direction after the first quick glance. When they too were seated at a table he stood up and strolled over to them. He smiled as he leaned over them.

'Perhaps it would save you some time if I mention that I'm going on to Four Seasons Hotel where I shall be having a chat with Senator Watkins about the tour of an American basket-ball team to Moscow and Kiev.' He smiled again as he laid the book he had bought on their table. 'I thought, Mr Laufer, you might like this as a reminder of our time together.' He nodded, and said, 'Have a nice day,' and walked away.

Laufer picked up the book. It was an abridged translation of Karl Marx's *Das Kapital*. For a moment he was silent then he showed it to the girl and laughed. 'The cheeky bastard.'

She laughed too. 'At least it's something to meet a Russian with a sense of humour.'

Laufer said, 'I hope Larry Getz thinks that too.'

'He even knew your name. Maybe they're not so dumb as we think they are.'

He shrugged. 'Or maybe we're not as good as we thought we were.'

Getz's face was impassive as they told him what had happened. When they had finished he said, 'What did you learn from that?'

Tom Laufer said, 'First of all that we weren't as good as we thought we were.'

'And?'

'And I don't see a man like that being the case-officer of one of our people.'

'Why not?'

Laufer shrugged. 'Too easy-going, too laid-back. Too sure of himself. Not trying to hide that he was from the embassy.'

'Just the kind of man I'd use to handle an American,' Getz said. 'I'll put another team on him and I'd like you two to brief them on your surveillance so far.'

'I'm sorry if we let the side down.' Laufer said it hoping that Getz would deny that they had let the side down. But Getz stood up and opened his mouth as if he was about to say something, then closed it and walked away. So far as he was concerned they *had* let the side down and they needed to learn the lesson. Surveillance isn't a game, but lecturing them was too easy a let-off. They'd have to be sent back to Langley for redeployment.

Chapter 19

James Parfitt phoned Getz for a meeting after ten days' working on the bank accounts and the credit card records. He added that he wanted a week in Switzerland to see what he could squeeze out of the Zurich banks.

Parfitt was in his late thirties, an energetic and enthusiastic young man whose several years of experience working against the Mafia money-launderers made his task in dealing with Jarvis's attempts to conceal his finances much simpler. When working against the Mafia, almost the only pressure he could apply to reticent bankers was the fact that if they didn't co-operate with him they were virtually protecting major criminals. And that the government was aware of it. To be able to claim that he needed the information he asked for because it involved the security of the United States, put him in a different league with the bankers.

It was mid-evening when Parfitt shared sandwiches and coffee with Getz in his office at Tysons Corner.

'What's the state of the game, Mr Parfitt?'

'Pretty good, sir.'

Getz looked surprised. 'You mean that?'

'Of course, sir. I haven't even had to use the warrants except in a couple of cases. And that was a banker I'd met before and he wasn't too happy about our previous encounter.'

'What happened?'

'We gave him the choice. Co-operate or we'd leak the story to the *Post*.' Parfitt grinned. 'He co-operated but he didn't like it.'

'So tell me what you got.'

'Most people read about the Financial Crimes Enforcement Network when it announced that banks would now have to report to it any suspicious deposits.' He smiled. 'And in case they weren't too sure about how much was suspicious, the law said they had to report all deposits above ten thousand dollars. After some time the slimeballs figured they could get round the law by depositing large sums in multiple lots of ten thousands. What most people still don't realise is that in the late seventies Section 5324 of the Bank Secrecy Act was passed and that made what was called "structuring" of deposits illegal.

'Then the boys thought up a new game. They got a crooked banker, who was prosecuted, to claim that he didn't know that what he had been doing was illegal. And the Supreme Court found that the government had to prove that the offenders in future did know that what they were doing was illegal. And that was almost impossible to prove. But the banks found that they were getting all sorts of flak from the IRS and they were given pretty broad hints that maybe it would be easier if they reported structuring of deposits voluntarily. They screamed blue murder and said they would lose half their clients that way. And then some bright spark in IRS came up with a suggestion. Why not computerise the banking deposit system and notify the IRS automatically as part of the program. And that's how it is today, but it's never been in the media so ordinary folk don't know about it.' Parfitt smiled. 'Friend Jarvis didn't know about it and he's gone on his merry way structuring his deposits without knowing that they were all going to the IRS.'

Parfitt pulled out a typed sheet and a pile of papers as he paused. Then he looked over at Getz. 'Jarvis was reported to IRS several times for suspicious deposits. But they weren't big enough to interest IRS. At least twice Jarvis's name appeared on computer databases created to throw up signs of illegal activity. But no action was ever taken against him.'

'Why didn't *we* do something about it?'

Parfitt shrugged. 'For a very simple reason, chief. We didn't know. Nobody regularly checked those databases. Not us and not the FBI.'

'But it should have been an automatic source for both agencies.'

'Yeah. But it would have meant applying in every individual case for the permission of the Financial Crime Prevention Agency. Nobody wanted the work. So nothing was done.'

'Was the material about Jarvis any use to us?'

'Oh yes. We have documented evidence of nine transfers of large sums of money from overseas, purchases of large sums of foreign currency and a substantial number of deposits over ten thousand dollars.

'His credit cards alone are damning. Big amounts paid out for Meissen china, Chagall prints, china figurines, gold jewellery including six gold necklaces, stacks of designer clothes, watches from Gucci and Rolex and several thousand dollars a month of gourmet food from places like Dean and Deluca. In the last twelve months just his credit card debts have amounted to four or five times his gross pay from the agency.'

'Is all this documented?'

'Yes, sir.'

'And authenticated in some way?'

'Yes.'

'So why the need for a trip to Zurich?'

'We aren't dealing in thousands of dollars, sir. We're talking several million dollars and not a cent of it comes from his in-laws.' Parfitt paused. 'Just for the record, sir. His in-laws are very influential people in Bogotá. The President of Colombia dines with them frequently. But they haven't got a dime between them. Jarvis's big money will be in Switzerland. I want to see if I can identify at least where it is. And if I'm lucky I'll find out how much.' Parfitt pushed across a plastic file-cover stuffed with documents. 'Perhaps when you've read them, sir, you'd put them in safe-keeping.'

'How long will you be away?'

'About a week. Could be ten days.'

'The Swiss are pretty tough about non-disclosure, aren't they?'

'Very, very tough.'

'You think you might persuade them to co-operate in Jarvis's case?'

'I think I've got a good chance. They're in business. They wanna trade.' He shrugged. 'I'll trade.'

'What can you trade?'

'I don't know. But they'll have things they want to know. They'll have problems. They pretend to turn a blind eye to the criminals who bank with them. But there's always a point where they could go in the slammer themselves if they make a mistake. I can point out the dangerous ones.'

'Thanks for all your good work. It's great news for me. One more nail in the bastard's coffin.'

Parfitt nodded. 'I'll keep in touch.'

Getz asked Tom Welby to check if there was someone on the team who had experience of market research or polling. Three names came up. Two men and one female. The men's experience was statistical analysis with no contact with the public but the girl, Sally Bailey, had done two years on product and advertising groups. She was bright and responsive and Getz liked her immediately. She was twenty-seven and married. No children. And she had worked for a large advertising agency. They had chatted about the psychology of colour in pack design and the benefits of unstructured talks with potential users about the product or service being offered.

'Let me tell you what I want you to do. We've reduced the suspect names to a handful and I've made one of them, a guy named Art Jarvis, my own favourite. I've told Tom Welby to give you a thorough briefing on Jarvis and that means you'll be privy to very high-security information.' He paused. 'OK so far?'

'Yes. No problem.'

'I want you to contrive some research project that allows you to talk to this guy's neighbours. You could be researching for a social studies project for a university or government social services people. A study of a small community. How they live? Their jobs. How they spend their time? How they get on with their neighbours? Who decides what? Hobbies, how they spend their money on pleasure things? Who's in charge of the money? Who they bank with?' He shrugged. 'A picture of their lives with special attention to anything they can tell you about the Jarvis family.' He paused. 'And you'll have to interview the Jarvis family too. Or people will wonder why they're not included.' He smiled. 'I want everything. Gossip as well as fact. And in the end I want your assessment of Art Jarvis himself. OK?'

'Yes. How long do I have?'

'How long do you want?'

'At least a month. I've got to allow for people on vacation or just not available for some time.'

'OK. Anything else?'

'Yes. It's usual when you do this kind of project that you offer

136

some token benefit. A gift or something. Any ideas what we could offer?' She paused. 'What sort of district is it?'

'Arlington. Upper middle-class. Average house price half a million bucks. Good standard of living.'

'How about a bottle of Jean-Paul Gaultier for the lady of the household?'

'No. Not booze in this case.'

She laughed. 'It's not booze, it's a very expensive perfume. A couple of hundred bucks at least.'

Getz smiled. 'That's fine. I'd better remember that name.'

'When shall I start?'

'Right now. I've told Tom to expect you. It'll take a few days to read through what we've got.' He stood up and walked her to the door. 'Keep me posted on how you're doing.'

She smiled and nodded. 'I will. All the gossip shall be yours.' Then she paused. 'As a matter of interest, what do *you* think of this guy?'

'Jarvis, you mean?'

'Yeah.'

Getz hesitated. 'No word I could use in front of a young woman.' He paused. 'Not a nice man.'

'Because he might be a traitor?'

'Even without that.'

Maria had become more and more dissatisfied with her life with Art Jarvis. His drunken behaviour would have been enough but telling her of his relationship with the Russians had made her an accomplice. She had thought many times about informing the FBI or the CIA, but that would affect her and Peter as well. It would finish her life of luxury and break up the whole family.

She spent hours trying to work out where her loyalties lay. They certainly didn't lie with Art Jarvis. But why the hell should she care about the USA? It wasn't her country. And she didn't give a damn for the CIA. Her duty was to Peter and herself. If she exposed Art Jarvis, Peter would grow up without a father and a family. She came to the conclusion that all she could do was to involve herself enough in what Jarvis was doing to keep it under control. But Maria didn't have a temperament for keeping even herself under control let alone Art Jarvis who went on his way ignoring her warnings and threats.

Having decided to stay silent, she gradually but inevitably became an accomplice. Jarvis used her now to make comparatively small deposits to various banks. Deposits around $7000 or so.

Jarvis informed the Russians that he had information to give them of considerable importance and suggested a meeting with Volkov or others in Caracas, Venezuela. A city Jarvis knew quite well.

When he hadn't heard from the Russians after two weeks, Jarvis was worried. The Russians always responded quickly even if it was a negative.

On the twentieth day without contact Jarvis used the KGB system and left a small check-mark on the top strip of a wooden bench in a park and later the same day drove to a churchyard and left a package of documents and a letter in the overgrown grass by one of the headstones. The next morning Jarvis checked the park bench. The check-mark had not been rubbed out and was still there, which signalled that his package had not been picked up. He hurriedly drove to the churchyard and retrieved the letter and the package.

All this left Jarvis in a state of utter confusion. He could imagine no satisfactory reason for the Russians' lack of co-operation. It was crazy that just a check-mark on a park bench, apparently ignored by Volkov, was the tenuous and only thread that kept him in communication with the KGB. For the first time Jarvis was desperately scared. It suddenly seemed possible that they could be abandoning him. Maybe even worse and they were selling him to the wolves. But why? What had he done wrong? Maybe they knew that the CIA had finally spotted him, and the KGB were ready to let him go. Or trade him for something or someone else. Instinct told him he was on his own now. He'd got to cover his own back. Nobody else was going to do it for him. As Jarvis drove back home he felt very cold and very lonely. Inevitably he drank himself into his usual escape from reality, oblivious to the angry tirade from his wife.

When Volkov got the radio signal from Moscow he was apprehensive. It was signed by Fomenko but it lacked the security code-word that they used between themselves. His phone-calls to Moscow were fruitless. He was told to stick to the instructions in the signal. The instructions said that he was to break off all contacts with Jarvis. When he asked why he was told not to question his orders.

It was almost a month before he got the instructions to make contact with Jarvis again. And this time the security code-word was included. Moscow suggested that the first meeting with Jarvis should be in Bogotá and then in Caracas. He should arrange to be in Bogotá forty-eight hours before Jarvis arrived. Volkov had to go through the elaborate system to reactivate his contacts with Jarvis who was sufficiently angered at the way he had been treated to be in no hurry to collaborate. But he had said in his response that if he was to go to Bogotá he would expect a substantial cash funding. This was readily agreed to on Fomenko's orders.

The embassy had sent an unmarked car to the airport to pick up Volkov who was surprised to see Fomenko himself in the back seat. Fomenko put his hand to his mouth to signal that it was not safe to talk. Fomenko told him that he was staying at the Hilton and that an adjoining suite was booked for Volkov.

When they were eventually alone in Volkov's suite, he turned on Fomenko barely concealing his anger.

'What the hell's been going on, Viktor?'

Fomenko waved his hand. 'Sit down for God's sake. I've got a lot to tell you.'

Volkov sat down and watched Fomenko light the habitual cigar. As he put the spent match in an ashtray on the small table beside the armchair, he looked across at Volkov.

'Are you sure our friend will be coming?'

'His message said he would. I've had no personal contact with him. The tone of all his messages has been unfriendly and vaguely aggressive.'

Fomenko sighed. 'When Gorbachev went and Boris Yeltsin took over there was no interference with our operation. But about three months ago there were cronies of Yeltsin who started wanting to probe into what we were doing. I refused on the grounds of security of the asset and a week later I was arrested. The usual crap. Knock on the door in the early hours of the morning. Arrested because I was an enemy of the State. Hauled off to the Lubyanka, stripped and body searched and then Oskar Panov came to see me. I've known the bastard for years. Plays tough but underneath the bluff he's shit-scared he might be doing the wrong thing.' He paused. 'How about you get us a whisky?'

Volkov, his anger diffused, walked over to the bar and looked at the bottles.

'Bells or Haig? That's all they've got that's real whisky.'

'Bells.'

Volkov walked back and handed one of the glasses to Fomenko and then sat down. Fomenko took a good slug of the whisky and then put down the glass.

'Panov demanded to know where our documentation was. I told him to go to hell. He said – OK, if I didn't co-operate I'd be executed. I pointed out that the trial itself would be a gross breach of security to the detriment of the State. Panov smiled and said – no problem. There'd be no trial. I told him that when he chopped me they would have closed down the finest source of secret information the State had ever had. He just shrugged and said – so be it.' Fomenko smiled. 'So I called his bluff. I said – OK, go ahead.' Fomenko sighed. 'He saw me every day, desperate to find out if anyone else knew about the operation. I refused to answer any questions about the operation.' He held up his empty glass and Volkov walked over to the bar and brought back the bottle. When Fomenko had poured himself another drink he held it up.

'*Na zdrovye.*'

Volkov, appeased, did the same. '*Na zdrovye.*'

Fomenko went on. 'I realised after a few days that Panov was scared. He'd been given a job to do and he wasn't going to make it. He told me what had gone on. Somehow they had found that Gorbachev himself was involved in the operation and they told Yeltsin that Gorbachev might still be involved. Yeltsin wasn't interested except that he was going to raise hell if our guy in the CIA was not going to be keeping up the flow of CIA material that had helped them so much. So there was a compromise. Panov was going to threaten me and get the details they wanted and once I'd spilled the beans one of them, probably Panov, would take over the control in Moscow. If I co-operated I'd get my full pension and a *dacha* anywhere I chose so long as it was far from Moscow. Then, thank God, Nikovsky took over the KGB.' Fomenko smiled. 'By the way, it's considered an insult to the organisation these days if you refer to it as the KGB instead of its new name – the SVR.' He took a deep breath. 'I had an interview with Kinovsky and he was angry that the operation had not only been inactive for three months but had been in danger of collapsing.' Fomenko shrugged his broad shoulders. 'So now let's hear your belly-aches.'

'It's still a secure operation?'

'Absolutely. We're back to square one. And I've brought a sackful of dollars for our friend who must be shit-scared by now.'

'I'll smooth him down.' He paused. 'A favour, Viktor.'

'What is it?'

'Let me arrange things so that I can have a week away.'

'Where?'

'Paris.'

'I knew that bitch would mean trouble. You've kept in touch with her have you?'

'Just letters and a few phone calls.'

'OK. I leave it to you. You work it out with your little friend in Washington.'

'Are you moving on to Caracas with me tomorrow?'

'Do you want me to?'

'Yeah. He'll be impressed. But for Christ's sake don't get him drunk. He's crazy when he's drunk.'

Fomenko smiled. 'You've never seen me drunk, Yuri, have you?'

'No. You're different.'

'Oh. In what way?'

'You're all of a piece, solid. He's weak and near enough an alcoholic.' He paused. 'Any problem he's got with us will be solved by the money.'

'Where are you meeting him?'

'In a park. It's our "iron" RV.'

'Why do we have to go to Caracas?'

'That's where he's going officially.'

'I'll go down to Caracas. Spend an hour or so with our friend and then head back for Moscow.'

'I shall only stay one full day provided he seems committed again.'

*   *   *

For once Jarvis was on time. Looking a little defiant. Querying why it was necessary to go to the Hilton but obviously impressed that Fomenko had come over especially to meet him. In fact Fomenko and Jarvis got on remarkably well despite Fomenko's terrible English interlaced with Russian. They drank innumerable beers and Fomenko talked vaguely of changes and intervening intelligence operations that Fomenko had felt could affect their set-up unfavourably. He assured Jarvis that Moscow were impressed with what he was providing and fully behind him. A bit of an administrative hitch but everything sorted out. Volkov would go over all the new routines with him the next day when they were in Caracas.

They had flown separately to Caracas and had spent only two hours together before Jarvis had to leave for his meeting with the local CIA whom he knew well from his time in South America.

Volkov gave him $100,000 and hinted at more to come once the operation got going again. Volkov had worked out new recognition signs and new drops for letters or packages and had supplied photographs of new marker sites, most of them over the river in Arlington so that they would be handy for Jarvis.

Volkov took a late-night flight back to Washington and was satisfied that Jarvis accepted the new arrangements. It was obvious that dollars in large numbers would cure any problems with the American.

Getz sat on the edge of his camp-bed, slowly and awkwardly undressing as he watched a News Review of the week on a small Sony TV they had rigged up for him.

The screen showed the blazing fire at the Waco installation as the FBI stormed the buildings. The commentator said there were casualties but as yet nobody knew how many. The picture cut to more burning buildings and lines of frightened women refugees. The Serbs had attacked Srebrenica, there had been many casualties in hand-to-hand fighting and reports said that thousands of Muslim men had been captured and subsequently slaughtered in the heavily wooded hills to the east of the city. A newsman, hair blowing in the wind as he tried to read the agreed statement, reported that officers of the LAPD had finally been found guilty by the courts of beating up a Negro named Rodney King. He switched off the TV and sat with his face in his hands. He was so tired. Tired of thinking. Tired of analysing bits of information. Tired of making decisions without enough facts to go on. Tired of the world of mirrors they called intelligence. And he was tired of people. Tired of listening. Tired of smoothing down ruffled feathers. Still wearing his denim shirt he pulled the blanket over him and was asleep in minutes.

She was wearing a gingham dress. Red and white squares. It was very Vermont. Very pretty. They had just finished eating their Saturday lunch. Bobby was at the cinema with friends and their own kids.

'We need to talk, honey,' she said but she avoided looking at his face.

'OK. Talk to me.' He smiled. 'I guess that's what you mean isn't it?'

'Why do you always have to be flippant about serious things?'

'First of all I don't think I was flippant. And secondly I didn't know we were about to talk about serious things.'

'You always have an answer for everything, don't you? Always the lawyer.'

He smiled. 'Come off it, kid. What's it all about?'

'You've no idea have you?'

'No.'

'We've talked about it enough times. I don't seem to ever get through to you.'

'Tell me again, now.'

She sighed. A heavy sigh. 'I've tried to tell you, Larry, that I can't take our life any longer. I don't see you in the evenings. Sometimes I don't even see you at the weekends. I used to stay in in case you came back unexpectedly. But I've learned my lesson. If you come back unexpectedly it's because you need a fresh shirt. I'm lonely, Larry.'

'But we've got lots of friends, Joanie. They're people who are very fond of you. Invite them around. Some of them too have husbands who have to work strange hours.'

'I'm not interested in other people and how they live. I want to live my own way with a proper marriage and a family life. Like my parents and your parents had.'

'But we're not our parents. And times have changed. In my kind of work you can't just knock off at five-thirty and let the world get on with destroying our country.'

143

She laughed sharply. 'You really believe that what you people do saves the country from destruction. You must be kidding.'

'Trashing the CIA won't solve our problem.' He paused. 'Maybe my inconvenient hours aren't the real problem.'

'So what is our real problem?'

'You want me to be your father and my father.'

'What's wrong with that?'

'Nothing, but they're them, and I'm me, and it's today not forty years ago. My father always wanted to own a store for farmers. I don't. Your father always wanted to own the bakery he worked for. I don't.' She saw his fist clench before he banged it on the table making the crockery tinkle as he said, 'You might as well get it straight, Joanie. I intend keeping my job and living in this year, not the past.'

For long moments she was silent and then she said, 'At least you've simplified the problem.'

'What's that mean?'

'You have to choose between me and CIA. It's as simple as that.'

'No way,' he said angrily. 'It's the reverse of that. It's a question of a wife supporting her husband in his chosen field of work.'

She shrugged her shoulders. 'The choice is yours, Larry, it's me or the job.'

'You're wrong. It's you who's making the rules and you who is making the choice. Not me, my dear, not me.'

Sally Bailey was never quite sure whether May was the end of Spring or the beginning of Summer. So far as Washington weather could decide it was summer and she wore a lime-green linen dress and jacket. It was nicely cut. It could have been Chanel but it wasn't. She was blonde and pretty and twenty-seven years old and it wasn't easy to pitch how you dressed to be attractive but not devastating. She'd had a quick reconnaissance a few days earlier to see how the women in the North Randolph Street area were turned out. She was reminded of a constant saying of her father, an ex-US marine sergeant – 'clean, bright and slightly oiled'. He admitted that it was really meant for personal weapons but he maintained that it applied universally. It was a fair description of the local ladies. No drop-dead beauties but still attractive enough to be obviously full of self-confidence.

As Sally Bailey rang the first doorbell and explained that she was doing research on small communities for a group of mid-west universities, she was listened to with an amiable smile and invited in.

She made a mental note of the decor of the room but made no notes on her clip-board. As she said, this was a survey of people. Did they like where they lived? Why? Did they get on with their neighbours? Relationships between husbands. Relationships between wives. Entertainment and hobbies. Was it a good environment for children? Was there mutual entertainment between families?

Mrs Iris Maloney was a lucky first strike. Outgoing, humorous and observant, she gave a vivid picture of over a dozen neighbourhood families. She not only gave her own opinions freely but introduced Sally Bailey to one family after another. She spent ten days with Iris Maloney and arranged for a private tour of the White House for all the wives who had been involved. They all said that it had been a wonderful time and that they were going to miss Sally Bailey and her questions about their lives. It took her two weeks to assemble what she had learned about Art and Maria Jarvis. She typed it up herself and insisted that she presented it to Larry Getz herself, in person.

Getz took her to tea at the Marriott to hear her report. Her opening words were his reward for making the small effort.

She looked at him smiling. 'I'm sure he's your man, Larry. I don't have any doubts.'

Getz smiled. 'OK. You've done the tease, now tell me the details.'

'Right. I interviewed fourteen families. But two of them had never heard of the Jarvis family so my information is based on twelve families. Ninety per cent of the material came from the wives of the families.

'Most of the women found Maria Jarvis a bit strange but tolerable. They didn't like all the heavy gold jewellery but several of them commented that if they were stuck with Art Jarvis they'd want a lot of gold bracelets to make up for it. They were all of the opinion that it was a bad marriage. Their neighbours on both sides had heard shouting and screaming but at least one thought that was because Maria was South American and that's how Hispanic women behaved.

'None of them had a good word to say about Art Jarvis himself.

But it was interesting that at least half of them saw him as a nonentity. A bit of a creep. Only two of them knew anything about his job. One thought he was probably IRS and the other thought he might be a private detective. No reason given except that he looked like one.

'The Jarvises gave a couple of parties every year at Christmas and Thanksgiving but they were avoided where possible because they were just canapés and gallons of booze. It was taken as read that Jarvis had a real drink problem. They'd seen him sleeping it off in his car in the driveway of the house and they'd seen him carried home drunk by men friends.

'I asked them what they thought of him and the most constant words were unreliable, shifty, arrogant and weird. Most of the men were ruder. Asshole and scumbag was the general opinion.' She paused. 'Am I talking too much?'

Getz laughed. 'No way. Just keep going.'

'Have you ever met Jarvis?'

'No. I went and had a look at him from the next office but I've never spoken to him.'

'I had two visits to the Jarvis household. The first time was just with Mrs J. She not only doesn't like her old man, she positively hates him. Every word she uttered about him was critical and disparaging. When I pointed at the jewellery she was wearing and said he must at least be generous, she said something very interesting. She said he just gave her that to keep her quiet. Now that could mean just to stop her from complaining. But it might be a kind of Freudian slip. I didn't pursue it. I'd guess that whatever he's up to she knows about it and probably plays some part in it. There was only one thing they have in common. That's the boy, Peter. I'd say they both really love him. He's a nice kid. Very bright.

'The second meeting Jarvis was there. A real creep. When she wasn't around he was chatting me up. He talked about his Jaguar and the foreign holidays they had.' She smiled. 'By the way, he gave a substantial amount to Democrat funds at the last election. I asked him what his job was and he didn't hesitate. Said he was working as an adviser to the State Department. Specialised on South American affairs. All his body movements are give-aways. Arms crossed defensively. Can't keep still, constantly touching things. Moving ornaments, shifting chairs. Real weird. He obviously fancies himself with the ladies but I doubt if he does anything about it apart from talk.' Finally she said, 'The whole atmosphere in that house stinks of tension and conflict.' She smiled. 'That's about it.'

'It's far more than I expected. You did a great job. Thanks for all the effort.'

'Are you OK?'

'Why do you ask? he said, half smiling.

'You look tired out.'

He smiled. 'You're giving me the research treatment. It's time you stopped and got back into real life.'

She laughed. 'Yes, captain. As of now.'

Volkov had warned Jarvis that he would be away for a week, maybe even ten days. He didn't give any explanation.

She was wearing the bracelet he had sent her from Bogotá when she met him at Charles de Gaulle and their pleasure in seeing one another was obvious. He had only one bag so he had no need to wait at the carousel. They went to the restaurant for a coffee and a chance to talk. But for long, long moments they sat silently enjoying just holding hands across the table, and looking at each other's happy faces. After a couple more coffees she said, 'Why did you book in at the Georges Cinq?'

Volkov looked surprised. 'I contacted our embassy here and they gave me the name and telephone number.' He smiled. 'Why, is it no good or something?'

She shrugged. 'It's OK. But you must stay at my place.'

'But I didn't know that.' He shrugged. 'I wanted to do whatever would please you.'

She smiled. 'Anyway I cancelled it and fixed you a nice room at a really nice hotel called Hotel d'Angleterre. It used to be the British Embassy. It's very charming and very civilised. You'll like it.'

He smiled. 'I'm sure I will.'

She laughed. 'Don't look so serious. I've only booked you in for one night.' She paused. 'How long can you stay?'

'Officially four days but I intended to stretch it to a week if that's OK with you?'

'Of course it is. Let's get a taxi and go and book you in. We're having drinks this evening at my parents' house.' She stood up. 'Just one bag, yes?'

'Yes. I thought I might buy some clothes while I'm here.'

She laughed. 'I suppose I ought to warn you . . .' she said as they walked along '. . . that Papa is blue denim shirt and blue denim trousers. He's very handsome, but he looks more like what we call a "gopher" than the head of a big firm.'

'And your mother?'

'Ah yes. Maman. My father is great at motivating people. Using their talents and making them even better. He's never strident or aggressive. He smiles them into doing what he wants. But Maman is more aggressive. The product comes first and everybody has to go by the script. She does mainly documentaries. Battered wives. People with terrible afflictions.' She laughed. 'Maman has just as soft a heart as Papa but she will fight like a tiger to prevent some politician from watering-down the impact of some story.'

'What made them both go into the film business?'

'I don't know. They were both the same apparently, even when they were kids. Both sets of parents said they never wanted anything else.' She smiled. 'They're still totally committed and it's part of their lives together. Always discussing, always arguing, but always caring about each other.'

The taxi had dropped them at the hotel and when Volkov had signed in they'd gone up to check his room. He was delighted with both the room and the hotel.

He sat facing her as they drank the ubiquitous Cokes. 'Tell me about you. What have you been doing?'

'I've been working on the script of a film about two young people. The girl is a country girl and longs to live in Paris. The guy loves the countryside and hates having to live in the city. He meets her when she is working as a waitress at a cafe.' She smiled and shrugged. 'They fall in love. So what do they do about it?'

He smiled. 'It sounds very you. Are you enjoying it?'

She sighed. 'You can never enjoy a script. Everyone agrees that it is great, then the money people want a bankable star for the girl instead of an *ingénue*. The actor playing the guy wants to use his dialogue, not yours. The producer complains that the budget is too extravagant. And it rains when we need the sun.' She shrugged, smiling. 'But I love it. All of it. It's never out of my mind. Even now when I look at you I'm wondering what you're thinking.'

He laughed. 'I'm thinking how lucky I am to be here with you.' He paused and shrugged. 'And I'm wondering what your parents will think of me. Wondering if they disapprove of you being pursued by a Russian. And even more disapproving if they knew what my job is.'

She laughed. 'You're not on trial, my boy. You're my nice friend Yuri Volkov and you come from the same country as Tchaikovsky, Rachmaninov, Glazunov, etcetera, etcetera.'

'But I'm an officer in the KGB?'

'They don't know that, and all they do know is that you are a diplomat at the Soviet Embassy in Washington.'

'What about you? What do you feel about it?'

'The KGB bit you mean?'

'Yes.'

'I can't imagine you torturing people or sending them to a Gulag but I think it might worry me if you were doing your job here in Paris instead of in Washington.' She smiled. 'I always remember what your mother said apropos of you. A quote, she said, from Nietzsche – "a great man is only an actor playing out his own ideal".'

'Ah well, dear Mama, always ready to damn with faint praise.'

'She's very fond of you in her own peculiar way.'

He smiled. 'I'm sure you're right.' He paused. 'Can I ask you a very foolish question?'

She laughed. 'Try me.'

'Do *you* like me?'

'I more than like you.'

'But not love?'

She smiled and shrugged. 'Somewhere very near that. Only time will tell. And what about you with me?'

'I never stop thinking about you. Wishing you were with me to talk about the day's happenings for both of us. Love is a wicked word. A little word that can explode in your face. Or a big word that can mean so much. For me I'm sure I love you but I want to be sure for both of us.'

'Sure of what?'

'That it's love and not in-love. One lasts for ever, no matter what happens. The other can melt away.'

For a moment she was silent, then she looked at her watch. 'We'd better get on our way.'

The apartment of the parents was in walking distance of the hotel. The top two floors of a beautiful old house near St Sulpice. The decor and furnishings were old-fashioned and valuable. Every wall was lined with shelves crammed full with books and there was a Blüthner baby grand in a corner near the tall windows.

In appearance her father was rather like Fomenko. A magnificent Roman head and observant eyes. But there the likeness ended. Mr Fleury was warm and welcoming, talkative and amiable. His wife had clearly provided the genes for Sabine's calm beauty and jet-black hair. She was soft-spoken and tactfully moved from the sofa so that Sabine and Yuri Volkov could sit together.

There was much talk of the troubles at the Opéra and of Mitterand's health. And, inevitably, talk of films.

It was her father who said, 'What was the last film you saw, Yuri?'

'I don't often go to the cinema but the last film I saw was *The Battleship Potemkin*.'

'Really now.' And Fleury leaned forward, interested. 'And how did you come to see that?'

'There's a club for film buffs that meets weekly at the Library of Congress. They contacted me to see if I could get an unedited copy for showing to members.' He smiled. 'Moscow insisted that I shouldn't let it out of my sight. So I had to be there.'

'What did you think of it?'

'As a film I thought it was magnificent. The technique was far ahead of its time. But of course it was a fabrication. The so-called massacre never happened. It was propaganda.'

'I see. Propaganda, eh. A strange word. What does it mean? It is always used pejoratively. Propaganda is always a bad thing. But it has a religious foundation, from the eighteenth century when Rome created the *Sacra Congregatio de Propaganda Fide*, the Sacred Congregation for Propagating the Faith.' He smiled. 'I suppose a Muslim or a Buddhist or even a Protestant could claim that it was just propaganda.' He turned to his wife. 'Could make an interesting feature, my dear.'

She laughed. 'Sounds more like an examination question to me. Propaganda is always bad – discuss.'

Fleury turned to Volkov. 'She's so clever when she's saying she disagrees. So disarming. When I win an argument she says it doesn't make what I say correct. It just means I'm a better arguer than she is.'

'You are, dear boy. You are. How about you pour us more drinks?'

As Fleury filled their glasses, he said, 'Where are you staying, Yuri?'

'I had booked in at the Georges Cinq. But Sabine said I'd prefer the Hotel d'Angleterre and she booked me in there instead.'

'D'you like it?'

'Very much.'

Volkov had been in the game too long not to recognise the rather amateur attempt to check whether he was staying with Sabine. But he was aware that it gave him a plus point that he wasn't so far as her old man was concerned. Subconsciously maybe. But there.

They were asked to stay to dinner but Sabine had said no and they left ten minutes later.

Sabine had slept with him that night at the hotel and he had moved into her apartment the next day. It was quite small but two rooms had been converted into one. And that one room said it all. It was a writer's room. Two tables. One with stacks of scripts and notebooks and the other with a PC and keyboard, and a modem cabled to a phone. Just one wall was books from floor to ceiling. There was a small table with four fold-up chairs in the kitchen and a comfortable-looking bed in a room whose walls were covered with photographs and prints; the walls were burgundy red and the window curtains were white.

'Well, my boy,' she said, 'that's the grand tour done.'

'It's very cosy.'

She frowned. 'It's not supposed to be cosy. It's for working.'

'And it says – I belong to Sabine Fleury. Warm, red, heart-on-sleeve Sabine Fleury.'

She looked at him and said slowly, 'That's very odd. Very

perceptive. My father said something like that the first time he came here.'

'What did your mother say?'

'She took it all in but made no comment. She would be able to describe it accurately and in detail but it wouldn't be related to me. It might be related to her.' She shrugged. 'That's the real difference between them. She's the intellectual of the two but, unlike Papa, she's not creative. She lacks imagination.' She smiled. 'Find some place for your bag and we'll go and eat.'

They had visited all the traditional tourist attractions and there were things about Volkov that surprised her. He had asked that on the last day of his visit they should go again to the *Musée de l'Orangerie* and he had stood there in the oval room on the ground floor and she'd seen tears on his cheeks as he looked at Claude Monet's paintings of the water-lilies. The gentle light from the windows invested the whole room with a kind of purity that was usually only found in a cathedral.

She had said nothing at the time but as they had their last dinner together she had asked him why he liked the Monet paintings so much.

He was silent for long moments and then he said, 'I don't know. But I felt that that was how the world should be. So calm, so beautiful and so . . . I don't know what. It was a sort of sanctuary against the real world. If I lived in Paris I would go there every week, or when I felt depressed.'

'I can't imagine you being depressed, Yuri.'

'Why not?'

'You always seem so positive, so self-confident.'

He shrugged and smiled rather wryly. 'Maybe that's because I don't live in the real world.' He paused. 'I don't belong. I play a part.' He looked at her. 'But not with you. That's why I like so much being with you.' He sighed. 'Are you sure I don't bore you?'

'Don't be an idiot. Of course you don't bore me.' She paused. 'Are you worried about something?'

'Yeah. When we were in the *Orangerie* the first time I wanted to ask you if you would marry me. But when I thought about it I wondered what I was offering you. When we went back the second time I felt it was too little.' He paused. 'And I wondered what I could do to change it.'

She put her hand on his. 'I love you, Yuri Volkov, but like when you asked me to go with you to Bogotá it was too soon.' She smiled. 'I wouldn't hesitate if you asked me to go to Bogotá tomorrow. I'm glad you want me to marry you. I think I would enjoy it but we do have problems. Your job is one of them. How would I fit into that life? My career, and where we should live. We need to think about it. Being married is more than just loving one another. We need to be sure that we have a decent chance to make it work and make it last.' She smiled up at him. 'Do you agree?'

'Of course I do. And I love you very much. Just being with you is like being in the *Orangerie*.'

She laughed. 'Maybe I should write a film-script based on the *Musée* and its influences on different people. Anyway, thanks for the lovely thought. Let's go home.'

Volkov had a window seat on the plane and as it circled Paris to head out to the Atlantic he could see the lights of the city winking and glittering below, and he felt sad. He had fallen in love with the city as well as the girl. There were echoes of Russia in Paris. Despite his dreadful French he had felt at home there. Music, art and literature were important in Paris and part of everyday life. Not just a special occasion as they made it in Washington or New York.

He had phoned Fomenko twice from the Paris embassy and there was nothing new. But the last batch of Jarvis's information was, it seemed, vitally interesting and well worth the dollars.

As they started rigging up the screen for the in-flight film, Volkov leaned back in his seat and closed his eyes. The girl had had more sense than he had. He wasn't sure what 'love' actually meant. He hadn't said anything that he didn't believe to be true. He found her attractive both physically and mentally. She was very perceptive and she obviously liked him. Maybe actually did love him and wanted to be with him. But they had only been together when he wasn't in Washington and wasn't working. The KGB didn't post you somewhere because your wife wouldn't mind living there. They told you and you went. Now that he was a key figure in the KGB's most important current operation he could argue, and they might condescend to try and please him, but

Fomenko was no fairy godmother. And moving to be with him in Washington would mean giving up her work in Paris. Nobody in LA was looking for love stories set in rural France in French. Of course he could give up his job. Just resign and stay in the States. But how would he earn enough to support them both? His last vague waking thought before he slept was that maybe he should do what that creep Jarvis had done. Sell his knowledge to the other side.

Chapter 20

Getz and the search team sat around the table waiting for the call from the radio car that was circling a couple of blocks near the Jarvis's home. Getz was looking at his watch when the call came through. It was 01.30 hours and the car confirmed that all lights had gone off in the house at 23.54 hours. He hung up the phone.

'It's OK. Let's go.'

The target that night was an easy one – Jarvis's office on Floor G of the main building at Langley. Getz used a bunch of master-keys to open the office door and the three-man team took over. One was a computer expert and the other two specialised on documentation. They had expected to stay about half an hour but had been occupied for nearly three hours. There were dozens of reports and summaries of a high-security nature that were nothing to do with Jarvis's present duties or with his work in the past. It was obvious that he was collecting a mass of documents of vital interest to the Soviets. Even items of naval intelligence concerning the detection of Soviet submarines and radio codes. The tests on Jarvis's computer revealed the authorisation that gave him access to top-security information.

Photographs were taken of every aspect of the office and of a number of typical files of top-secret information, none of them relevant to Jarvis's current assignment. Most of them so confidential that he would not have had access to them in any of the posts he had held in the CIA.

Although Getz was pleased with the damning evidence that had been revealed, he was bitterly angry about the lack of internal security that had allowed it to happen.

He waited until midday and then phoned O'Hara for a meeting that afternoon.

*   *   *

O'Hara looked at Getz's hastily typed report and at photocopies of some of the documents involved. He looked across his desk at Getz. 'It's incredible. What do you want to do next?'

'I want warrants for "searching without occupant present" for his home, his car and trash cans. Unspecified and unlimited occasions and dates.'

'What are you after?'

'Anything that shows that he's working with and for the Soviets.'

'Just showing won't be enough, Larry. Proves is the word that matters.' He paused. 'Have you spoken to any of our legal people?'

'No.'

'I'll make an appointment for you to have a meeting with Joe Shapiro. Their boss. When you've talked to him come back and see me again and I'll see what I can do about the warrants.'

Shapiro was another O'Hara. Big-built and a craggy, handsome face and a brain that was reported to be four moves ahead of any opponent. He was a careful listener but no communicator except about the law. He ran a course at the university law school on 'The structure of successful prosecution'.

Shapiro sat with his chair turned to face the window as he listened to Getz outlining his evidence against Jarvis. When he finished Joe Shapiro just sat there for long moments before turning his chair to face Getz across his desk.

'It's Larry, isn't it?'

'Yes, sir.'

'Joe.' He paused. 'When you're looking at this sort of operation it's always wise to look at the ending before the beginning.' He looked at Getz. 'What do you see as the ending?'

'The arrest of Jarvis.'

Shapiro shook his head. 'The arrest of Jarvis is not much more than half-way down the track. What we're looking for is Jarvis being found guilty by a Federal court and going in the slammer for the rest of his life. And before you get anywhere near that there's gonna be a little snag. Friend Jarvis is going to have a lawyer. Either one he appoints or one the courts appoint. And either way he's going to be the best there is. You say Jarvis has got a lot of money and that means he'll go for the best. If the court appoints an attorney they'll be queuing up for the job. The publicity will be worth millions to any good law firm. Agreed?'

'Yes.'

'So let's look at a bit of what we've got. First the big sums of money. OK. Very suspicious but how do you prove it came from the KGB? He denies it flatly. And he doesn't have to say where it *did* come from. That's your job to make the connection.' He paused. 'Then you've got that damning material you've just found on the search of his office. Says he always wondered why it kept coming to him. Just put it on one side until somebody claimed it. No matter how pathetic and unlikely his lies are, it doesn't matter. Your stuff is just circumstantial. OK. You say – it may be circumstantial but there's a ton of it for heaven's sake.' Shapiro shook his head. 'Doesn't matter if there's fifty ton of it – it's just unconnected to our friend, Jarvis.' He shrugged. 'What you need is proof of a connection with the KGB. Some things from them to him.'

'I was hoping that the search of his home would supply that.'

'You think he's that careless?'

'Yes. His actions have shown that time and time again. CIA security is bad or he wouldn't have got away with it for so long.'

'I hope you're right.' He paused. 'I'll recommend to O'Hara that he get you the warrants.' He shrugged. 'If he can.' He paused. 'I don't know how he thinks he'll do it.'

'Why not?'

'All the judges I deal with would say it's too circumstantial, too speculative.'

'That's what we hope the searches will provide. Solid proof of a connection.'

'Do people still believe that communism can work? The Soviets have abandoned it. Who still carries the ball?'

'Castro, North Korea, China.'

'Castro and North Korea are bankrupt. They won't last long. China – well,' he shrugged, 'depends on what you call communism.' He stood up. 'Anyway. Best of luck. If there's anything that comes up that I can help with, just let me know. I'll have a word with O'Hara.'

Getz was amazed when two days later O'Hara showed him two

warrants. Between the two of them it meant that the team could virtually search anything that was part of the Jarvis household. And O'Hara in his wisdom had added the name of Maria Jarvis to the warrants.

Chapter 21

It was the last time that he would be able to be away for two days until the Jarvis operation was finished one way or another. He had taken her back to his past in Vermont and they had stayed at a small hotel on the edge of Lake Champlain.

They sat on the last evening watching the boats on the lake. It was mid-week and too early for the small towns around the lake to be busy. She smiled as she watched him with the country-boy's stalk of grass in his mouth, and the breeze from the water lifting the blond hair and making him squint into the sun. He wasn't handsome but he was good-looking and attractive in a Robert Redford sort of way. Still young-looking, no wrinkles except the smile lines at his eyes and mouth. He turned to look at her, catching her smiling.

'Why are you smiling?'

'Just affection.' She watched him as she said, 'Have you been happy these two days?'

He nodded. 'I've not been so happy for years. And you?'

'I'm always happy just thinking about you, and being with you is wonderful.' She paused. 'How long before we can do this again?'

'Not too long I hope.'

'Is this job you're doing permanent?'

He smiled. 'I hope not but it's taking a long time. It's very complex.'

'Are you in any danger?'

He shook his head. 'No. Absolutely not.'

They stayed until it was dark, and then drove the hire car to Burlington International and took the late flight to Washington where they went to Getz's place, had breakfast together and Getz dropped her off at the embassy on his way to his HQ.

*   *   *

Sam Harris had got hold of prints of the architect's original plans for the Jarvis house. They showed every room on both floors on the house and were to scale. All windows and doors were shown and the position of all electrical sockets and fuse-boxes. Somebody had got details of the telephone installations in the house and those positions had been marked in red on the plans.

It was going to take at least fifty highly-trained surveillance personnel to monitor Jarvis twenty-four hours a day. And a lot of high-tech equipment. Directional microphones, lasers to pick up inside traffic using the windows as diaphragms, a range of cameras and the usual picks and rakes for lock-picking with a special key-pattern device that would allow them to make duplicate keys for old-fashioned ward locks.

What they needed now was information that would prove to the satisfaction of a court that not only was Jarvis passing top-secret information to the Russians but that Moscow was controlling the operation.

At the group meeting it was decided that two immediate targets would be the setting up of a miniature video camera somewhere to cover the Jarvises' house continually, and a regular check of the item that all surveillance operators went for – the trash barrel at the Jarvises' residence.

The only house opposite the Jarvises' place that could cover the property even with a wide-angle lens was the house of a family with five kids and it was reckoned that an observant child would soon notice the addition to the face of the house.

The solution they came up with meant hiring a truck with a lift from a local tree-trimming company. The two men from the team who were raised up on the lift had used a small chain-saw to lop off a few branches and the camera was lifted to the telephone lines that ran in front of the tree. It gave a clear and full picture of the Jarvises' house that was relayed back to the HQ at Tysons Corner.

Checking trash cans and barrels was such a common exercise that there were drills for carrying out such operations without arousing suspicion.

It was confirmed that the Jarvises' trash was collected on Wednesday mornings and the trash team spent a week checking the neighbourhood pattern of late-night dog walking and similar activities.

On the first Tuesday night a custom-built, unmarked van with a specially silenced engine and exhaust pulled up to the trash barrel which was lifted quickly into the van and an exact replica with similar household rubbish was left in its place. Back at Tysons Corner the trash was sifted by specialists who photographed anything that looked as if it might be interesting. Two hours later the barrel was returned and the substitute reclaimed. The sifting team even made notes of what was on the top of the garbage so that it was replaced in exactly the same way.

It had taken a week of careful checking to establish when the whole Jarvis family would be out of the house long enough for a team to bug the place. It turned out to be a PTA concert at their son's school. It was estimated that they would be limited to fifty minutes only. They bugged every room and were out in thirty minutes. The Jarvises' phone was a routine bugging. The local switching station were given orders to attach an additional circuit to the number and that ensured that all calls in or out of the Jarvises' house were monitored and recorded.

On the same day that the Jarvises' house was bugged, Larry Getz received a photocopy of Art Jarvis's joint income-tax report for himself and his wife. He reported a total joint income of $67,577.90. With the details he had of Jarvis's bank deposits it was damning evidence. But because he had once been a lawyer himself he knew that a sharp attorney could claim that the only offence Jarvis had committed was to make a false income-tax declaration.

A team of six document experts had been checking out the contents of dozens of bundles of documents found in Jarvis's office. None of them were of legitimate interest to him in his job at the Counter-Narcotics Centre. They covered almost every aspect of top-security operations against the Soviets and particularly the KGB. And what was even more damning was that most of them were dated after his transfer to Counter-Narcotics, which meant that he would have no possible legitimate reason for having even seen them, let alone removing them. And yet the records showed no single instance of the legitimate users having reported the loss of any document. Jarvis must have been picking up documents and reports from a dozen or so areas like a housewife picking interesting-looking items from supermarket shelves. The CIA's carelessness was criminal and incredible.

Getz had so many people working on different aspects of the surveillance of Jarvis but the rewards seemed small for so much effort. But Getz knew that this kind of operation was a bit like a farmer ploughing and harrowing, then planting the seeds before a long time later the crop was there to be harvested. Any one of the small pieces of evidence that was being logged and examined could be vital to some aspect of a court case. The last nail in the coffin.

Getz read the report of the number two team monitoring Jarvis's movements. It was evidence that showed Jarvis involved in typical trade-craft used by the KGB. There were colour prints of the four sites mentioned in the report.

Team: Ockerson and Thomas
Date of surveillance: May 26, 1993
Subject: A. Jarvis

Subject left his home in Arlington, North Randolph Street in Jaguar car, approx. 08.24 hours. Did not take usual route to Langley but went to the mailbox (photo A) at Thirty-Seventh and R Streets where he put chalk mark (photo B) on mailbox. He then drove to pedestrian footbridge at Little Falls Parkway where he left small package. Following our routine instructions the package was not examined but left in place.

Team: Ockerson and Thomas
Date of surveillance: 30 May, 1993
Subject: A. Jarvis
Subject stopped at telephone pole on corner of Military Road and Thirty-Sixth Street, Arlington. He may have left some sign but we could not identify such a sign. At 18.17 hrs. subject stopped in Wheaton Park and removed package from drainpipe. Contents of package unknown.

The telephone monitoring team had provided new information on the Jarvises' money from a long telephone communication between

Maria Jarvis and her mother who was informing her daughter of money problems with properties owned by the Jarvises in Cartagena, Bogotá and Guajira. It sounded as if Guajira was a farm on the coast somewhere in Bogotá. Getz had passed the transcript to James Parfitt with a note asking him if he could track down any details of the properties and their registered owners. Either in the Jarvis name or that of the in-laws, dos Santos. He could use any facilities or leads that the Bogotá CIA group could provide.

At long last there had been sighting of an actual contact between Jarvis and Yuri Volkov. Jarvis had been standing with a glass of beer at the crowded bar of the Brickseller and fifteen minutes later Volkov had appeared. Looking around the dense crowd for Jarvis. When he had spotted his quarry he had pushed his way to the bar alongside Jarvis who turned and looked at Volkov, saying something before turning away again. A few minutes later Jarvis laid a folded copy of a newspaper on the bar counter, keeping his hand on it until Volkov picked it up. It looked as if there could be a package inside the paper.

It had already been decided that if Jarvis was seen making an obvious contact no action should be taken. In this case they could have taken in Volkov and examined the package if there was one. But Volkov had diplomatic immunity and in any case it would have blown the operation to Jarvis himself. They needed a lot more before they could even consider going for Jarvis. The only sour note so far as Getz was concerned was that Volkov had managed to give the slip to the surveillance team that was detailed to monitor him. But Getz had no doubt now that the massive operation was beginning to pay off.

What still needed to be done was to establish more evidence of Soviet involvement.

But there was more bad news the next day. Jarvis was a man of fixed habits and they used his routine to avoid having surveillance cars near his home when it didn't seem necessary. It was meant to give extra security to avoid being noticed by Jarvis. But on that day Jarvis had left home early, two hours before his usual time and before the CIA cars were in place. When they moved in at the usual time they were shocked to see him not leaving his house but returning from what had obviously been Jarvis servicing one of the dead-drops. To make matters worse, instead of leaving Langley at 5 p.m., his regular time, he had pulled out of the parking area at 4 p.m. and by the time the surveillance team had got their cars together they had lost him.

The same evening Jarvis and his wife had gone to a meeting at their son's school and this time the surveillance team were on full alert. He had driven a strange, seemingly pointless route that eventually crossed the Memorial Bridge and up Massachusetts Avenue, around the Naval Observatory and then back along Garfield. He turned into Garfield Terrace, a cul-de-sac, backed into a driveway to make a turn and drove straight back to his house.

Extra personnel had been called in to search the whole area for any signs that could have been left by either Jarvis or the Russians. It was a hopeless task and was more a kind of absolution for their earlier failures than anything more realistic. Getz was furious with the carelessness of the surveillance team that had missed what could have been a damning piece of evidence.

Chapter 22

Volkov had checked the time difference between Washington and Paris and had phoned her mid-evening. She sounded pleased to hear him.

'Thanks for your letters, Yuri, and thanks for the earrings, they're really beautiful. How are you?'

'I'm fine. And how are you?'

'I had a cold last week but I'm OK now.'

'You said if I contacted you after a couple of months or so we might be able to get together again. Any chance of doing that?'

'Why not? Where should we go?'

'How about Turkey, on the sea coast. It's very beautiful.'

There was a long silence and then he said, 'Are you there?'

'Yes. I'm here. But I wouldn't feel happy in a country that treats its people so badly.'

He groaned. 'So draw me a map, my love, showing all the countries that we can go to that are democratic and civilised.'

She laughed. 'You're right of course. There's nowhere left.'

'How about you come over here? I can get you a flight and we can take an apartment. No problem.'

'OK. Why not?'

'When can you come?' She smiled at the young-boy's eagerness in his voice.

'When would suit you?'

'Tomorrow.'

She laughed. 'How about in two weeks' time? I can clear up my current work and be able to relax.'

'I'll phone you in a couple of days with the flight details.' He paused and when he spoke his voice was softer. 'I miss you so much, Sabine. Everywhere I go I try to imagine you're with me. There's a park near the embassy and I take a walk there most days. I found myself talking out loud to you the other day. There were mothers with kids who hung on to them obviously thinking I was a dangerous lunatic.'

She laughed. 'You are a dangerous lunatic. But I miss you too.'

'Tell me what you miss.'

'Your arm round my waist. That grin of yours. Your optimism and your belief that there's nothing you can't deal with.'

'I've learned the words of the song on that tape of Charles Trenet.'

'Which song – "*La Mer*"?'

'No. "*J'ai ta main dans ma main*".'

'Let me hear it. Sing it to me.'

'I will when you're here.'

'You're chicken.' She paused. 'My parents have just arrived. I'll have to go. Call me like you said.'

'I love you, Sabine.'

'I love you too. *Jusqu'àu bout de ma vie.*'

Getz set out on his late-night walk around the block just after midnight. He looked up at the sky. It was like a stage set. Deep blue with a full moon. The perfect backdrop for a musical. Something by Rodgers and Hart. *The Follies of 1993* maybe. It had been hot and humid all day and the night breeze was a relief. The weather-girl had said there could be rain the next day. Which meant today.

They had been able to do four checks on the garbage from the Jarvises' home over a period of three months. It was too tricky an operation to do more often. It had been six or seven weeks since they had last done the garbage run and he had agreed that they could run it again that night. Despite meticulous checking nothing had been found from the previous pick-ups.

Back at his HQ he undressed slowly and set the alarm beside his camp-bed for 6 p.m. The radio-phone and a glass of fresh apple-juice were on a small table beside the bed. He reached for his paperback. It was Irwin Shaw's collection of short stories – *Girls in their summer dresses*.

The phone rang at 4 a.m. It was the trash searchers and it was good news. Amongst the kitchen refuse they'd found a scrumpled yellow page from a Post-it self-stick pad. It was obviously draft notes for a message to Jarvis's KGB contact. It covered dates and coded meeting-places and complaints that messages had not been found where they were supposed to be. When the FBI specialists had examined the note they had filled in the blanks and the most important factor was that Jarvis wanted to meet his contact in Bogotá on October 1 and wanted the meeting confirmed.

On the 19th September Jarvis booked a reservation on a flight to Bogotá.

Four days later they monitored a phone call from Jarvis's office to his wife. It was a very guarded conversation. He wouldn't be making the trip. He told her to warn her mother that the visit was off. She asked him if he'd received anything and he was obviously irritated as he said he had. This transcript connected Maria positively with her husband's treason.

A few days later another telephone tap indicated that Jarvis was finally going to Bogotá. He finished up by saying, 'Everything's OK', and she said, 'Financially too?' He said, 'Yeah. When I get there.'

Another trash check the following week produced another note. Handwritten by Jarvis himself.

It read: 'You have probably heard a bit about me by this time from your (and now my) colleagues in the MBRF.'

This was very interesting. All Jarvis's contacts had been with the SVR, the old KGB, and the SVR were only concerned with direct espionage, but the MBRF was solely concerned with counter-espionage inside Russia. It was puzzling as to why he should be connected to the Soviet equivalent of the FBI rather than the SVR, the Soviet equivalent of the CIA.

Then, as if a reward for their massive efforts, Getz's team pieced together random telephone calls that indicated that the whole Jarvis household would be going to a wedding in Pensacola, Florida. They would all be away for the whole weekend.

A special team was assembled to go in at the weekend of October 8. They were all experienced experts and it was planned that to avoid alerting neighbours they would go in after dark and leave before daylight.

They filtered in quietly in couples at 12.45 a.m. and the last of them had left by 4.00 a.m. They left silently on foot and made their way to the coach that was waiting for them two streets away.

The computer expert broke Jarvis's amateurish computer password in minutes and downloaded the entire contents of the hard-disk onto the lap-top computer they had brought with them. Every document was photographed, every drawer and cupboard searched professionally, stubs for airline tickets logged and every item of expensive jewellery photographed.

The computer expert had sat at a table checking the information he now had on the lap-top and couldn't resist using his security cell-phone to report to Larry Getz that Jarvis had kept almost every message he had received on floppy disk from the Russians and every file he had ever made for them. To complete the haul there were details of the KGB street-craft methods, including a list of all dead-drops and their code-names, signal sites and their instruction markings.

It was hours later when cheerful teams laid out their hauls on the long table. The photographers had taken their loot to Langley where the facilities were more sophisticated. Even with those facilities it took a dozen technicians two days to provide what was needed.

Getz hadn't slept for two nights and days and he had gone back to his apartment to get a good night's sleep. He had handed in a note in the early hours of the morning at the embassy for Gabriella, suggesting that she should come to the apartment and let herself in if he was asleep.

She was sitting on the edge of his bed holding his hand when he woke up.

'Hi,' he said. 'Lovely to see you. What time is it?'

She looked at her watch. 'Ten thirty-five and it's cold outside but sunny.' She leaned over and kissed him. 'I'll make us some coffee.'

He put on his bathrobe, showered and shaved and they sat with their coffee at the kitchen table. As he stirred his coffee, she said, 'What happened? You look quite human again. Is that job finished at last?'

'Afraid not. But we're nearly there.' He paused. 'What day is it?'

'Monday. Have you got to go back?'

'I'll stay until this evening if you'll be here.'

'I'll be here as long as you want.'

'What have you been doing?'

'Hanging around, waiting for you. Sorting out Mama's music

scores, teaching Papa how to use Internet and handing round drinks at cocktail parties.'

'You're not only very beautiful but you're a very versatile young woman too.'

She smiled and accepted that Americans didn't go in much for irony.

They spent the day routinely as couples do, but for Getz it was a wonderful break from the treadmill of Jarvis and his villainy. It was like a short leave he'd had from Vietnam when just seeing civilians and shops and drug stores was an incredible treat. He had bought her an Hermés scarf with roses on it instead of saddles and stirrups and she had bought him a Sheaffer fountain pen.

They had had drinks with her parents at the embassy on his way back that night to his office.

Getz had called a meeting of the main team and section leaders to hear what new material was available. He had asked Joe Shapiro to arrange for one of his senior people in Legal to attend the meeting. To his surprise Shapiro had come himself.

After the introductions, Getz asked Theo Papas, the computer expert, to report on what he had found.

Theo Papas opened a box file and passed out typed sheets, four at a time, stapled together.

'Those sheets give you a menu of what I've got off the target's computer. It's incredible that the guy should have recorded so assiduously everything that could prove that he was paid huge sums by the KGB, that he gave them thousands of copies and sometimes originals of top-security CIA documents, that he did it all so arrogantly, so indiscriminately that it shows that he assessed the CIA as an organisation so careless and so lax that he could get away with anything.' He looked at Getz. 'I find it embarrassing to have to report this, Mr Getz. And I find it outrageous that we made it so easy for him.

'You'll find page references of the menu and the supporting documents are available. For the sake of economy of size I've printed paper on both sides.' He paused and looked around. 'There are approximately nine thousand pages, plus my summary. There are ten sets of reference copies and I've left the distribution for you to decide, Mr Getz.'

'Thank you, Theo.' He looked around. 'Any questions?'

Somebody said, 'Some of us have already seen relevant parts of the material. What about the rest of us? When do we get to see it?'

'I'll tell you about that at the end of the meeting. Anything else?'

'May I put a question, Larry?' Shapiro spoke very quietly just as he used to in court when he was an attorney about to make a point that would ruin the opposition's case.

'Of course, Joe. Go ahead.'

'Mr Papas. I can only stand in awe of what you have been able to construct from a few computer disks and a lot of hard work and skill. Forgive my stupidity in asking the question, but would it be possible to delete any of it, or add to it or even change it?'

Papas smiled. He was used to these grey-haired old boys with their stately courtesies. They always knew a lot more than they let on. He hadn't said anything about disks in the report he'd just given the meeting.

'All I can say, sir, is that depends on what you want to do.'

'Let's say I want to alter the dates on a couple of documents.'

'That wouldn't be a problem, sir.'

'And if the opposing counsel suggested that you had put all this stuff on a computer yourself and that it had never been near the defendant's computer, should we be embarrassed? Or worse?'

Papas hesitated. 'There would be two problems in doing that, sir. This material has been put on the computer over a period of two or three years. And gathering up the documents would have taken a hell of a lot of people working for months.'

'But forgetting the time – it could be done?'

'I guess so.'

'Interesting. Very interesting.'

Getz nodded at another man, Rowley Shears.

'You go next Rowley.' Getz looked around the table. 'Rowley is our documents king for the operation.'

Shears smiled and shrugged. 'We've got a mass of documentary evidence. I've reproduced a message we've got that ties Jarvis to the KGB and asking for money from them. Maybe you'd like to read it. It's quite short – just an extract.'

Shears passed copies of the message to each of them.

170

My most immediate need, as I pointed out in March, is money. As I have mentioned several times, I do my best to invest a good part of the cash I received, but keep part of it out for ordinary expenses.

Now I am faced with the need to cash in investments to meet current needs – a very tight and unpleasant situation! I have had to sell a certificate of deposit in Zurich and some stock here to help make up the gap. Therefore, I will need as much cash delivered in PIPE as you think can be accommodated – it seems to me that it could accommodate up to $100,000.

As they monitored the phone calls from Jarvis's house there were more and more angry phone calls from Maria to Jarvis at his office. She was obviously now deeply involved in his relationship with the Soviets. She found his dilatory response to the KGB messages left at the sites asking him to make an appointment enough to enrage her to urge him, as she put it, to 'Stop behaving like an asshole and get on and do it'. But Jarvis went his own way. Finally there was a meeting in Bogotá which the team monitored from the moment he stepped onto the plane until he returned four days later. Even while he was in Bogotá he was harangued from home about whether he had problems there. When he denied this there were guarded queries about whether he had been paid. The team had photographs of him with all his Soviet contacts and with his in-laws. Even on the day he was returning Maria had been insistent that he should deposit the cash rather than risk his baggage being searched. The team found the scenario of the wife instructing him on field-craft almost incredible.

It was in the second week of February that the monitoring team heard her phone Jarvis at work to say that she was worried that their phone might have been bugged. When he asked her why she thought this she admitted that she had no grounds for thinking this but she 'just had a feeling' about it. Jarvis had laughed and hung up.

On the evening of February 17 Getz held a meeting with his team leaders with O'Hara sitting-in and they decided that it was time to call it a day. They would arrest Jarvis on the morning of February 21, 1994. They were convinced that they had more than enough material to satisfy any court.

171

PART THREE

Chapter 23

Larry Getz had tried to make the day as normal as possible. He and Gabriella had lunch at the Italian restaurant and then went back to his place. They were looking at the Cosby Show and after ten minutes she used the remote to switch off the TV.

She turned her head to look at his face. 'How long before you're back?'

'I'm not sure. A week at least. But I'll be in Washington and I'll try and phone you and maybe sneak out for an hour if it's possible.'

'I'll have a number for wherever I go and they can transfer you.' She paused. 'Is this the thing you've been working on for so long?'

'Yeah. It should be the end of it.' He kissed her. 'I'll drop you at the embassy on the way but I'd better get moving.'

She smiled as he stood up. 'I don't often see you in a suit. But you look very handsome.'

He reached in his jacket pocket and pulled out a small tissue-paper wrapped package. 'I bought this for you.'

She unwrapped it carefully. It was a ring with a beautifully set opal. She looked up at him. 'Our birthstone. We sensible Scorpios. I love it. It's beautiful.' She kissed him and then drew back to slide the ring onto her finger. 'Mama will be very jealous, she loves opals.' She kissed him. 'I love it. Thank you.'

Getz smiled. 'I'll buy one for her for our wedding day.' He paused. 'It won't be long.'

'I can't wait.'

It was just after 9 p.m. on the 20th February 1994 when Getz cleared the security lock on the entrance to his control room.

Like a wife on holiday who worried about whether she had turned off the gas, he found himself constantly checking out the things that were pinned to the cork tiles that stretched from one side of the long wall to the other.

There were three typed pages naming all the people working on the operation with a column for their tasks. There were fifty-two names. There was a hard core of sixteen names that were vital, and a handful of specialists. The rest were drivers, guards, telephonists, technicians and archivists. All under the strictest security and aware that there were others whom they didn't know who would be checking their security day after day.

There were photographs of Jarvis's home in Arlington. Views from front and rear and an aerial shot showing its relationship to other houses. There was a large-scale map marked to show where the car would be stopped and positions in surrounding streets where cars would be blocking roads. There were a dozen photographs of Jarvis and several of his wife, and one picture of his son, Peter.

There was a time schedule of all the stages of their activities from the point where Jarvis left his home to the time when he was to be arrested by Getz and taken back to the team at the safe-house. There was a colour shot of Jarvis's latest Jaguar.

Getz was aware of the FBI's resentment that he was in charge of the operation but they had not let it interfere with their co-operation on the investigation of Jarvis. The fact was that it was incumbent on the CIA to notify the FBI of suspected traitors. The CIA was for active intelligence, not spy-catching. But he equally understood the CIA's reluctance to notify the FBI of the treachery of one of their own men. As O'Hara had said way back, 'Telling the FBI that one of your own guys is a traitor is a bit like expecting Ford to inform General Motors of the shortcomings of Ford's most recent model.' But Getz had been in the espionage business long enough to realise that the FBI's co-operation could also be an insurance policy against them taking all the blame if the whole thing collapsed. Between the two agencies they seemed to have either deliberately or by default made sure that he would personally carry the can if anything went wrong. But he'd kept a war-diary for the whole time he'd been in charge and the investigation had stuck to the rule-book. Warrants for everything that called for a warrant. Even for searching the trash bins in the back-yard when the family were away. And he had ten box-files of the documentation. Originals or photocopies.

Getz looked at his watch. It was ten minutes past midnight. It was already the day. President's Day, a federal public holiday. The day that Jarvis would go in the bag. Signed, sealed and delivered.

He was looking forward to interrogating Jarvis. He had got away with so many blatant breaches of security that he must have felt that he was immune from the law. He himself had been hammering away for two years at the almost complete lack of even basic security inside the CIA and nothing had improved. Maybe Jarvis had made the same assessment and he wasn't as stupid and feckless as he appeared to be.

It would be four hours before any of Getz's arrest team appeared. Then an hour for one last briefing. Each one already knowing exactly what he had to do. Expecting no physical resistance but prepared for any eventuality that trained units could imagine. And it would be he himself who actually arrested and charged Arthur Jarvis. Kirsty would arrest Maria.

His HQ for that day was in the FBI building at Buzzard Point, one of the city's grimmer areas, and, despite the hour, there was considerable activity in the rest of the building. Activity not concerned with his operation. Not even aware of its existence. Solely carrying on the routine duties of the FBI's Metropolitan Field Office.

His thoughts went to Gabriella. O'Hara and others had hinted at a major promotion once the Jarvis case was tied up but he had no idea of what such a promotion would entail. He was determined not to let his job ruin another relationship. But Gabriella was very different from Joan. Gabriella had been brought up accustomed to the constant moving to new countries and the absences that being a government servant entailed. But more than that, she loved him, not as the boy next door, but as a man. Passionately, and fundamentally uncritical. Ready to poke fun at some of his habits but always with a broad smile of affection. All that Italian passion suited the boy from Vermont very well. He had once said, smiling, that being with her was like lying in a warm bath listening to Ella Fitzgerald singing 'Manhattan'.

He stood at one of the windows looking out at the silhouettes of grim buildings. A few with lights in the windows but still cheerless and foreboding. It was a strange city, Washington DC. Areas of magnificent vistas and fine old public buildings that had been designed and built with real affection for the city that they hoped would one day be a worthy capital. Beautiful suburbs like his area of Georgetown where strangers had recognised the value of time and history. Parks and lakes that few cities could equal and then the sheer weight of people assembled to govern the United States of America. Philosophers, lawyers, musicians, actors and good day-to-day Americans who had, by misfortune or neglect, contrived their own purgatory of hucksters, drug-pushers, thugs and hustlers, fraudsters and psychopaths.

There were fifteen agents at four different locations reporting back by radio to the control centre from strategic points that kept Jarvis's home under constant surveillance. A small team sat in a cubicle at the FBI building listening for sounds on the microphones and telephone taps in Jarvis's house. At six-thirty everything was still quiet inside. They knew the patterns of Jarvis's life as well as he knew them himself. If he was sending a message to the Russians he would go out early but he seemed to be sticking to his normal routine.

Getz went over his own check-list and phoned O'Hara from the FBI's office at Tysons Corner, Virginia. The warrants for the arrest of Jarvis and his wife had been signed and were already on their way to him and he checked with the radio group that the forward team was already in the carpark at the Italian delicatessen a quarter of a mile from the house on North Randolph Street.

Jarvis was due to fly to Moscow the next day on an official visit and it was essential that the arrests took place that day. Getz's greatest fear was that the preparations and surveillance might have alerted Jarvis and that he'd find some way to avoid the trap that had been so elaborately organised and head for Moscow. Just after 7.30 a.m. Getz phoned Jarvis's boss at Langley and asked him to make the pre-arranged phone call, and Getz moved over to the monitoring team.

Jarvis yawned and looked at his watch as he reached for the phone beside his bed.

'Yeah.'

'Hi, Art. Something important has just come in that you'll need to clear before your Moscow trip. I think you'd better come in right now and check it out.'

Jarvis sighed. 'OK. I'll be over in about an hour. See you.' Then he hung up.

When he had shaved and dressed he woke his wife and told her that he was going to Langley and expected to be away for about two hours. She barely acknowledged the news and rolled over to go back to sleep. It looked like a chilly morning and he took a windcheater from the rack in the hall, checking as he went to the car that he'd got cigarettes and a lighter. Nobody else was allowed to smoke in the Jaguar but he sometimes lit up a Benson and Hedges himself as a small reward for an early start.

He turned right on North Randolph and right again on Quebec, lighting a cigarette as he settled back in the leather seat. When he got to the junction where Quebec crosses into Nellie Curtis Drive he saw two sets of tail-lights ahead of him. The cars were side by side and Jarvis braked to a stop, waiting for the idiot in the right-hand lane to turn. But the car didn't move and then more cars turned into Quebec behind Jarvis.

When one of the cars behind him put on a red flasher light and then a siren, Jarvis did what a good citizen should do and pulled towards the curb.

The eight agents from the four cars got out of their vehicles and stood to one side as Larry Getz tapped on the window of the Jag. Jarvis lowered the window and said, 'What's going on?'

Getz said quietly. 'Keep your hands in sight and get out of the car.'

In a sudden flash of anger Getz reached forward, removing the lighted cigarette from Jarvis's lips and tossed it into the gutter. When Jarvis still sat there Getz jerked open the car door and hauled him to his feet. Getz sensed that even now Jarvis didn't understand what was happening, as he said angrily, 'What the hell's going on?'

'Arthur Casey Jarvis you are under arrest and charged with espionage. Turn round and put your arms behind your back.'

As Getz handcuffed him, Jarvis was still protesting. 'You're making a mistake. You've got the wrong man.'

Getz was not amused and he shoved Jarvis into the back seat of his unmarked car and nodded to the driver to get moving. Jarvis, traitor and millionaire, sat crouched down in the car as it sped on its journey to the FBI office at Tysons Corner.

Twenty FBI agents had surrounded the house on North Randolph Street. When the doorbell rang Maria was busy putting on her make-up in the bathroom. Her mother, on a visit from Bogotá, was asleep in the guest bedroom.

When the doorbell rang she slipped on a silk dressing-gown and made her way downstairs, giving a quick adjustment to a stray lock of hair before she opened the door. The young woman standing there was in her mid-thirties, dressed in a dark blue jacket and skirt.

'Are you from the bridge club or . . .'

'My name's Kirsty Westrop and I'm an FBI special agent.' The young woman held up her card and badge.

'I can't read it without my glasses. What does it say?'

'It's my identification, Mrs Jarvis. I have to tell you, Mrs Jarvis, that I am arresting you on charges of conspiracy to commit treason. Your husband is already in custody.'

'You're joking. My husband is a CIA officer.'

'May I come in, Mrs Jarvis?'

Maria stood back to allow her visitor to enter. Kirsty Westrop closed the door behind them.

'Mrs Jarvis, I can give you half an hour to collect a few things then you'll be taken to a prison before going in front of a magistrate to be charged. One of my colleagues will stay at your house to assist your mother. Is there anyone you wish to give power-of-attorney to so that your son can be cared for properly?'

Maria shook her head slowly, her voice barely audible as she said, 'Is this really all true?'

'I'm afraid so, Mrs Jarvis. Now, a guardian for your son.'

'It had better be Art's sister until I'm let out.'

'How about you phone her to come across right away?'

'Yes,' she whispered. 'Yes, I'll phone her.'

It was nearly an hour later when Special Agent Westrop escorted Maria to the waiting car. She had given her mother and sister-in-law joint power-of-attorney concerning their son and their possessions. A search team were already going over the house as they left.

Getz had taken Jarvis to the control room at Tysons Corner so that he could see the notice-boards covered with photographs of his house and a number of sites used for dead-drops and messages.

He even heard the voice on the loudspeaker say through the static – 'The second party is now under arrest and the dwelling is under our control – out.' He put his bowed head in his hands, shaking it from side to side as he said, 'You bastards. You mother-fucking bastards.'

Gabriella was at the embassy drinking a mid-morning coffee with her mother. They were watching the ABC morning show when a news-flash broke in and as they turned up the sound they heard the words – '. . . arrested today on charges of treason against the United States of America', and then a steadycam shot of a group of men, one of them in chains, and the comment continuing '. . . taken before a magistrate at Alexandria to be . . .'

It was only then that she realised that the man holding the prisoner's arm was Getz.

'Mama, look, that's Larry. See him . . .'

Then the news-flash commentator passed the viewers back to the studio and an interview with an actress who had just divorced her sixth husband.

It was a mid-evening clip on CNN showing Jarvis on his way to be charged by the Federal magistrate.

Volkov was manicuring his nails as he sat looking at the CNN news round-up. He was on his way to a cocktail party at the Dutch embassy. As the trailers came up for the review, Volkov used the remote to bring up the sound. He hardly absorbed the words like – 'espionage' – 'treason', but the shots of Jarvis in chains on his way from the prison to the court in Alexandria seemed like something out of a terrible nightmare. He had to wait twenty minutes to watch another repeat and it still seemed incredible. When he had watched it again he knew he had to make some quick decisions. Nobody else at the embassy even knew Jarvis as a name and the commentary had not specified which country Jarvis had sold out to.

He spent the rest of the evening packing his bags and considering where to head for. Perhaps inevitably, he decided on Paris. There were two night flights but he would have to wait until the banks were operational the next day for he needed all the money he had in his several bank accounts. He also put two passports in his bag. One

Canadian, the other British. Both containing his own photograph. And both very nearly genuine. The passports were genuine. Only the identities were false.

He made no phone calls from the embassy and didn't sleep that night. The next morning, downtown, he booked a flight to Toronto and a follow-on flight to Paris. When he had withdrawn all his money it came to $70,000. He thought of the many times he had handed over more than that in cash to Jarvis.

Back at the embassy he told His Excellency that he was taking a couple of weeks' holiday in Florida and as a precaution he sent a message to Fomenko to say that he was moving out of Washington until he had had the chance to assess the new situation. He would clear all the dead-drops before he left. In fact he had no intention of going near any of the sites. He was quite sure that the FBI or the CIA would be watching them for months.

As he waited that evening for his flight to Toronto to be called, he wondered if they knew enough about him to pull him off the plane. He wondered too what Jarvis was doing. Was he talking to save his skin or saying nothing for the same reason? He felt no sympathy for Jarvis. He was just a traitor for money. They always were, even if they claimed that it was belief in the socialist revolution. Gorbachev and Yeltsin had wiped out all that crap. You didn't even have to pretend anymore.

As he took his window seat on the plane he looked out at the activity on the tarmac. There was no sign of anything unusual and he took the newspapers offered him by the cabin crew. Jarvis's arrest and photographs were all over the front pages with columns of background on Javis's career and comments from people who had known him over the years. It was interesting to see that they were all shocked to learn of his arrest. He hadn't seemed anything special when they had known him. Tense as he was, Volkov was amused at the comments. People seemed to imagine that spies and traitors had horns growing out of their foreheads. He remembered the words of wisdom from some old hand at the KGB training school who said that the best spies looked much like your favourite uncle.

He wondered what Sabine's attitude to him would be. And what should he tell her. And even more important, what was he going to do next. Should he try to maintain a relationship with Fomenko or should he reckon that his career with the KGB was over. He was not responsible for Jarvis's arrest. Jarvis was careless about his own security and Moscow knew all about that. Moscow should welcome him back, thankful that he had been able to get them what they'd had. But he knew from experience that a welcome from Moscow was the last thing that would happen to him. Angry at the loss of Jarvis Moscow would make him their scapegoat. There was one other alternative that came to mind but he refused to consider it.

Maybe Sabine could suggest some way for him to earn a living in France. With his British passport he could have all the benefits of being an EU citizen. There would be nearly two hours between flights at Toronto and he could have a meal and maybe phone Sabine. For the first time in his life Volkov found that his usual sophisticated, laid-back persona had deserted him. He wouldn't have admitted it. Not even to himself. But Volkov was close to the edge of panic.

Chapter 24

O'Hara picked up the phone as he read the latest summary on Jarvis.

'O'Hara.'

'Justice Richards speaking. Who passed the copies of the warrants on the Jarvis operation to Judge Klein?'

'I've no idea. I neither sent them to him nor authorised him to see them. I saw him way back when I wanted warrants but he threw my application out. I came to you about a couple of hours later.' He paused. 'How do you think he got his hands on them?'

'I've no idea but you'd better come over here right away.'

'What's the problem?'

'Not one you talk about on the telephone.'

'OK. But I'll be about an hour.'

'So be it.'

It was beginning to snow as O'Hara drove across to the Supreme Court buildings. Richards' office was in one of the countless alleyways at the back of the building, on the ground floor. When he knocked on the door he heard several locks being turned before Justice Richards himself opened the door and beckoned him inside, pointing to a chair in front of the desk as he took his own seat behind it.

'Tell me something, O'Hara. Is Jarvis going to plead guilty and make a confession?'

'He's saying nothing at the moment. I understand the Court are going to assign him an attorney.'

'I heard that it's going to be Ira Shulman. I don't know who you're using for prosecution but Shulman is red-hot. He won't miss a trick.' He paused. 'Who sent you to me way back?'

'I'd spoken to the Director about the operation and the need for

185

warrants. He asked me who I was consulting. I said Judge Klein, and he kind of shrugged then said if he threw me out I should go to somebody who'd dealt with warrant applications before.' He paused. 'That's what I did.'

'When you contacted me you used a number as your introduction. Who gave you that number?'

'It was in our file against your name.'

'Can you remember the number?'

'Yes. 12949.'

'Was there any indication as to what that number represented?'

'I gathered that it was the number of a Presidential Executive Order.'

Richards leaned back in his chair looking away towards the shelves of law books on the far wall, his hands palms down on his desk. Then, sighing, he leaned forward.

'O'Hara, I got to tell you. You're in deep, deep shit.'

O'Hara had assumed that being called to see Richards was not good news. But he didn't expect to have it laid out so crudely by a man like Richards.

O'Hara shrugged. 'You'd better tell me why.'

'If I told you that all your bugging, house-breaking and financial investigations were illegal, what would you do?'

O'Hara was beginning to lose patience. 'First of all I'd ask you not to make such a mystery of whatever it is you're telling me. And secondly, I'd ask you why warrants signed by you are suddenly void and illegal.'

Richards looked for long moments at O'Hara's face and O'Hara knew by instinct that what he had just said had made him an enemy. Or at least, an adversary. He wasn't sure what Richards' status was. He was obviously in some no-man's-land between CIA and Justice. He remembered the odd feeling he had had when having been refused warrants by Judge Klein he had just carried out the usual procedures and then gone straight from the records to Richards. Richards hadn't appeared to even read the applications. He had just signed them. A dozen or so. And there had been some sort of guard or security man outside Richards' small office. Richards' crisp voice brought him back to present realities.

'Right, Mr O'Hara. The facts of life. The number you quoted

to me is the number of the Executive Order signed by President Clinton on February 9. It relates to a secret court created by the Foreign Intelligence Surveillance Act. Sometimes referred to as the FISA court.' He paused. 'The Justice Department on behalf of the FBI and the CIA can apply to the FISA court for warrants for any kind of surveillance they deem necessary. There are no published orders and no public record. It was exempt from any Fourth Amendment restrictions. The court is known to only a handful of people and will never be challenged or tested in the courts. The FISA court has authorised just under ten thousand applications to carry out electronic, telephonic and other means of surveillance since its inception. There are seven judges authorised to approve such applications and they do it in turn. Only one being involved at a time. It was my turn to approve warrants when you came to the court.'

'So what's the problem so far as I am concerned?'

'That none of the evidence that you and your people came by in the course of benefiting from the warrants is technically legal and you will never be able to use it in court.'

'Why not? If it's legal, it's legal.'

'Mr O'Hara. I'm told that you are an exceptionally successful intelligence officer. I'm sure you are. But you're being very naif if you think that the government are going to allow you to expose a secret of state concerning the existence of a court that nobody, not even Supreme Court Judges, has ever heard of.'

'We're talking about treason. This man has callously sent a dozen men to their deaths – just for money. Are you suggesting we set him free?'

'Calm down, Mr O'Hara. I've not suggested anything of the sort. There must be other ways to settle that account.'

'Such as?'

Richard shrugged. 'Get him to confess and plead guilty.'

'He shows no sign of doing that. Why should he, he's holding all the aces even if he doesn't know it – yet. A good lawyer will probably realise that there's something fishy and start ferreting around.'

'Do a deal with him. He pleads guilty. Confesses, and a month later he bolts and is never caught. Happy ending all round.'

'And when he's safe in some country where we have no extradition agreement he sells his story to a publisher.' O'Hara shook his head. 'No way.'

'Maybe he commits suicide. Shame, remorse, etcetera, etcetera.'

'That kind of man has neither shame nor remorse. Neither do they kill themselves.'

'With a little help, maybe?'

'Does Joe Shapiro know what you're telling me?'

'Of course.'

'Did he know right from the start?'

Richards half smiled. 'You must ask him that yourself.'

'How would I be stopped from using the warrants as justification in court?'

Richards said briskly. 'The warrants are in safe custody, my friend.'

'We have copies of all of them.'

Richards smiled. 'You did have.' He paused. 'Don't press me, O'Hara. There are a dozen ways to stop you. God forbid that it should be necessary, after all the sterling work you and your people have done.'

Richards stood up to mark the end of the interview and O'Hara headed for the door, beside himself with anger, and only half believing what he had just been told. As he got to the door he turned to look back at Richards.

'Why did nobody warn me?'

Richards shrugged. 'I guess that, like you, they were desperate to find the evidence and ignored the problem of how to use it if they got it.' He paused. 'You wanted to get the evidence didn't you?'

'There would be no point if we couldn't use it.'

Richards smiled. A knowing smile. 'You would still have wanted it, wouldn't you? Even if it was only to prove that you were right about Jarvis.'

O'Hara opened his mouth to speak, changed his mind and closed the door behind him, glancing at the young plain-clothes man standing beside the door.

As he left the building the snow was thick on the streets and as he walked to where he had parked his car he wondered what Getz's reaction would be to the news. But first he must talk to Joe Shapiro. When he dialled Shapiro's number, Shapiro answered himself.

'It's O'Hara. I need to see you.'

'I know. Richards phoned me and told me he'd seen you. Where do you want to meet?'

'Are you in your office?'

'Yeah.'

'I'll come over but I'll be about an hour, the snow's beginning to build up.'

'Don't rush. I'll be here.'

It was, in fact, almost two hours before O'Hara knocked on Shapiro's door and went in. The main lights in the room were out, leaving the place in near darkness, except for a pool of light from the reading lamp on Shapiro's desk.

'They've got the snow-ploughs and the gritters out. Do you have far to go?'

'I'll bed down here for the night. How about you?'

'I've warned Maggie I'll be very late. But I may stay the night too if they can find me a bed.'

'There's a spare one in my room.' He paused. 'How about a whisky?'

'Fine. But a small one.' He shrugged. 'You're almost cheering me up.'

'Let's sit over there.' Shapiro nodded to a group of armchairs around a low glass-topped table. He was silent as he brought over glasses and a bottle of Glenlivet, and poured them each a full glass. As he sat down he said, 'Richards filled me in, so just a few questions. OK?'

'Sure. Fire away.'

'Who sent you to Richards in the first place?'

'We've got a file on judges and warrants. Past experience of what they'll go with and what they won't. I wanted to keep it away from our usual list and I came across a file with Richards' name on it. It was plastered with "Eyes only" stickers and stamps and there was just a single page inside. It was obvious that we'd never tried him before but the notes said he was the guy to submit warrant applications to that involved Fourth Amendment problems and the suspect could not under any circumstances be informed.' O'Hara shrugged. 'It looked perfect for what we wanted. When I got no joy from Judge Klein I just went to Richards, the guy in the file.' He paused. 'No questions, no queries. I'm not even sure that he read any of it. Told me to come back in an hour, which I did. He handed me back the application signed and dated. It gave us all we asked for.'

'Have you still got that original file?'

'So far as I know we have.'

'Did it have a signature on the notes?'

'I don't remember. I vaguely remember initials on some of them.' He shrugged. 'Maybe there were signatures too.'

'I advise you to take over that file and put it in a very safe place. We might be glad of it before we've finished.'

O'Hara noticed the 'we' and was grateful. Shapiro looked across at O'Hara. 'What do you intend doing?'

'Have you decided who's going to prosecute?'

'I've been thinking about it. Going over names. But we've got a major problem here and we've got to stop it from getting out of hand. I don't want to take it on myself, the prosecution, but the more I think about it the more it comes down to that.' He sighed. 'The fact is that those warrants gave us full authority to do everything we did. But we can't use the evidence if the other side discover how we got the warrants.' He paused. 'Can you imagine what damage it would do if it came out that there was a secret panel of judges constituting a secret court that could ignore every aspect of the Fourth Amendment and ride rough-shod over any citizen's rights just on the suspicion that there was a security risk attached to that person. I doubt if even Clinton himself could survive it.' He shuffled the papers on his desk and then looked at O'Hara.

'If we appoint an outside attorney we're going to have to level with him or the other side will kick his butt in public, in court. The only virtue in me taking it on is that we keep the whole FISA court business in-house. But, by God, it riles me that I have to do it.'

'Does that mean that you were against Clinton signing the FISA order?'

Shapiro shook his head. 'No. It means I'm a lousy hypocrite like the rest of 'em. I want us to have the powers but I despise the way we got those powers.'

'Maybe there's some other way to give us those powers.'

'I'm sure there is but right now isn't the time to discuss it. I'll let you know tomorrow if I'm going to take it on myself or not. The story for the PR people is that I'm so incensed by what Jarvis has done. A lust for money. A traitor for a Jaguar and a half-million-dollar house.' He sighed. 'We've got to stretch this out as long as we can. Delays, misunderstandings, lost documents – all that bullshit to wear the others down.' He paused. 'Let's go and find something to eat. Do you want to phone Maggie that you'll be staying here for the night?'

O'Hara shrugged. 'I guess so.'

Getz had taken over a room at the Alexandria Prison for his initial interrogation of Jarvis. It was a converted cell without a window. Just a table bolted to the concrete floor, four basic chairs made in the prison workshop and a printed copy of the prison regulations in a metal frame fastened to a wall.

There was a tape-recorder on a trolley alongside the table but it was switched off. Two of Getz's team were with him and when a warder brought in Jarvis, Getz pointed to the empty seat.

Jarvis looked pale and drawn and very apprehensive.

Getz took his time before he started the interview but after a long, tense silence, he said, 'You know why you're here, Jarvis. You are charged with treason. Aiding and abetting the actions of a foreign country against the security of the United States of America.'

Jarvis just shrugged his shoulders but said nothing. Getz pushed across a sheet of paper that outlined Jarvis's legal rights. Jarvis just shoved it back at him.

'Just a few preliminary questions, Jarvis.'

'Is this interview being recorded?'

'No. But I can record it if you so wish.'

Jarvis shook his head. 'No.' He paused. 'You can ask all the questions you like but I'm not answering any of them.'

'That's up to you, Jarvis. But you'd better remember that your wife is being interrogated too. She's here in this prison under the same conditions as you. We shall get the answers we want one way or another.'

'What's happened to my son?'

'Your sister and your mother-in-law were given power of attorney over your son and your property and your son is with them at the moment.'

'When do I get an attorney?'

'The court has already appointed one. I think they are just waiting for his acceptance.'

'Who is he?'

'They'll tell you officially in due course.'

'Why do we have to go through all this bullshit?'

'We don't have to if you plead guilty.'

'You must think I'm crazy.'

Getz smiled. 'As a matter of fact I *do* think you're crazy. After seeing what you've been up to this last year or so you must be. How the hell did you think you could get away with it without being caught?'

'So why did you take so long?'

Getz shrugged. 'Due process of law.'

'Don't give me that crap. If you'd had anything on me you'd have jumped on me a long time ago.'

'We have to be sure when there's murder involved.'

'Murder. What murder?'

'The murder of ten or eleven men who were assisting the CIA. You sold their identities to the KGB so that you could drive around in a Jaguar car and buy a half-million-dollar house for cash.'

'That was my wife's parents' money, not mine.'

'Your parents-in-law haven't got two dollars to rub together and never have had.' He paused. 'And we've got details of most of your accounts both here in the States and overseas.'

Jarvis shook his head. 'You'd need special warrants for that so don't try bluffing me.'

'We'll go over them with you later.' He grinned. 'You should have headed for the *dacha* the KGB wrote to you about.' He shrugged. 'Too late now though. A life sentence for treason really is a life sentence. You should remember that. Your wife's sentence will be at least fifteen to twenty years.'

'You really are a pack of shits, the lot of you.'

Getz stood up. 'On that elegant note we'll call it a day.' Turning to one of his assistants, he said, 'Press the button for the guard, will you?'

There was a message for him in the prison governor's office to phone O'Hara. When he contacted him O'Hara asked him to come over.

*   *   *

192

O'Hara looked tired but more alert than at their last meeting.

'First things first, Larry. Joe Shapiro phoned me and asked me to let you know that he's taking over the prosecution of Jarvis himself. There are several reasons for this that I'll go into later. It will be announced tomorrow at the same time as Ira Shulman accepts the court's request for him to act for Jarvis.' O'Hara smiled. A not very convincing smile before he went on. 'That's the good news. The bad news is a mixture of politics and the media.' He paused and sighed. 'I hate having to tell you this but the warrants I obtained have become a bit of a problem.'

O'Hara stopped just to see what effect his news had had on Getz. But Getz's face showed nothing.

O'Hara hunched up his shoulders with his elbows resting on his desk. Getz noticed the instinctive self-defensive attitude.

'Let me put it as briefly as I can.' He paused. 'The warrants I got you I got by applying to a secret court that has been authorised by the President to issue warrants without the usual Fourth Amendment requirements.'

Getz said, 'When you say secret, how secret?'

'There are seven judges who take turns acting on their own to sign warrants. It really is secret. There are Supreme Court judges who will have never heard of it.'

'If the President has authorised it why does it need to be secret?'

'Put bluntly, Larry, he signed away every citizen's rights of privacy if somebody felt it was necessary for reasons of intelligence or counter-intelligence.'

Getz was silent for long moments and then he said quietly, 'You're right. This is going to be real trouble. If the media or the politicians get hold of this, Clinton's finished. And so is the government.'

'What would you have done if I hadn't got those perfectly legal warrants?' He paused. 'Would you have called off the operation, because I can tell you right now that we didn't stand a cat in hell's chance of getting warrants under the normal rules. What would you have done?'

Getz smiled. 'You remind me of my mother and father whey they argued about something and my father won the argument, my mother used to say that that didn't make him right. It just made him a better arguer.'

'So what's your answer?'

'You know my answer as well as I do. I'd have used the warrants. If they hadn't been available I would have instructed my team to ignore Fourth Amendment restrictions and get on and bug and intercept and generally abuse the constitution; and if I had been caught I would have appealed to Congress to bless what I'd done on their behalf and for the security of the State.'

O'Hara smiled. 'Would make a good film-script but if there's one thing I've learned in this business it's never, repeat never rely on any politician to do the right thing. By the time the media have put you through the mincer you'll learn who your friends are – the boy who delivers your papers at home and the cleaning lady.' He paused as if considering what he was going to say and then he said it. 'And don't expect any support from this place. Langley will only have one thing in mind – coming out looking like they're the injured parties. Inefficient maybe, but good ol' boys to the end.'

'At the moment there's no chance that Jarvis will plead guilty but given time I think I can wear him down if you can keep his attorney off my back.'

'I know Ira Shulman from the old days. He's a very good lawyer. He phoned for a meeting and we're meeting tomorrow. He's a ferret and I suspect he'll be planning to take all our evidence and make it look like coincidence or subject to other, non-treasonable interpretations. Have you talked with Jarvis's wife yet?'

'I had a brief chat with her on day one.'

'What was her attitude?'

'Cursing Jarvis as a complete fool and seemed ready to talk but that won't last. Once the court and lawyers are on the scene it always brings home what could happen to them.'

'OK. Let's meet every day and exchange what we've got.'

Getz nodded. 'Yes, phone me, but remember I'm the other side of town at the prison. I'm going to move back into my own place tonight. You've got all my numbers haven't you?'

'I'm sure I have.'

Getz had been able to phone her the day Jarvis was arrested and she had moved the next day into what was now 'their' place, so that she could get it ready for them to move in together permanently.

They ate at their Italian place and were amused that now that Larry Getz had been seen time and time again on the TV newsflashes of Jarvis being taken in chains and shackles to the court at Alexandria it was he, as the celebrity, who was asked to sign a menu. He had told them, not strictly truthfully, that he wasn't allowed to sign anything for security reasons.

Back at the apartment Getz had changed into an old towelling bathrobe and they sat together watching a rerun of the Cosby Show followed by a late-night rerun of *Casablanca*. When they finally switched off the TV, she said, 'How often will you be able to come home?'

'Every day for at least four or five weeks. When it gets to the last stages of presenting the case there may be some all-night sessions. The same applies if the other side want to drag out the actual trial. That means overnight work.' He paused and looked at her. 'Is that OK with you?'

'Of course it is. This is your home. You belong here.'

'For me it's your home as well. I hope that we can get married as soon as this case is over.' He paused and looked at her as if he were slightly embarrassed. 'There's talk of a promotion for me and that could mean living somewhere overseas or somewhere else in the States.'

She smiled. 'Maybe they'll make you an ambassador.'

'Ambassadors here are political postings. The White House, not Langley.'

'What would you like to do?'

'What made you ask that?'

She shrugged. 'Because I feel you're dissatisfied with your life somehow. Ever since I first knew you. Way back I thought it was just the problems with Bobby but more recently you've seemed very tense – kind of strung up but I assumed that was the case you were working on. But now I'm not so sure. Maybe I'm just being stupid.'

'No way are you stupid. I *am* in a kind of limbo about what I want to do and you're very perceptive to have diagnosed it.'

'What's wrong with what you do now?'

'I couldn't explain it. I don't even know but my instinct says that I'm in the wrong business. I see people like my boss. O'Hara.

A lovely man, a good man. Shrewd, a good citizen, but he's wasted in that job. He's too good for it. I don't want to end up like that.'

'What about going back to the law?'

He smiled. 'It's one of the two things I've seriously thought about.'

'What's the other?'

'You'll think I'm crazy.'

'I doubt it. Tell me.'

'I thought of going back to Vermont. Taking over the family business. I own all the stock. But I'd run it and expand it.'

'What is it that appeals to you about doing that?'

'I know the people in those parts. I know about farmers. When you are concerned with growing things, you do no harm to people. You are just part of the natural order of things.' He laughed and shrugged. 'I'm talking a lot of nonsense. Let's go to bed.'

She kissed him but made no comment. She called to him from the bedroom.

'What time do you have to leave tomorrow?'

'About eight to allow for the traffic.'

Getz interviewed her alone. She sat facing him, dressed in a blue prison gown, her hands still handcuffed.

'Good morning. Would you feel easier if I got them to take off the handcuffs?'

She shrugged. 'I guess so. It's up to you.'

Getz called the guard who unlocked the handcuffs and took them away. For a few moments he waited as she rubbed her wrists.

Then he said, 'This isn't a formal interrogation, Mrs Jarvis, but you can have a female guard present while we're talking if you want.'

She shook her head. 'Just do me one favour, mister. Don't call me Mrs Jarvis, call me Maria. Maria dos Santos.'

'OK. I'll do that.' He paused. 'You obviously feel that your husband has been extremely stupid. Am I right?'

'I told him again and again that he would be caught. I warned him about his drinking and his carelessness. He thought he was above all that. He knew better. Your people were all fools. You'd never get onto him.'

'Did you ever think of turning him in?'

196

'Yeah. Dozens of times.'

'Why didn't you?'

'I didn't want to break up the family and for my son to grow up with no father.'

'Have you got your own lawyer? Did the court appoint one for you?'

'No, his guy is supposed to look after me.'

'I think you'd do well to have your own attorney. You can apply to the court for one.'

'What reason should I give?'

'That the facts in your case are very different from his.' He paused. 'You have to realise that if you're found guilty you'll get a very long sentence. Jarvis will get life but you'd get ten or fifteen years.' He paused. 'You could opt to give evidence against Jarvis.'

'I thought wives couldn't give evidence against their husbands?'

'They can if it's voluntary.'

'No. I wouldn't do that. Not even against that bastard.' She looked at him. 'I thought you were the one who was supposed to prosecute us?'

'I'm only the investigator, but none of what we've talked about is official. It's off the record. Can't be used against you.' Getz stood up and called the woman warder and turned to Maria. 'Think about it.'

As he drove back to Langley, Getz knew that he had been cheating the wretched woman. He was the investigator not the prosecutor and he was entitled to interrogate her. But there was a fine line between interrogation about past misdeeds and present intentions. And he knew he'd gone over that line several times. There were things that he had learned that could be very useful to the prosecution case but he ought not to have learned them. Or did the end justify the means?

'Where shall we meet?'

'I guess it had better be at your office, Joe. That's what protocol says. We defenders have to kow-tow a bit to the prosecutors.'

Shapiro laughed softly. 'Should be quite a sight, Ira, you kow-towing. But sure. When and what time?'

'How about your place this afternoon?'

'Fine. I look forward to seeing you.'

Shapiro had cleaned his desk of papers and his assistant had arranged comfortable chairs around a coffee table. When Ira Shulman arrived he was made warmly welcome. They had known one another for years. They had gone to their first school together in Brighton Beach. They were not exactly friends but they had an amiable relationship and got along well whenever they happened to meet as they grew up and their lives went their different ways.

The hugs were routine but genuine, and then Shapiro pointed to the chairs. 'Make yourself comfortable, my friend.' He grinned as he looked at Shulman. 'You still on vodka?'

'Just a touch, Joe. Just a touch.'

When they raised their glasses and both said *Na zdrowie* it was a Polish *Na zdrowie* not a Russian one.

'You start, Joe. But I'd better say I haven't yet had the time to go through all the statements.' He shrugged. 'Been cleaning up current cases so that I can concentrate on this one.'

'We'll be going for the death penalty. Are you defending his wife?'

'She withdrew this morning. Got herself some guy she knew from our embassy in Bogotá. I've not heard of him except that he specialises in plea-bargaining.' Shulman smiled. 'Should be fun.'

'What's your general feeling about Jarvis?'

Shulman shrugged. 'Let's say, not my kind of guy. A third-rater in every respect. I've only had ten minutes or so with him. Now that the first shock is over he's quite cocky again.' He shrugged. 'But I'll do my best for him. Due process of law and all that.'

'Any idea of when you'll be ready to start?'

'How about four weeks' time for the preliminaries?' He looked across at Shapiro. 'How the hell did you weasel your way into those Swiss bank accounts?'

Shapiro smiled. 'Collected a few old debts.'

'You'll still have a problem proving that they're his.'

'His name's on them.'

'Maybe somebody else put the money in, in his name, and he knows nothing about it. Could be your guys in CIA playing games again.'

'There's nearly a quarter of a million bucks in those accounts, Ira.

We don't have that kind of dough for playing games.' He smiled. 'Of course, if you could prove it's ours to satisfy the court and the Swiss bankers, we could draw out the money immediately.'

'You bastard. You would too.' He sighed. 'Well, always a treat to see you again but I'd better get back. You look pretty fit. Family OK?'

'They're fine thank you, Ira.'

He said nothing about Ira's family which was a human disaster area.

There had been no answer to his phone call to her from Toronto and as he waited at the carousel for his bags he wondered what her reaction would be. She'd obviously been surprised when he phoned from Charles de Gaulle and told her that he was already in Paris. She made him write down her address and told him to come over; and she asked him how long he was staying. He'd said evasively that he wasn't sure.

When he arrived at her place it had taken three journeys to get his kit up the stairs to her landing. She'd hugged him, laughing, saying it looked as if he was moving in for good.

As they sat in the small kitchen sipping hot chocolate she said, 'Tell me what's going on. You look kind of funny.'

'I've got a problem and I haven't sorted out what to do.'

'What's the problem? Tell me.'

'Have you seen anything in the media here about an American CIA agent who was selling secrets to the KGB?'

She thought for a moment and then said, 'Yeah. There was a piece about a week ago. I think it was in *Le Matin* or *Le Figaro*. I didn't read it properly.'

'I've been controlling that guy for nearly four years and when he was arrested I decided that I'd better get out in case the CIA made some move against me.'

'But you're a diplomat. They couldn't touch you.'

'Honey. It doesn't work like that in these games. There aren't any rules and diplomatic immunity doesn't always count. I didn't want to risk it.'

'What did your people in Moscow say?'

He sighed. 'I haven't told them that I've left.'

'Are you going to tell them?'

'I don't know. I need some time to think about what the hell I should do.' He looked at her rather plaintively as he said, 'I've got a British passport so there's no problem about being here.'

She looked at him as he sat there and suddenly he wasn't the dashing KBG officer any longer. He was just a small boy who'd run away from home. She reached over and touched his cheek. 'Don't worry. We'll work something out. Anyway, it's lovely for me to have you here.'

'Are you sure? I could find a room.'

'No way. It's going to be great.'

Chapter 25

Joe Shapiro had watched a repeat of *The Godfather* with his wife and spoken to his daughter in Carmel about his grandson who had cerebral palsy but who was the brightest boy in his class. His wife noticed that he was restless but that was nothing unusual. He had been like that in the days when he was a DA. And he'd been even worse when he had been offered a judgeship in Sacramento. Typical of the man, he had turned it down because he thought he wasn't good enough. She had never tried to influence him in any of the decisions he made about his career and their life. Not even to comfort or encourage him. She totally trusted his judgment and she had always been right.

Shapiro woke in the night and looked at the illuminated digital alarm clock on the bedside table. It was 3.17 a.m. and although he was tired he wasn't sleepy and he slid out of bed quietly, reached for his well-worn bathrobe and headed downstairs for the kitchen. When he'd made himself a coffee he sat down at the table and then got up again and went to his small study for his clipboard. Shapiro was a great believer in the pragmatic approach. If you've got a problem describe it in not more than four lines and then list the pros and cons.

As he took the top off his favourite writing instrument, a PILOT Hi-techpoint V7 finepoint roller-ball, he squiggled a bit on the paper and, as always, it ran freely. He squared the clipboard in front of him, then closed his eyes and thought.

Ten minutes later the paper was blank. Not because he didn't know what the problem was or how to describe it. But because he couldn't bring himself to write it down and expose it to light and judgment. Finally he brought himself to write one word in capital letters – WARRANTS.

When Larry Getz and his staff had been working on the Jarvis

201

business, the pursuit itself was justification for almost anything. All's fair in love and war was the motto. But now another hackneyed old proverb was taking pride of place. The one about chickens coming home to roost.

It wouldn't be true to say that he hadn't given a moment's thought to how he was getting the warrants that Getz wanted so badly. But it had been only a moment's thought. And suddenly, in the midst of what seemed to be success, there was a much worse scenario than failure would have been.

It was obvious that if Jarvis didn't plead guilty he would have to rely on the warrants to prove Jarvis's guilt. And if he did that, it was certain that Ira Shulman would eventually spot that they were not normal warrants. So it meant finding some solution before Shulman got that far. The picture of a secret court with seven judges each working and deciding solo would be bad enough, but the fact that Clinton had signed an order allowing them to completely ignore all the requirements of the Fourth Amendment would cause the biggest scandal that Congress had ever had to face in its history. A secret court that even the judges of the Supreme Court had never heard of, let alone sanctioned.

There was an obvious, straightforward scenario. OK. He had used warrants issued by a secret court. But they were legal warrants issued by a legal court. Clinton's Executive Order 12949 made it so. If Clinton was prepared to sign away the citizen's rights, who was he to query it. Clinton must carry the can.

So you then come to *why* Clinton signed that order. And Joe Shapiro knew what would have happened. Both the FBI and the CIA had been raising hell for months about the impossibility of seeking out and preventing sabotage, insurrection and murder, because the Fourth Amendment had been passed to protect the rights of every citizen. After the bombing at Oklahoma the pressures on the President must have been irresistible. If you want to stop more Oklahomas you give us the freedom to go after the perpetrators, most of them well-known but protected by the law. If you don't sign, the responsibility for future deaths and destruction will be all yours.

There would have been protests in the Oval office and threats to take the whole issue to Congress. And Congress would have eaten the lot of them. Abandon every man's basic rights? Never.

It would make the hullabaloo over the gun laws look like a spat over a backyard fence.

However he wrestled with it, Shapiro knew there was a question to answer that would make clear what he should do. It was a simple question. If he had been Clinton, would he have signed that Presidential Order giving free rein to the FBI and the CIA? He knew without doubt what the answer was – it was yes. He would have signed that order.

So what did that mean? It meant that every effort had to be made to prevent the provenance of the warrants being brought up in court or otherwise made known to Congress and the public. And that meant that he and O'Hara and Getz had to be prepared to go to any lengths to make Jarvis plead guilty. He walked slowly to his study, sat in his leather armchair and switched on the TV. It was Ginger Rogers and Fred Astaire in black and white. That's where he was, sound asleep and snoring when his wife found him when she came down to make breakfast.

That afternoon he had a meeting with O'Hara and Getz and told them of the dilemma and that they now had to concentrate on pressuring Jarvis into pleading guilty. Although Shapiro didn't mention it, he had at the back of his mind the possibility of doing some deal with Ira Shulman.

It was nearly a week later when Shulman asked Shapiro for a meeting. They met as before at Shapiro's office. He noticed Shulman's bulging brief-case but people sometimes did that to indicate how much material the defence had.

'Could this little chat be off the record, Joe?'

'What's the subject matter?'

'Unproven circumstantial evidence.'

Shapiro shrugged. 'OK. Sounds interesting.'

Shulman pulled out a file from his bag and placed it carefully on Shapiro's desk.

With his hand on the cover of his file, Shulman said, 'Swiss bank accounts in Jarvis's name.'

'If you say so. What's the problem?'

'How are you going to tie them to Jarvis?'

'They're in his name for God's sake. What else do you want – fingerprints?'

'Joe. An account in a guy's name isn't proof of anything. Maybe somebody else opened those accounts and used the name Jarvis as a privacy device.'

'Why should he pick on that name?'

'Maybe that *was* the guy's name. Another Jarvis. I gotta tell you there's over a hundred Jarvises in the Washington DC and Maryland phone books. It's not an uncommon name.' He shook his head slowly. 'I'll have to make you link him up positively, Joe.' He paused and then went on. 'Can I ask you how you tracked down those accounts? Swiss banks don't reveal details of accounts without a hell of a lot of pressure. What did you trade for this stuff?' He waved his hand over the file.

'I'm not prepared to reveal that. At least not at this stage.'

'Why not?'

'For reasons of national security.'

'Joe, Joe. We're old friends. You don't have to give me that sort of bullshit.'

'Anything else?'

'Yeah. That goddamned car. The Jaguar. Why do your people make such a song and dance about it? Right this minute there's six Jaguar cars down in your parking lot. Why is it so important?'

'It isn't, unless you bear in mind that the bastard only earned sixty thousands dollars all year and he paid over forty thousand in cash.' He paused. 'Have you ever paid cash – dollar notes – for a car? Of course you haven't. How could *he* do it?'

'It was a lifelong ambition. Maybe he saved that dough for years. Anyway that was only the price of that one Jaguar out of three. There must have been trade-in allowances on the others.'

'You got any proof of that?'

Shulman smiled and then, looking serious, he said, 'I've insisted that Mrs Jarvis has her own attorney. It's better that way. Their interests don't necessarily go together.'

'Have you spoken to her yourself?'

'Very briefly. She could cause us some problems.'

Shapiro chuckled. 'Cause *you* some problems. Not me. Anyway I got your message.'

Shulman looked surprised. 'What message was that?'

'That you're going to be a pain in the ass every inch of the way about evidence.'

Shulman stood up, putting the file back in his case, turning to look at Shapiro, smiling as he said, 'Maybe we can compromise here and there.'

'If we don't, my friend, we shall still be in court next Christmas.'

'So be it, old friend.'

They shook hands and Shulman left. When he was alone Shapiro was relieved that there had been no query about the warrants.

'Now you're getting your own lawyer, our talks will have to be more formal. With your attorney present. Is there anything you want to say right now?'

'What kind of sentence will Art get if he's found guilty?'

'He'll be in for life with no parole.'

'And me? What would happen to me?'

'I said before. It would be quite a long sentence. At least ten years.'

'What if I pleaded guilty myself?'

'You shouldn't do that, Maria. Wait and see what your attorney recommends.'

There were tears in her eyes as she said, 'I miss my son so much. I can't believe I'll never see him again.'

'I'm sure there will be visits when the case is over.'

'I can't bear to think of him on his own.'

'I'm sure your parents will care for him.'

'It's not the same. I'm his mother.' She reached for the box of Kleenex and said, 'Is there anything I could do not to be in prison?'

Getz hesitated for a moment and then said quietly, 'How much influence do you have over your husband?'

She shrugged. 'It was a lot but I don't know about now.'

'What were his feelings about your son?'

'Oh, he loved him. He was a good father in his own way.'

'What are his feelings about you now?'

She smiled and shrugged. 'He swears he loves me and bitterly regrets involving me in this mess.'

'Would he be prepared to take all the blame and claim he forced you to help him?'

She smiled wryly. 'Not if it made it worse for himself. He swears he won't answer any questions in court or out of it.'

'How about if you asked him to?'

'It wouldn't make him change his mind. He sees himself as the tough guy. Won't talk to the cops. Point of honour and all that.' She shrugged. 'I think he always sees himself as a kind of James Bond. The master-spy. Ought to have been an actor.'

'I'll see if I can arrange for you to have a brief meeting with your son. Away from this place.'

Her voice quavered as she said, 'I'd be very grateful.'

The counsel chosen by Maria Jarvis was a bilingual American from the Bogotá embassy. She had known him socially before she had met Jarvis. He had been mainly concerned with litigation on commercial deals and had never dealt with either domestic or criminal cases in court. But he had a good reputation in Bogotá and in the State Department. And he was the one she wanted.

Shapiro had phoned him as soon as he set up an office in Washington and had been friendly and helpful. After giving the new man a week to study the papers in the case, Shapiro had suggested that they should have a preliminary meeting. Shapiro himself, O'Hara, Getz and the new boy, Nielson.

The setting was informal, coffee, beer and sandwiches and jackets on backs of chairs to point up the arrival of May sunshine through the big windows.

It was Joe Shapiro who got them down to business.

'Have you had a chance to talk with Mrs Jarvis?'

'Yes, we've had several meetings.'

'And you've had a quick look at the evidence and summaries?'

Nielson nodded. 'Enough to talk but not enough to decide on our approach.'

Shapiro smiled. 'Fair enough. Have you got any thoughts on procedure?'

'I think my client would be best served if her case was treated entirely separately from that of her husband.'

Shapiro nodded. 'I think you're right. But what makes you feel that way?'

'I think she should be kept clear of the treason charges. She was

206

just an unwilling spouse who was bound to do what her husband told her to do.'

'Could that be the basis of a plea bargain?'

Nielson shook his head. 'No way. There'll be no deals on my side.' He paused. 'I doubt if she'd go along with a deal anyway. She's a very bitter woman.' He paused again. 'Apart from that I don't see any benefit for her.'

Getz said quietly, 'You'll have difficulty establishing that she wasn't an integral part of Jarvis's operation. There was no indication that she was forced to co-operate. And how could he have forced her? What was the threat?'

'I think I can make a jury understand the pressures on a wife that a husband can bring.'

'Is there anything else you want to raise, Mr Nielson?'

'Yeah. She's fretting about her son. What chance is there of access before the trial?'

Shapiro said, 'That would be for the court to decide.'

'Would there be any objection from your side?'

'Let's see what the court has to say first.'

'They won't accede without your approval.'

'Let's just see what happens. Yes?'

Nielson shrugged. 'OK. If that's how you want to play it. I was looking for co-operation.'

Shapiro nodded. 'Me too. Co-operation's a two-way thing.'

And that was how the meeting had ended. When Nielson had left, O'Hara said, 'Why not work out some deal with access as part of it?'

'And what do we get?'

'She persuades Jarvis to plead guilty and the question of warrants never comes up.'

'And what do we offer?'

'If she persuades him to plead guilty she gets four years instead of a likely ten. So she'd be out with good behaviour in three years. Meantime she has regular weekend access in suitable circumstances outside the prison every other weekend.'

Shapiro and O'Hara both looked at Getz. 'D'you think she'd play?'

'What if she refuses?'

'Then there's no deal.' It was O'Hara who said it.

Getz said nothing and then O'Hara said, 'What's the problem?'

Getz shrugged. 'I just don't like it.'

'Why not?'

'She was a fool and she benefited from KGB cash but she didn't initiate or play any part except blame him for doing it and doing it badly.'

'So?'

'So we tear her apart because she loves her son so much. If she doesn't play she knows it will be a long sentence. Few visits and the child will be a twenty-year-old when she comes out.'

'So she goes along with what we want and she's got it made. No problem. Jarvis sold a dozen men down the river so that the pair of them could live like millionaires. The wives of the Russians who were helping us didn't have such a choice, God damn it.'

Shapiro intervened. 'Think about it, Larry. There's no hurry. Maybe there's another way.' He paused. 'I can understand your reluctance but it would solve all our problems.'

'And if she refuses I've got to live with what I've done for the rest of my life. I don't like it. But I guess I'll do it if it's the only way.'

Shapiro said. 'Fair enough, but remember we are offering her far more than she and Jarvis deserve.'

'I know. But I'm not a Jarvis.'

Shapiro stood up. 'Just think about it and any alternatives you can come up with. Like I said. We don't have to rush into it.But it would solve our problems with the warrants, and Jarvis would get what he deserves.' He paused. 'Let's go out and have a meal together.'

Getz said, 'I'm taking Gabby out to dinner tonight. But thanks for the invitation.'

Chapter 26

They were having breakfast at a nearby restaurant and Volkov said, 'Where's Avenue Gabriel?'

'It's alongside the Champs Elysées gardens. Very posh. Big houses. Why do you want to know?'

'That's where the American embassy is. I thought of paying them a visit.'

'What on earth for?'

'If I get a job will you marry me?'

She frowned but smiled at the same time. 'Tell me more.'

'There isn't anything more to tell.'

'Come on, Yuri. What's it all about?'

'What kind of job do you think I could get here in Paris?'

'I don't know. It won't be easy because of the language.'

'But if I got the job where the language isn't a problem would you go there with me? To another country.'

'You mean Russia?'

'No way. I mean America.'

'But you've just left there because you'd have problems because of being KGB and that guy they've arrested for treason.'

'If I went back I wouldn't be KGB.'

'This is getting crazy. Tell me what it's all about.'

'I'm thinking of doing a deal with the Americans. The CIA. I know how to do it but not if it means losing you.'

She looked at him and said quietly, 'You are an idiot. You really are. Tell me something.'

'What?'

'You must have had a lot of girl-friends, did you love any of them?'

'No. I liked them, but my job made getting emotionally involved impossible.'

'Did any of them love you?'

He laughed. 'I'm sure they didn't. I was just a guy to have a good time with.Why do you ask about that?'

'Do you think I love you?'

'Yes. But it worries me that I don't deserve it and that you'd stop if you knew more about me.'

'Do you love me?'

'Yes. Absolutely.'

'How do you know?'

'Because I'd rather be a road-sweeper in Paris with you than be anywhere else with a lot of money but without you.'

She laughed softly. 'Always practical, my Yuri.' She paused. 'Yes I'll marry you and yes I'll go and live with you wherever it has to be. But I earn enough to keep both of us from road-sweeping if your CIA friends won't play. You don't have to go along with anything you don't like.'

'What about your work if we were in the States?'

'I'd have to come over fairly frequently but I can use faxes for scripts and revisions.' She laughed. 'They'll probably get them quicker than they do when I'm here. I've got a lot of contacts in LA as well.'

The taxi had dropped him off at the Rond Point but it was a longer walk than he'd expected to the US Embassy. He tried to get used to his thoughts of what it would feel like to be treated as a 'dangler'.

There was a US Marine standing just inside the main doors and he had pointed Volkov to the reception desk. A middle-aged woman smiled and said, 'Can I help you?'

'I'd like to speak to a senior CIA officer.'

She showed no sign of surprise as she said, 'May I ask what it's about so that I can be sure you're talking to the appropriate person?'

'Tell whoever you speak to that it's about Art Jarvis.'

'How are you spelling that?'

He watched her write it on a slip of paper as he spelt it out.

She looked up at him. 'Excuse me for a moment but do please have a seat, it may take a few moments.' She paused. 'What name shall I say?'

He shook his head. 'If you give them my message that'll be good enough.'

It was ten minutes before two men appeared. One, a big older man without a jacket and a younger man in a light-weight suit. They walked towards the main doors where they shook hands and the older man turned and walked slowly towards Volkov and sat himself down in the chair alongside the Russian.

'How can I help you?'

'Are you CIA?'

'I'm just a senior member of the embassy staff but if you want to talk about the Jarvis business I'm the one to talk to.'

Volkov smiled. 'I'm your "dangler" for today. I'm offering to help you.'

'Have you any identification? A passport maybe?'

'My passport's British. The genuine thing except for my name and the fact that I'm a Soviet citizen.'

'My name's Frazer and I must congratulate you on your English. You've even got an American accent.'

'Do you think we might go somewhere more private?'

'By all means.' Frazer stood up and led Volkov through big double-doors. There was another US Marine inside the corridor. Frazer said casually, 'I'll just have our young man check that you're not armed.' He smiled. 'Just a formality.'

The Marine did a quick but efficient body check and then nodded to Frazer. As the two of them walked down the corridor Frazer said, 'When were you last in the States?'

'I left just over a week ago.'

They came to a door near the end of the corridor, Frazer pushed in his smart-card and opened the door, standing aside so that Volkov could go inside.

It was a large important-looking office, a miniature Oval Office with windows onto a garden that were laced with metal wires. Frazer waved his guest to a chair at his desk and pulled up a chair to face Volkov.

'Now, sir,' he said. 'Let's get down to business. I understand you want to talk about the case of Mr Jarvis.'

'OK. My name's Yuri Volkov and I was Jarvis's controller in Washington for nearly five years.'

'When did you stop being his controller?'

'I guess on the day your people arrested him. Two days later I flew over here to Paris.'

There was a knock on the door ten minutes later and a young woman came in and handed Frazer a card. He looked at the card intently and then handed it back to the girl with a smile and a nod. When she had left Volkov smiled and said, 'After the mike picked up my name they can only have had six minutes at the most to check on me. That's pretty good going even with computers.'

Frazer smiled. 'Why did Moscow order you to Paris? Why not back to Moscow?'

'I didn't contact Moscow.'

'Why not?'

'Because I was pretty sure that I should carry the can for Jarvis's arrest.' He smiled and shrugged. 'Things in Moscow are a bit mixed up these days.'

'Who was your controller in Moscow?'

'A guy named Fomenko. Viktor Fomenko.'

'*The* Fomenko?'

Volkov nodded. 'Yeah. I guess you've heard of him.'

'When did you last speak to him or communicate with him?'

'We don't have speech communication. I spoke to him last several months ago when I paid a short visit to Moscow.' He paused. 'We used super-fast coded tapes on short-wave. RTTL. I haven't had a message from him for about two weeks.'

Frazer looked at Volkov for several moments and then said, 'Did you like him?'

'No. But we got on well together. But he was under a cloud because of the failed KGB coup against the Kremlin. I think he only survived afterwards because of his close work with me on the Jarvis affair.'

Fraser nodded and then said, 'I'm afraid Viktor Fomenko is no more. Our people in Moscow informed me that he was executed the day after Jarvis was arrested. Our Moscow people said that we could safely assume that he must have had something to do with the Jarvis operation and was paying the price for failure.'

Volkov sighed. 'Jarvis was the only one responsible for his arrest. He was an arrogant man who came to believe that he had some magic touch. The security rules didn't apply to him.'

'Tell me what you had in mind for helping us?'

'I was hoping I could do a deal with Langley.'

'What kind of deal did you have in mind?'

'I would give the CIA a complete picture of the Jarvis operation and they would employ me in some capacity with a new legitimate identity so that I could live in the USA.'

'I know you'll understand that I'll have to consult my colleagues in Washington and they'll need a day or so to sort out their thoughts. How can I get in touch with you?'

Volkov thought about it for several moments and then said, 'How about I phone you in a couple of hours and you can tell me how long it will be before they make up their minds and then I can maybe give you a phone number?'

'OK. Let's do that.' He searched for a pen and a pad. 'You ring me on this number. Wherever I am it will come through.' He handed Volkov the slip of paper. 'Let me show you out through our garden entrance.'

It was a small garden with high stone walls and alongside the massive wrought-iron gates was a guard-house and two US Marine sergeants, both carrying side-arms with the holster flaps open.

Frazer watched his guest depart and then hurried back to his office.

He put in the call to Langley using the double-scrambler but still talking in the usual jargon that intelligence people use when there's nothing safer. It was O'Hara who took the call.

'O'Hara.'

'Are you using the scrambler?'

'Yeah.'

'I've had a dangler in. He's just left. I think you'd better see him.'

'I can't get away just now. I'm on the J thing.'

'So is this. This guy was J's controller in Washington DC.'

'What's his name?'

'You want me to say it in clear?'

'Yes if you have to.'

'Volkov. Yuri Volkov.'

'My God. I can't believe it. What the hell's he doing in Paris?'

'When you picked up J my friend here thought that his friends in the frozen north might give him the chop, for making a cock-up of it.'

'What's he offering?'

'Anything we want.'

'Would he go in court as a witness in the case?'

'I don't know. I imagine from what he was saying that he would do anything we want.'

'What's he want in return?'

'New legitimate identity and a job or some sort of provision for the rest of his life.'

'He'd be worth every cent, Tom. He really would. Will he come over here? All expenses paid.'

'He's calling me back in just over an hour, shall I ask him?'

'You bet, sunshine. Next plane to DC and I'll meet him in myself. My God, you don't know what good news this is. Call me back when you've made the arrangements. If we've got an air-force plane at one of the Paris fields use it. Tell 'em to contact me for authority. Well done, Tom.'

Frazer laughed. 'Cut it out, Mike, cut it out.'

Volkov had begun to have doubts about what he was doing. Not for himself but for the girl. He was uprooting her from her life in Paris, her job, her friends and her parents. All in the hope that everything would turn out all right in the end. Twice he had stopped himself from completing Frazer's number but finally he pressed the last button.

'Frazer. How can I help you?'

'It's Volkov. What did they say?'

'No problem. They want you to fly over immediately. Tonight if possible.'

'Can I come in to see you for a few minutes right now?'

'Sure. I'll wait for you.'

It was nearly 4 p.m. when Volkov was shown into Frazer's office for the second time that day. The big American had put him at ease and told him that the embassy had made a provisional booking on the night-flight to Washington from Charles de Gaulle.

'Now tell me how I can help you.' He paused. 'Just one thing. Am I right in thinking that you're willing to appear to give evidence in

214

court at Jarvis's trial so long as we look after you as you mentioned? Identity, security and finance?'

'Yes. That's no problem.'

'OK, so go ahead.'

Volkov related his concerns about his fiancée. Frazer had asked several questions about her family and background and then said, 'Would you be happier staying here in Paris instead of living in the States?'

'Yes, but there's the language problem in getting a job.'

'Listen, my friend. If you co-operate with us on this Jarvis case, we'll give you proper American citizenship and a substantial pension. In addition, you'd work here in the embassy for me as a consultant. And it'll be a real job, not a sinecure. How about that?'

'You're sure Langley will agree?'

'Quite sure. Take it as an official offer.'

'That's great.'

'No time to celebrate, my friend.' He paused. 'The guy who'll meet you at the other end is an old friend of mine. His name's Mike O'Hara and you'll like him. He's in charge of the Jarvis thing. So . . .' he smiled, '. . . have a quick glass of champagne with that girl of yours, then get on your way to the airport.'

Sabine went with him to the airport and after he had checked-in they went to the bistro for coffee. Desperate to be the bearer of some good news for a change he had told her of his possible deal with the Americans so that they could stay in Paris and she had been delighted.

Neither of them noticed the young man from the US embassy who was acting as an anonymous 'minder' for Volkov on Frazer's careful instructions. He was to observe and report regularly but take no action no matter what happened. Once Volkov was on the plane the observer's job was over.

It was mid-afternoon in Washington DC and O'Hara phoned Larry Getz on his portable. Getz was on his way back from a session with Jarvis that had put him on edge and when O'Hara heard the tiredness and tension in Getz's voice he said, 'How about we meet at your place, Larry? Save you the journey.'

Getz shrugged, even though there was nobody there to witness it. 'Thanks. That'll suit me fine. That bastard really pisses me off. Gabby won't be there but I'll put the kettle on for us. See you,' and he hung up.

When he opened the door half an hour later to O'Hara, he was aware that O'Hara looked as tired as he felt himself.

'Come on in. I found some fruit-cake in a tin. Looks good – with cherries.'

When they were sitting, facing one another, O'Hara said, 'Are you doing anything special tonight?'

'Yeah. Getting to bed early.'

'I want you to come with me to Dulles to meet somebody in.'

'Oh my God. Do I have to?'

'Yeah. He's your good fairy.'

'What's that mean?'

'You ever heard of a guy named Volkov? Yuri Volkov?'

'Yeah. Of course I have. He's on our suspect list. We've always suspected that he was Jarvis's handler. Why? Where's he popped up from? We lost track of him about three or four weeks ago. And he spotted one of my surveillance teams. He was a very careful operator. Stuck to the rules that Jarvis ignored.' He paused. 'You said we were meeting him in. Why and where?'

'Like I said, he's your good fairy. He's going to solve both our major problems.'

'Which particular problems?'

'The warrants and your conscience.'

Getz laughed. 'My conscience – what's he got to do with that?'

'He'll be giving evidence for the prosecution so there's no need for you to go on fretting about putting the pressure on the Jarvis woman.'

It took some time for Getz to absorb O'Hara's news but eventually he said, 'Thank God for that.' Then, as his job took over again, he said, 'How are we going to look after him? My people will still be looking out for him and so will his old mates from the KGB. As soon as they know he's going to give evidence against Jarvis he'll be on their hit list.' He paused. 'What made him come over to us?'

'When Jarvis went in the bag, Volkov was sure that he would be carrying the can so far as Moscow was concerned. So he did a bolt. He's got a girl-friend in Paris and that was where he holed up.'

'Where are you going to put him up tonight?'

'He can stay at my place tonight and after that we'll take a house somewhere in your area. There'll have to be meetings with Shapiro and other lawyers, so he's got to be local. When it becomes public then we'll stash him away somewhere in the countryside. Maybe we could bring his girl-friend over.'

'There's an apartment up for rent three doors away from my place in Georgetown. Bigger than mine.'

'Take it, Larry. As soon as we've picked up our friend.'

'How long shall I take it for?'

'A year should be ample.'

They sat in the airport coffee bar listening to the arrivals announcements. Volkov's Air France plane had a half-hour delay.

O'Hara said, 'As soon as you've fixed that apartment, come over to Langley. We'll have to discuss things with Joe Shapiro and at some stage, as a bit of fancy footwork, with Shulman.'

'Will Shulman do a deal?'

'Doesn't matter either way. If he refuses, then Volkov's evidence is enough. Our surveillance and all that doesn't need to be mentioned. Volkov is enough on his own. If Shulman agrees to a deal, then we'll do a deal on the wife. No pressures. No bad feelings.'

Getz smiled. 'You sound very generous all of a sudden.'

O'Hara nodded. 'I am, my boy, I am. I just want to see the back of this case.'

'They're calling the flight. We'd better go.'

They had kept Volkov in his seat on the plane until all the other passengers had gone. Then they bypassed immigration and customs and walked him to O'Hara's car which was alongside the aircrew reporting office. Volkov only had one piece of hand-luggage and when it had been put in the boot of the car, O'Hara held out his hand. 'Welcome back to Washington. My name's O'Hara. Mike O'Hara and my colleague here is Larry Getz.'

Hands were shaken all round and Volkov still holding Getz's hand, smiled and said, 'Tell me just one thing. Why did it take you so long to get Jarvis?'

Getz smiled back. 'It's not like Moscow, Yuri. It's called due process and we have to obey our own laws and constitution.' He paused. 'Most of them anyway.' He paused again. 'Why did you decide you'd had enough? They ought to have rewarded you for all that stuff you got for them.' He smiled. 'They could at least have given you that *dacha* they'd got for Jarvis.'

'You know my friends in Moscow better than that, Larry. Your guy in Paris told me they've already executed my boss in Moscow.'

O'Hara took his arm. 'My car's over there and you'll be staying at my place tonight. We'll eat on the way and tomorrow Larry's getting you a place of your own.' He paused. 'We'll look after your security but I can't imagine that there'll be a problem until your rôle is made public. At that stage we'll move you out of DC to the countryside.'

It took nearly an hour to get to O'Hara's place, introduce him to Maggie O'Hara, and let Getz phone Gabbie to say that he would be at O'Hara's place that night.

It was just on midnight when they got down to business and it was Volkov who got them started.

He looked at O'Hara. 'Did your colleague in Paris tell you what he had offered me?'

'Yeah. When the case is over and you've done your stuff you are given American citizenship and all the documentation. We suggest in another name for security. You'll be hired as a consultant by our Paris office on a grade that pays about a hundred and fifty thousand dollars a year. And the usual benefits. You'll be doing a genuine job and your contributions will be important. Until the trial is over we shall look after your expenses and you'll have an allowance at the rate of twenty thousand dollars cash per month.' He looked at Volkov. 'That OK?'

Volkov nodded. 'And Langley have agreed to it?'

O'Hara smiled. 'I *am* Langley in this little episode. Don't worry. There are no problems.' He stood up. 'Let me show you your room. We shall have a busy day tomorrow, so get a good night's rest.'

When Volkov had been settled in, O'Hara came back and sat down with Larry Getz.

'How long do you need to fix that apartment?'

'About an hour. I can do it on the phone.'

'Shapiro will want to have a long talk with Volkov to deal with the legal niceties and then you'd better take over and debrief Volkov about his handling of Jarvis. It's going to be quite a shock for Shulman, and an even bigger shock for Jarvis. How long will you need?'

'About a week provided there are no interruptions.'

'D'you see any problems?'

'No. The only problem I've got is that I can't believe we've been so lucky.'

'Fifty highly-skilled people working like maniacs for over a year ain't luck, my friend. Volkov just means we don't have to worry about those darned warrants. The case itself was cast-iron otherwise. Don't forget it.'

'I rather like Volkov.'

'He's OK.'

'You sound like you've got doubts.'

'Not at all.'

'So why so non-committal?'

'Just the facts of life, my boy. Jarvis sold out for a Jaguar and all the rest of that crap. Volkov is selling out for a safe income for the rest of his life.'

'With the knowledge that if he had gone back to Moscow they'd have shot him within hours in the basement at Dzherdzinski Square.'

'OK. OK. Let's get to bed.'

Orlov sat looking at the two pieces of paper that had come out of the envelope from Moscow.

One piece came from the torn-off page of an official note-pad. It was hand-written. It just said, Sabine Fleury, and an address in Saint Germain. The note that came with it said that it related to Yuri Volkov and the person and the address should be checked out thoroughly. Orlov had no idea who Yuri Volkov was or why Moscow were interested in him and some French girl. But that was typical of Moscow. He put the note from Moscow and the other piece of paper into a folder and then into the pending tray.

Shapiro was playing it all with formality. Faintly irritated by the obvious elation of O'Hara and Getz. He sympathised with their feelings but they were now dealing with the law of the land and a capital charge of treason. At that moment he was more impressed by Volkov's diffidence than his colleagues' enthusiasm.

'Tell me, Mr Volkov. Was anyone else in Washington DC involved in the Jarvis business?'

'No, sir. It was top secret and I was the only person who knew what was happening. Not even the ambassador knew.'

'Did you, personally, hand over amounts of cash to Jarvis?'

'Yes, sir.'

'You actually saw the money?'

'Yes.'

'Did you count it?'

'It was mainly in banded amounts and I just checked the total.'

'How did you hand it over?'

'If it was a few thousand it would be in an envelope. If it was a large amount it would be in a brief-case or a packet.'

'And Moscow informed you of how much money you were handing over?'

'Yes.'

'Now the material that he gave you in exchange. What form did that take?'

'Mainly original documents or photocopies. He stuck them in bags of one kind and other. The first time there were three plastic Safeways bags stuffed to bursting-point with material.'

'Did you ever examine the material?'

'It depends what you mean by examine. It was always far too much to go over piece by piece. It wasn't part of my duty to evaluate the material but I generally looked at it out of curiosity. It was always high-security material.'

'On what subject?'

'CIA reports and papers on action in various countries against the KGB.'

'The denunciation of Soviet citizens who were assisting the CIA – did you see that material?'

'Yes and copies were microfilmed back to me for comments and information.'

'Were you aware that the KGB in Moscow would deal severely with such people?'

'Yes, sir.'

'What did you expect would happen to them?'

'I expected that they would be executed.'

'Tried and executed?'

'No, there would be no need for a trial. The information about Jarvis's arrest would have been more than enough.'

'Did you ever discuss their certain execution with Jarvis?'

'Yes, sir.'

'What was his reaction?'

'He was not concerned. He said it was part of the game. They knew what to expect.'

'Did you ever meet his wife?'

'No.'

'Did he talk about her?'

'Only very vaguely.'

'One last question, Mr Volkov.' Shapiro paused and spoke very slowly as if he were choosing his words very carefully. 'Why are you prepared to give evidence against Mr Jarvis who you worked with for several years?'

'I knew that I would be recalled to Moscow and almost certainly blamed for Jarvis's arrest and they would execute me. I asked for protection from the US government in return for giving evidence.'

'Do you really think that these days even Moscow would go so far as to execute you?'

'I understand from your colleague in Paris that my opposite number in Moscow, Viktor Fomenko, was executed the day after Jarvis was arrested.'

Shapiro leaned back in his chair and looked from O'Hara to Getz as he said, 'Mr Volkov will make an excellent witness. I'm quite satisfied.' He turned to look at Volkov and shrugged. 'You and I and Larry Getz will have to spend a lot of time together but you've been a good witness. Thank you.'

It was just over a week later that Shapiro called Ira Shulman.

'That you, Ira?'

'Yeah.'

'Could we meet?'

'When and where?'

'How about I get some sandwiches and we'll eat here. Some nice Napa Valley red wine, yes?'

Shulman laughed. 'You should be selling cars, Joe.'

*   *   *

221

'This . . .' Shapiro said, holding up the bottle, '. . . is Paul Masson Pinot Noir. You'll love it.'

'Why do I get the feeling you've got some bad news for me.'

Shapiro poured out the wine carefully and passed Shulman his glass. Holding it up to the light Shapiro said, 'Rabbi Huna said "wine helps to open the heart to reasoning".'

'Now I know I'm in trouble,' Shulman said as he sipped at his wine.

'Have you talked to Jarvis about what he was up to with the Russians?'

'No comment, Joe. That question's not only argumentative but it's totally out of order.'

'Let me put it another way, my friend. Has he ever mentioned a Russian named Volkov?'

'Joe. You're on a fishing expedition and I ain't playing.'

Shapiro sighed, a touch theatrically. 'Ira, I've got some news for you. It's gonna save us both a lot of problems.' He looked across at Shulman. 'Yuri Volkov was the KGB man at the Soviet Embassy, here in DC, who handled Jarvis from the first day he walked into the embassy offering to sell the CIA for cash, until the day we arrested your client. He is going to give, in sworn evidence, every detail of all the things that went on. Dead-drops, secret signs, meeting instructions, the top-secret material that Jarvis handed over for cash. Top-secret material that gave the Soviets a better view of what the CIA are up to than the Director himself had.' He paused. 'He'll be the State's only witness apart from some routine things. We had enough without Comrade Volkov. But with him it's all over bar the shouting.'

Shulman was looking at his wine, swirling it slowly in the glass. Then he looked up at Shapiro. 'How much you pay him, Joe?'

'The whole transaction will be stated in court where it doesn't affect the safety of Yuri Volkov.'

'Affect the safety . . .' Shulman said disparagingly. '. . . what safety? You've been reading too many spy stories.'

'You might care to pass on the news to your client that the man who was controlling the operation in Moscow, a Viktor Fomenko, was executed the day after your client was arrested.'

For a few moments Shulman was silent, and then he stood up clutching his leather case as he looked at Joe Shapiro.

'I'll apply for an investigation of how this matter has been conducted. There's something wrong somewhere.'

Shapiro laughed. 'Remember what your Mama used to say to us – "girls who can't dance always say the musicians can't keep time".'

Shulman didn't look amused or placated by the words as he headed for the door, turning to look at Shapiro for a moment as if he were about to speak, then changed his mind and let himself out.

Volkov had settled comfortably into the apartment. After ten days he felt remarkably at home despite the FBI plain-clothes man who shared his space, answered all phone calls and rings at the door. The FBI man was well-trained, amiable, capable and a non-communicator.

They were both watching the evening news on ABC and were impatient for the ball-game to start. Then they saw the crowds of journalists and photographers on the steps of the Justice Building clustering around a white-haired man. Volkov used the remote to pull up the sound and then realised with the head-shot that it was Joe Shapiro brushing aside thrusting microphones and speaking into an old-fashioned mike with no foam rubber.

'I can only repeat what I just said. The State's main witness in the Jarvis treason case will be the former KGB officer, Yuri Volkov, who controlled Jarvis from start to finish of his treason. Some of you will have met Mr Volkov when he was senior public relations officer at the Soviet Embassy. He knows the United States well and has lived here for almost ten years. He was a Fulbright scholar . . .' Joe Shapiro seemed to hesitate and then he said as an apparent aside, '. . . what the hell is it that makes Fulbright scholars so politically confused?' The dig at President Clinton got its small recognition from the assembled journalists.

'OK.' Shapiro said. 'Two questions, but only two.'

'Why has the Russian decided to testify?'

'He'll explain that in court, Tony.' He looked to one side. 'Joan – your question.'

'Can we have a picture of this guy Volkov?'

'Yeah. There's 10 × 8s in my temporary office in this building. Ask for Penny.' He adjusted his hat and looked down to check where the steps were and made his way to his waiting car.

Shapiro appeared on two chat shows that evening and annoyed both presenters by skilfully avoiding any response that might even vaguely answer their pointed questions.

Volkov and the FBI man were highly amused when callers to one of the programmes complained that the presenter had harassed his guest.

Shulman had agreed that now the whole thrust of the case against Jarvis had changed, Larry Getz could re-interview Mrs Jarvis. Getz had arranged for the meeting to be in an annexe to the prison governor's office.

'How're you feeling, Maria?'

'A bit confused. Mr Shulman didn't seem to know if this new witness would make any difference to my case.'

'That's what I came to see you about. To ask for your co-operation.'

She smiled wanly. 'How can I be of any use to your people?'

'Have you spoken to Jarvis recently?'

'Yes. About two days ago.'

'What was his attitude?'

She shrugged. 'You know Jarvis. Defiant. Going to bring down the government with his revelations.' She shrugged again. 'Just the same old Jarvis.'

'I spoke to him yesterday. I think he's ready to talk sense. Ready to face the facts and plead guilty. I think he needs a gentle push. And I think you could provide that push. You would in no way be making his sentence worse but you would be giving him a status he longs for. And I would see that it helped you and your son.'

'What would I have to do?'

'See him today or tomorrow. Make clear that if he pleads guilty that in your eyes he's a hero. And you'll tell the world. He's a guy who takes the load for the sake of his wife and son. You don't need to do anything more.'

'And how will it help me and my son?'

'If Jarvis pleads guilty and doesn't try playing games, I'll put in a report to the court asking for clemency for you on the grounds of your co-operation. The form of the co-operation won't be specified. That should bring your sentence down to roughly four years and parole and we'll arrange meetings with your son every other weekend in some non-official environment.'

She nodded her head. 'OK. I'll do it. He may not respond but I'll try.'

'Is there anything you want?'

'There was a pair of tortoiseshell hair-combs on my dressing-table. They've got my initials on in zircons. I'd like to have those if it's possible.'

'I'll get them for you.'

Back in his office Getz phoned Maria Jarvis's lawyer, Nielson, and told him the gist of his conversation with her. Nielson had had no objections to the meeting without him being present.

They were listening to a CD of *Phantom of the Opera* as they sat each side of a chess-board. There was a half-empty bottle of wine with two glasses on the floor beside the low table.

Getz looked up from the board as she made her move. 'Why did you do that?'

'Because two moves to come you could have forked my king and my castle.' She smiled. 'I don't want to lose my castle.'

'I've never been able to look that many moves ahead.'

'That's because you're not really interested in winning at chess.'

'So why do *you* always win?'

'I played chess with my father when I was a little girl. Every day without fail. I got my first roller-skates the first time I won a game. He's a good chess player but I can always beat him now.'

'Always?'

'Yes.'

'You must be bored playing against me.'

She laughed. 'On the contrary. Most of your moves are so crazy it keeps me on my toes.' She leaned out and touched his hand. 'You look brighter tonight. Are you?'

'Yeah.'

'Does this Russian guy coming on the scene make things easier?'

'It's the last nail in Jarvis's coffin.'

'Any news of what you'll be doing when it's over?'

'Not as yet. Everybody's too occupied with the case to think beyond it.'

'What will happen to his wife?'

'She's done a deal. She'll serve a couple of years. She wasn't really involved. But enjoyed the bucks that came in from it.'

'When does it go to trial?'

'Next week.'

Chapter 27

Shapiro had asked both O'Hara and Getz to the meeting although it was only Getz he was actually concerned with.

'This meeting is really for you, Larry. You will be required to give a certain amount of evidence particularly in the trial of Mrs Jarvis. Maria Jarvis. She has co-operated with us and Jarvis himself will be pleading guilty. Evidence by Yuri Volkov will substantiate his guilt without going into much detail. But Maria Jarvis is something else, and you'll have to give evidence covering certain things to make our case.'

Shapiro looked at Getz and went on. 'Now I want you to understand a bit of the law that will seem strange to you. It *is* strange. But nevertheless it is the law. Firstly, when she learned the truth about what her husband was doing she was under no obligation to report it to the authorities. It is not a crime to fail to report a crime. Secondly, there is no federal law against spending money from espionage. Even when she knew where the money came from, it was legal for her to spend the money because spending the money was not itself a crime. So don't waste time trying to establish those points.

'Finally Maria Jarvis's attorney, Nielson, obviously felt that his client was coming out looking pretty black so he arranged for her to have two interviews with women journalists. The thrust of the interviews will be that she was ignorant of what was going on and consequently could be considered as a victim of spousal abuse. There'll be discussion of their sex life and her attempts to get him to stop working for the Soviets. Don't agree with it but don't decry it because it will help public understanding of why she comes out of it so lightly. Doesn't matter if you destroy a couple of her points but don't go overboard.' He shrugged and leaned back in his chair. 'Any questions?'

Getz said, 'I'm beginning to regret the deal we did with her. I think we could have got Jarvis to plead guilty without using her.'

Shapiro smiled. 'It was you who offered her the plea bargain.' He paused. 'There's one more thing but it's nothing to do with the court case.' He paused again. 'What do you think of Volkov?'

'In what way?'

'How far is he on our side?'

Getz looked in query at O'Hara. 'I'd say he's committed. What do you think, Mike?'

'I agree. And he still needs our protection.' He looked at Shapiro. 'What's on your mind, Joe?'

'Did you see that piece in yesterday's *Washington Post* about Mrs Jarvis?'

Getz said, 'I saw it but I didn't read it. There's too much in the media to read it all.'

O'Hara said, 'I didn't see it at all. What was the angle? Another Watergate?'

'No. But somebody on their staff had been doing sums on the payments made to Jarvis and the amounts in the KGB letters to Jarvis about what they owed him. They calculate that the KGB still owe him well over a million dollars.'

O'Hara smiled. 'You gonna sue them for it, Joe?'

'Be an interesting case, Mike. If it's paid to a felon in jail it might not be legal.'

There was another twenty minutes of talk about details and then O'Hara had left for another appointment. Getz deliberately didn't leave with him. As he finished up his Coke, he said, 'What did you really have in mind when you asked about the money they owed Jarvis?'

'Who says I had anything else in mind?'

Getz shrugged. 'Your voice and your hands and your annoyance when nobody seemed to grasp what your real point was.'

'Did you get it?'

'No. I'm afraid not.'

'It passed through my mind that despite their reputations the Soviets have always taken care of their foreign agents. George Blake, Philby, Maclean and Burgess. Even those who weren't important they've always looked after them and any families they've left behind.' He shrugged. 'It's good propaganda anyway. Their guys who are still active know that they'll be looked after if they get caught or do a bolt to Moscow. I just wonder if they'll make an attempt to pay off that debt and who will they pay it to.'

'Will the money be mentioned in court?'

Shapiro smiled. 'Yeah. Both of them are being prosecuted for conspiracy to evade taxes.' He paused. 'Why don't you have a quiet word with Volkov?'

Getz laughed softly. 'You've got a very twisted mind, Joe.'

Shapiro shrugged. 'Just a passing thought.'

Chapter 28

Gabby was in the shower when the phone started ringing. She turned off the taps and clutching a towel around her she hurried to the phone.

'Yes. Who is it?'

A woman's voice said, 'Could I speak to Mr Getz please?'

'He's not here at the moment.'

'When will he be back?'

'I'm not sure but I'd better say that he doesn't give media interviews at least until the court-case is over.'

'My name's Mary Curtis. I used to be Larry's mother-in-law. I wonder if you could ask him to give me a ring. He's got my number.'

She hesitated for a moment and then said, 'Yes. I'll tell him you want him to call you.'

'Thank you very much.'

As she hung up the phone, Gabby sat down on the armchair beside the small table. It was a revealing voice, gentle and with a slight country accent. In fact it was a nice voice and she was a little bit jealous.

It was two hours before Larry Getz got home and when she gave him the message he looked surprised and vaguely apprehensive.

'Did she say what it was about?'

'No. Just asked if you would ring.'

Getz checked out the number in his phone book and tapped out the digits slowly.

'Mary Curtis.'

'It's Larry. Larry Getz.'

'Thanks for calling me back. You must be very tired at this hour but I need to talk to you about a number of things. Is that possible? It's rather urgent.'

'Is it something to do with Bobby?'

231

'Yes.'

'Is he ill or something?'

'No. He's OK. But I'd rather not talk about it on the phone.'

'OK. I'll be with you in about half an hour.'

'I don't want to offend in any way, Larry, but I'd heard that you were going to marry again. Was that the young woman who spoke to me on the phone?'

'Yes it was.'

'Can I suggest that she comes with you because one way or another she'll be involved.'

'What the hell's going on, Nana? Tell me.'

There was a long silence and then she said very softly, 'We've just come back from England, Larry. She's dead, Larry. She was killed in a car crash. We've brought Bobby back with us but we feel you should decide what he should do. I think he wants to be with you.'

'Is he at your place?'

'No. Dad's taken him up to Vermont showing him where we used to live and your family too.'

'We'll come over in about an hour.'

'Thanks.'

He hung up slowly and turned to look at Gabby.

'Joan died in England in a car crash. They've brought Bobby back here and they are ready to go along with whatever I want to do.'

'You mean you can have him permanently?'

'Yeah.'

'So what's the problem? We can fix him up a bed in the spare room for tonight.'

Getz sat down facing her. 'I love you so very much, Gabby. But think about it before we rush in.'

'You want him don't you?'

'Of course I do but you may not feel the same way about it.'

'He knows me for God's sake. We were friends. Get your damn coat on.'

'He's with my father-in-law in Vermont just giving him a bit of a tour around where I grew up.'

'Let's go and see her and she can phone him tonight and tell him.'

'I love you so much.'

She stood up looking at him. 'What did you expect? Did you think it was going to be another choice? Me or your son. I love you too Larry Getz, but I've got love enough to include your son too. Come on, let's go.'

They had eaten at their usual Italian restaurant after the meeting with Mary Curtis. She was obviously doing her best to hide her distress at her daughter's death, and at the same time to take some pleasure from Larry Getz's patience being rewarded by the return of his son. He was going to stay with his grandfather until the weekend when they would pick him up and bring him back with them. Gabby was going to fix a room for him for when he came back on Sunday night.

Back at the apartment they switched on the TV late news and heard President Clinton making a speech on the subject of relations with the Russians in the light of the Jarvis case. He said that he was anxious to minimise the impact of the case and not let it affect the financial aid to Russia to help establish a non-nuclear democracy.

The next news-clip was a spokesman on Mocow TV denying any knowledge of Jarvis. A heavily-bemedalled KGB officer added the KGB's denials to those of the Kremlin and sneeringly pointed out that in the evidence made public so far there was nothing to establish that they could link Jarvis with any aspect of the case, let alone Moscow. It was all circumstantial.

When Getz switched off the TV, she said. 'Does it make you angry when you hear that sort of crap from the Russians?'

'No way. In a couple of weeks' time you'll be seeing Jarvis pleading guilty to all the charges. It's just beginning to dawn on him what a life sentence with no parole really means. He's feeling very sorry for himself right now. He's in the Federal Penitentiary at Allenwood Pennsylvania, and his wife's in the federal prison at Danburg in Connecticut. Both in solitary with no phone calls and no visitors.'

'Will you be on TV at the court?'

'I will be when I give evidence in about ten days' time.' He looked at her. 'Are you sure that it's OK with you about Bobby?'

'Don't be an idiot, Larry. It's not just OK. It's a great pleasure, so please, please, no more doubts. Let's get on with our lives.'

He smiled. 'I'll enjoy taking you up to Vermont again.'

* * *

The next day in the court-room both Jarvis and his wife were there and both Shapiro and Getz noticed that they didn't look at one another. No recognition. No expression of affection or support. Nothing. Maria Jarvis sat there expressionless in her drab prison gown, her feet shackled and a female guard each side of her. Jarvis sat with his eyes closed as the two lawyers argued petty points of procedure before Judge Atkins. The hearing was to be put back another month on the grounds that Maria Jarvis's attorney needed more time to absorb the evidence offered by the prosecution.

Getz was aware of the dreariness of the whole proceedings. Over fifty highly-skilled people had spent over a year of their lives on the final stage of building the case against Jarvis and now the man who had been so lucky, so sure of himself, was brought down to the reality of being no more than a thief. Four million dollars was a lot of money but what good had the stolen documents really been to the KGB and Moscow? Their political system had collapsed dramatically in front of the whole world. Nevertheless they had learned more about the United States' doubts and intentions than the CIA had been able to find out about the Soviets. And despite the tracking down and arrest of Jarvis, Congress, the media, and even the White House were demanding a wholesale clean-out at Langley. Rumour had it that four highly-regarded men had been approached to take over as Director of the CIA. All of them had declined. The country had lost faith in their apparently ineffective and incompetent intelligence agency. The excitement of the chase suddenly seemed spurious as he looked at the two pathetic figures in the dock. No glamour there. More like clearing up the broken glasses and general detritus from a party that had got out of hand and gone on too long.

Jarvis had pleaded guilty but had asked to be allowed to make a statement. Judge Atkins reluctantly agreed. The thrust of Jarvis's statement was that the information he had passed to the Russians had been of no great value and had had no adverse effect on the security of the United States. It was listened to in silence by the court and then Shapiro had called Larry Getz to comment on Jarvis's statement. He had previously appeared for hours of evidence and so had Yuri Volkov.

The judge said, 'You are still under oath, Mr Getz.'

'Yes, sir.'

Shapiro said, 'Have you any comment to make on the statement by the accused?'

'Yes, sir.'

'Tell the court then.'

'It has already been established that the accused was directly responsible for the execution of at least ten Soviets who had given assistance to this country. He claims that this was just the wins and losses of what he refers to as the "intelligence game".' I want to take just one of those men he betrayed – Major-General Levin – and describe the debt we owe to him. He first contacted our people in 1959. He was a major then in the KGB. He was concerned that the Soviet Union and the USA were heading towards a military confrontation. We assured him that we in no way threatened the security of the Soviet Union. In 1962 you will recall that we had what became known as the Cuban Missile Crisis. Many of us recall the tension of those days. The terrible dilemma facing the President. It was the then Colonel Levin's insight into the Kremlin's thinking that allowed President Kennedy to maintain his stance and bring the situation under control. All the evidence shows that Levin never at any time betrayed his own country nor damaged the interests of the United States. He only co-operated in the hope that he could prevent a devastating war between the two countries.

'After the accused betrayed Levin he was executed without even the pretence of a trial. His widow was driven from their apartment and from her job as a child psychologist.' Getz paused. 'Why was this man betrayed and murdered?' He paused and pointed at Jarvis. 'He was betrayed and executed so that that man could drive around in a Jaguar car. He said in his statement that the material he passed to the Soviets was of no great value.' He paused. 'It was worth over four million dollars to Moscow and ten men's lives.'

Getz sat down and there was a short silence before Judge Atkins got on with the legal equivalent of tidying up after the children have gone to bed.

Three weeks later Getz had married Gabby in a ceremony at the French Embassy. A lot of people had been there including Mary

Curtis and half the staff of the Italian restaurant. Joe Shapiro had toasted the bride and groom at the reception afterwards.

Mary Curtis had offered to look after Bobby for a few days' honeymoon, but Gabby wouldn't hear of it. They had booked in the three of them for a four-day break on the shores of Lake Champlain and they'd stayed for two weeks.

PART FOUR

Chapter 29

Art Jarvis had served two years of his life-sentence when he underwent treatment for deep depression. He has no visitors and his cell is spartan.

Senora Maria dos Santos who used to be Mrs Art Jarvis has reverted to her former name and shares a house with her son and her parents on the outskirts of Bogotá. She was released early on humanitarian grounds and because of her good behaviour while serving her sentence. She seems to be well provided for financially but is no longer the big spender. Although the legal agreements made on her behalf and for her husband precluded both of them from publishing a book or agreeing to a film based on their lives she is, nevertheless, in negotiation through an agent for a ghosted autobiography and the rights for a film based on her life to be made by a film company in Prague. It seemed that United States' law on publishing restrictions did not apply to books or films published in another country. Legal threats were made from time to time but were ignored. Maria was a good mother and the next few years were the happiest years of her life. Few people knew of her background. Her son, Peter, eventually became a doctor. She still lives in Colombia.

When Dimitri Orlov was sent back to Moscow to face an internal KGB enquiry into his theft of KGB funds at the Paris embassy, the note with an address in St Germain was still in his pending tray. It was shredded and burnt along with most of his files of useless information. He served four years in a Gulag under its new name of Rehabilitation Centre.

Yuri Volkov and Sabine never married but they lived quite happily together. Rather like his parents did. Distance making the heart grow fonder and all that. Not that they spent all that much time apart. They enjoyed each other's company but both had work which absorbed them. Yuri had kept his forename but his passport now showed him as a US citizen named Yuri Venning, a full-time employee of the State Department on loan to the US Embassy in Paris. He was in charge of a special unit that had been set up by Langley at the Paris Embassy, where Yuri was responsible for the assessment of Russian documents obtained clandestinely by the CIA. Both sides constantly issued documents that were meant to confuse the other side and were for disinformation. It became a clearing-house for Russian documents from all CIA offices around the world. From time to time he gave lectures to small groups of agents at Langley on his view of current developments in Moscow. Listening to jazz was his main relaxation.

Sabine had become a full-time screen writer with far more work offered her than she could cope with. She spent at least a week of most months in Los Angeles. With an American woman as her agent she made a lot of money. Despite blandishments and threats she remained faithful to Yuri who surprised her by reciprocating. When he accompanied her to film parties and sometimes to Hollywood functions he was very popular. They have talked about marriage from time to time but have never felt that it would improve their relationship. Her parents were both supportive and helpful as a background for both Sabine and Yuri.

When Gabby and Larry Getz's four-day honeymoon was planned they had not allowed for the fact that Larry was now a public figure, his face recognised from TV. People were anxious to meet him. And Gabby was surprised and faintly amused to see her usually unsocial and non-communicative man so at home with the kind of people he so often talked about. She had never really believed that they could be all that different but they were. They were kind of old-fashioned but very lively and easy to get on with.

They had meals with several of Larry's old friends and he had phoned O'Hara to ask for his leave to be extended. O'Hara had told him to take as long as he wanted.

They had looked over the family firm and she had been impressed by its modern methods and the people who ran it. And she was surprised that Larry had not even referred to the possibility of taking over himself.

On the first Saturday they had been invited to a garden-party given by the Getz family's banker in Burlington. Larry had been taken off by a group of local worthies but Gabby and Bobby had been well looked after. It was late when they eventually drove back to the rented cottage by the lake. When Bobby was in bed they had sat on the porch.

'How do you like it here?'

'I liked it the first time.' She paused. 'Are you thinking about your idea of taking over the business?'

'No. I think it would bore me.' He paused. 'But I had an offer today.'

'Tell me.'

'The senior DA in Burlington is retiring. They've offered me the job.'

'What did you tell them?'

'That I would discuss it with you.' He paused. 'They would like a decision in the next week.'

'Do you fancy the job?'

'It would suit me well.'

She smiled. 'So let's say yes.'

'Would you miss Washington?'

She laughed. 'You're crazy. Nobody ever misses Washington. Vermont suits me fine.' She paused. 'What does a senior DA do?'

'I would be responsible for all prosecutions.' He paused. 'Let's look for a house tomorrow.'

Their son, Adam, was born a year later. Bobby ended up as creative director of a New York advertising agency, had many girl-friends but never married. Gabby slowly turned a good man into a happy man and gracefully fended off the amiable gallantries of the local worthies who were smitten by the accent and the beauty of the wife of the man who eventually became Judge Getz.